I0450864

DESTINY'S CALLING

YOUR FUTURE IS WAITING

TRACY BROEMMER

Destiny's Calling

Your Future is Waiting

by

Tracy Broemmer

Contemporary Romance

Published by Tracy Broemmer

Edited by Dawn Peters, 2nd Edition Lexie Broemmer

Cover Design: Designed With Grace

ISBN#: 978-1-7334023-4-7

Dear Readers:

I started this manuscript, which I called the pina colada story for a while, several years ago. The first time I worked on it, I wrote about ten chapters and stopped. I intended to submit it to a romance/time travel anthology. However, the word limit for the anthology was 25,000, and when I hit 25,000 as a word count, the story was just getting started. I tucked it away with the intention of writing it as a full-length novel someday. During the past couple of years, I opened the file occasionally and reread chapters. I decided it was kind of funny and that I should keep working on it, so I'd write another paragraph or two and then put it away again to work on something else.

Last winter, I finished writing it, but I had a lot of work to do to clean it up. When I first started working on it, I was going to set it in a fictional town. But as I wrote, my hometown, Quincy, Illinois kept popping up. I was envisioning Rae walking through Quincy, so finally, I decided to set the story in Quincy, 1980 Quincy. I was nine years old in 1980 Quincy. I remember a lot about what Quincy used to look like, but I don't remember it perfectly-kind of like remembering what your old bedroom looked like when you were a kid, but if you could actually go back, you might find something a little off. You remembered something bigger or smaller or a different color…

So while I remember the Quincy of my childhood, I can't say I remember exact dates for when particular businesses closed their doors and new ones opened. I did some research via the Internet, Carl

Landrum's Quincy books, high school yearbooks, and finally, I took it to the people of Quincy. I asked a lot of people a lot of questions about a lot of places and businesses in Quincy during the late '70s and early '80s. And, you guessed it; I got a lot of different answers.

I want to say a quick thank you to a few people in particular who helped me including Jim Broemmer, Rosie and Terry Madison, Dawn Peters, Sue Kapp, Christine Horman, Linda and Jim McNay, Kandi Ehrhart, Lori Vogel, Mary and Mike Foster, Lynn and Audie Breeden, and Tom Bueter.

Even with the research done, I am sure there are mistakes regarding Quincy, Illinois' timeline. Any mistakes made are mine, and I will apologize for them right here. First and foremost, I wanted to write a fun, happy love story, and second, I wanted to take my Quincy readers back in time for a little while. Also, I was told by both Terry Madison and Mike Foster that the Hi Hat Tavern on Broadway did not serve food, but for the plotline in this story, it did.

Also, I will never use a real address for any housing because I would never attempt to describe someone else's home, and I would never want anyone to think I was being critical of anyone's home. While I like using real street names and real business names because it makes the story so much more realistic, every home address, every apartment complex is made up. I drove the streets mentioned to make sure I used a fictional house/apartment number.

I hope you enjoy Rae and Chip's love story, and I hope Quincy readers have a little fun with a little throwback to 1980 Quincy. I certainly had a blast writing this one…though I suspect it will be the only time travel story I write! Far too much math and scientific thought (is it scientific if it's time travel??!!) for me!

Thanks for reading,
Tracy

Chapter 1

RAE WARNER SLOWS HER PACE AS A WAVE OF VERTIGO overwhelms her. In her rush to the courtroom earlier, she'd skipped lunch, and now it is nearing six in the evening, and she still hasn't eaten. She'd forgotten about dinner after she'd left the courtroom and headed back to the office. There's just always so much to do, she never seems to find the time to fit it all in. Her dad used to harp on her all the time, reminding her to take care of herself, and when he died, her brother Charlie had stepped in to take his place, as if Charlie is role model material.

Panic steals her breath when she glances around the sidewalk and doesn't recognize any of the storefronts or offices. She stops walking, moves closer to the building on her right, and lays her hand against the cool brick. A sign on the building proclaims it *Merkel's*. Merkel's used to be located here, but it seems it's been gone for quite some time.

She shivers, but she is not particularly cold. It is a warm summer day, and Rae's silk shell has been plastered against her back under her sleek taupe suit jacket most of the day. The sounds of traffic are distant, and yet she is walking down Broadway, the busiest street in town.

Deciding she needs to rest for a bit and maybe find a bite to eat, Rae takes a deep breath and begins walking again. She hates fast food, but there's a McDonald's just a few blocks down. She could sit down, drink a bottle of water and maybe eat a salad. Just enough to give her enough energy to get through her seven o'clock meeting at the hospital.

She should never have agreed to the meeting. Today had been too full already. The meeting with the PR director at the hospital could have waited another day. It's not as if they are launching the new community care program tomorrow.

Rae reaches the corner and steps into Seventeenth Street. An older model sports car zips past so close she thinks she sees the color of the driver's eyes. She scrambles back up on the curb and presses her hand against her chest to feel her heart's staccato beat.

She's not going to make it to McDonald's. Another four blocks. Another four streets she will have to cross while in this late afternoon funk and risk getting hit by a car. Rae turns her head and watches the cars zoom by on Broadway. The tavern across the street catches her eye. When she was in college a few years back, Barney's had served burgers and fries and other greasy, yummy bar food. She'd eaten her fair share back in the day. The thought of the juicy burgers makes her stomach growl now.

So she's going to have to wake up and get across Broadway without getting hit by a car. She'll have a burger and some fries and a Coke and then head down Broadway a couple more blocks to get to the hospital.

As she waits for a break in the traffic, she thinks of the old video game where the frog has to cross a busy street and then a stream, where it has to dodge being eaten by snakes and alligators. At least *she* only has to worry about the cars.

She laughs softly at the absurd direction her thoughts have taken. The breeze picks up a tendril of honey blond hair that has escaped her chignon. She lifts her hand and brushes the hair away from her face. The soft leather brief-case she carries on her left shoulder has grown heavy, and suddenly she can't wait to sit down in the tavern and rest.

The stoplight a block down changes to red, and Rae sees her opportunity to cross. She hurries across the wide street on taupe heels, careful to keep her stride small so she won't rip the slit in the side of her long skirt.

The smell of cigarette smoke hits her as she yanks the glass door open and steps inside the tavern. Cigarette smoke? The Smoke-free Illinois Act had been passed at the beginning of the year. She's been in gas station conve-nience stores in small towns and gotten a whiff of smoke, but she hasn't seen anyone blatantly ignore the new law. Until now, that is. Her eyes have not adjusted to the dark interior, and most of the people in here look like even darker shadows, but she can see tendrils of smoke curling up toward the ceiling from several spots in the tavern.

As her eyes adjust from the sunlit daylight to the dark-ness inside, Rae realizes several sets of eyes are watching her. She tries to ignore them—*what? Have they never seen a working woman before?*—and looks around for a place to sit. All of the barstools are taken, but she hadn't planned to sit at the bar anyway. Instead she lets the strap of her bag slip from her shoulder, and she sets it on a table just a few feet from the door. She tells herself she's not afraid of the clien-tele; she hasn't set foot inside this place for a long time, but she knows karate and she doesn't scare easily. Maybe it's just a good idea to sit close to the door, so she can eat and slip out quickly. She'll need the fresh air after sucking in all of this secondhand smoke.

She finally looks up again as she pulls a chair out and perches on the edge. No one is looking at her now. Not the workingmen on the barstools, nor the two young guys at the table across the room. Not even the bartender. Rae wonders if there is a waitress here. Maybe she will grow old waiting for someone to take her food order.

Sitting down seems to have helped. The dizziness is gone, but now she recognizes her hunger. She is famished. At any moment now, her stomach might start growling loud enough to grab everyone's attention. With a sigh of irritation, she stands again. Her long legs eat up the wooden floor between her table and the bar. The work-ingmen there all turn to look at her as she approaches.

"What can I get you, ma'am?" the bartender asks her. His hair is too long, and he wears a knit polo shirt with the collar up. Rae manages to control the urge to roll her eyes. She's only twenty-nine. It hasn't been that long since she was young. But really? What is this kid thinking, dressed like this?

And *ma'am*? She cringes. So he's polite, but twenty-nine! There should be an age limit before someone can call a woman *ma'am*. Like mid-thirties at least. Definitely not before thirty.

"Can I get a cheeseburger and fries?" she asks him. He grabs an order pad and writes her request down.

"Anything to drink with that?"

She realizes that ordering a diet soda with a greasy burger and fries would probably make the whole room full of men—there are no women in this joint—laugh at her.

"Just a Coke."

The bartender nods and walks over to the door to the kitchen. Rae glances around as he calls out her order, presumably to the cook. The man on the bar stool nearest her smiles at her. She nods and smiles back. He's nursing a draft beer, and he wears a plaid shirt with shiny, pearly buttons. The kind her uncle used to wear back when she was a kid.

Rae almost jumps when music blasts around her. She catches her breath, glances at the guy next to her again, and then sees one of the young guys at the table behind them sit down. Her gaze jumps from the guy to the far wall. Jukebox. Seems kind of odd that the song of choice for a young guy—he looks like he might be in college—is Eddie Rabbit's "I Love a Rainy Night."

The bartender returns to her with an icy Coke in hand. She taps her manicured nails on the bar as he figures her total and nearly drops the Coke when he announces the number.

"For a cheeseburger, fries, and a Coke?" Rae raises her eyebrows. "You're kidding me!"

"No, ma'am. The cheeseburger special is a lunch special. Price goes back to normal at four."

Rae flattens her hand on the bar. *Is he serious? He thinks I think the food is too expensive?* She hasn't eaten such a cheap meal, other than Ramen noodles, in years.

"No, I…" She shakes her head. "I thought it would be more." She clears her throat and motions back toward her table. "I left my purse over there. Do you take debit cards?"

"What's a debit card?"

"You're kidding me." She smiles uncertainly. "Right? You're kidding about the debit card?"

"I swear to you I am not kidding," the bartender says sincerely. "I take cash."

Rae feels a rush of heat in her cheeks, but at the same time, the blood drains from her face. Even though she once again feels she might faint, she is glad for the latter as it might hide her blush.

"I only have a debit card." She taps her fingernails again on the bar. "I don't have cash."

"What's a debit card?" the bartender asks again.

Rae cocks her head to study the kid. He's cute, but when she really looks at him, he seems so young. Definitely sincere. He honestly has no idea what a debit card is.

"It's plastic like a credit card. You swipe it in a little machine and the funds are transferred automatically—"

The guy shakes his head.

"Just a second," she mumbles. Aware that every man in the tavern is watching her again, Rae goes back to her table and opens the leather briefcase. She grabs her Coach wallet and her cell phone. Maybe she can catch Charlie at home. He could bring her some cash.

The men all watch curiously as she dials the phone number on her cell.

"What in the world is that?" One of the men at the bar stands as if he is going to approach her and take the phone.

"It's a cell phone," she answers absently. Maybe most of the clientele in here don't own a smart phone, but Rae is sure that all of them have a cell phone of some sort. Who in this day and age doesn't carry a cell phone? When seconds have passed and the phone is not even ringing, Rae looks at the screen. No service.

She groans. It's like the *Twilight Zone* here.

"Do you have a pay phone?" she asks the bartender quietly, all the while trying to remember when she last saw a pay phone *anywhere*.

"Sure do!" The guy seems excited that he can finally give her the answer she wants to hear. "It's back that way, by the restrooms."

"Lovely," Rae says with a nod. She touches the screen to end the attempted call and ducks her head, ready to find the pay phone and call Charlie. Maybe she should skip the meeting at the hospital. She's already going to be late, and the last hour has been surreal. What might happen if she does go to the meeting? Maybe William Shatner will show up and beam her up to the *Starship Enterprise*?

Rae groans as she collides with what feels like a brick wall. She looks up, unnerved to find herself face to face with a drop-dead gorgeous kid. He looks like he could be romance novel cover model material with his longish, dirty blond hair that curls around his neck and his ears. His brown eyes. Rae is so close to him, she can see tiny little flecks of gold in them. His tanned face looks soft, but the line of his jaw is firm. Five o'clock shadow covers his lower jaw and chin. Rae finds herself wondering what that five o'clock shadow would feel like if he kissed her. Maybe if he kissed her neck. Her stomach.

Embarrassed, she ducks her head again. What on earth is wrong with her? Fantasizing about kissing a total stranger, one who doesn't even look legal to be in a bar as a matter of fact. She swallows hard, reminds herself she needs to get in touch with Charlie so she can get some cash to pay for her dinner. She really needs to eat.

"Hi." The kid's voice is gravelly and sexy. Much too sexy for his age. And for her good. "Let me help you out," he offers.

"No, thank you. I just need to call my brother."

"Really," he says and smiles as he reaches to pull a bill-fold from his pocket. "Lemme get it for you."

Rae watches as he pulls out the bills to cover her meal. She looks back at the bartender who is watching her with more interest than suspicion. He's not concerned she's going to bolt out the door without paying for the food she's ordered.

"Okay," she concedes. "But let me go ahead and call Charlie. He can bring me the cash to pay you back before you go."

"Whatever."

Rae steps around him and remembers the feel of his body up against hers. Lean and hard with muscle. She shakes her head again and hurries to the back of the bar. Now *this* makes her nervous. Standing in the back of a tavern with a bunch of men in the room behind her and the men's room two steps away. She might be a black belt, but she's not too excited about needing to use those moves.

She looks back over her shoulder. Money Boy is watching her. He offers her a reassuring smile. It should make her feel better that *someone* is watching her back. But she can't help but picture his lips again, so soft-looking, and the five o'clock shadow and the way it might feel to kiss him. To hear his sexy voice say her name.

A wave of heat tingles inside her. It starts in her belly and crawls lower. She feels it out to her fingertips. How ridiculous. It's not like it's even been that long since she's seen Paul.

Not like Paul has ever made you burn with anticipation over a simple kiss, either.

"Stop it!" she hisses to herself. She digs for change and curses when she chips a nail. She drops the coins to assess the damage. A bit of the burgundy is now gone from the acrylic tip of her index finger.

"Dammit!"

"Everything okay, miss?" Money Boy calls.

"Yes!" she snaps and then feels bad. He's only trying to be helpful. "Thank you."

She grabs the coins again and drops them in the slot,

trying to picture her schedule so she can fit in a fix for her nail. She dials Charlie's number, shocked when a girl answers. Charlie is cute, but he's messy and absent-minded and oblivious to the opposite sex. Rae would wager that if he's lost his virginity, it was a surprise to him. She's seen a few women try to catch him, seduce him, but he's never seemed to get it. He's always too busy with his next invention.

For the sake of science, not money. Another reason most women don't stay interested in him for long.

"I need to speak with Charlie." She holds the phone with one hand and smoothes the other over her chignon. Her hair feels messy and unkempt. She hates that feeling.

"Charlie who? There's no Charlie here."

"Charlie Warner," Rae says patiently. "This is his sister, Rae."

"Sorry, no Charlie," the girl answers and laughs obnoxiously.

Rae takes a deep breath. *Happy place. Go to your happy place.* It's what her therapist would tell her. If she had one.

"Is this 555-0982?"

"Yes, it is. But there ain't no Charlie here. Never has been."

Rae cringes over the use of *ain't* and then again when the phone is dropped loudly on the cradle.

"Dammit."

She gently replaces the handset of the pay phone and lowers her head to rub the back of her neck. What a day. It's the absolute day from hell. Should have known when Judge Carver ruled against her this afternoon in court and then Mike Sellis, the sleaziest divorce attorney she knows— no wonder he'd failed as a corporate attorney, the guy wore his breakfast on his tie every day and dated girls young enough to play with his daughters—had hit on her. Touched her butt. *As if.*

Rae shivers involuntarily. *Paul.* She'll have to call Paul. She reaches for the handset again and remembers two things at once. She's just used her last dimes (now she has nothing but pennies) on a call to her brother—*how had she not reached him at his phone number?*—and Paul is in Chicago until Friday.

So she'll either have to do dishes here or send Money Boy a check. She'll just make sure to get his address.

Okay, Rae, she thinks. She begins walking back to the front of the bar. Eat the cheeseburger. Walk outside and call the PR person at the hospital. Reschedule the meeting. Go home and take a hot bath. Sip a glass of wine. Go to bed. Pretend today never happened.

She reaches up and unclips her hair. When she looks up, Money Boy is watching her shake it out. She drops her hand and smiles uncertainly, feeling like she's in a shampoo commercial.

"Get a hold of your brother?" the kid asks.

"No, I'm sorry," she answers. "If you give me your address, I'll mail you a check."

"Don't worry about it," he answers. She starts back to the bar, but he touches her elbow. "It's ready. Tony put it on the table for you."

She looks at her table, pleasantly surprised to see her cheeseburger and a huge plate of fries.

"Mind if I join you for a minute? You look like you could use some company."

She smiles and nods slowly. "Actually, I think I could use some company. Thank you."

"So what is this thing?" Money Boy points at her cell where it sets on the table. Rae sits down and takes a big drink of her Coke before she answers him. The cold soda on her throat feels great, and the taste of the Coke, which is normally too sweet for her, is delicious.

"It's my phone," she answers. She nods at the chair next to her and waits until he sits down to start eating.

"It's a phone." He frowns and picks it up. "Like those new car phones. Okay." He grins at her. "I see what you mean."

Rae looks around the tavern again. Ronnie Milsap is singing now, saying there's no getting over him. She stares at the neon beer signs hanging on the walls and from the ceiling. Something isn't right, but she's too hungry to care much about it at the moment. She picks up her cheeseburger and takes a big, unladylike bite.

"What's your name?" Money Boy asks her.

She tries to laugh, chews the sandwich in her mouth, and then tells him her name is Rae.

"What's yours?"

"Chip."

Chip? He doesn't look like a Chip. A *Dylan*, maybe. Or *Nick*. But Chip? She hasn't heard that name in a good fifteen to twenty years. She'd gone to grade school with a boy named Chip.

"It's Chase Andrews, but I go by Chip," he admits.

Ah. Nicknames she can understand.

"My name's actually Desirae, but I go by Rae. I think it sounds more professional."

Chip lifts an eyebrow in appreciation. "You certainly look professional, Desirae."

She rolls her eyes and pops a fry into her mouth.

"What do you do, Chip?"

"I'm a junior at the college," he tells her. Of course he is. Any good-looking, nice guy would have to be too young or too old or gay or married or something. Rae feels a pang of guilt; after all, she is dating Paul. They've gone to dinner twice, and he took her to an art show two weeks ago. Kissed her goodnight once.

Rae realizes she is staring at Chip's mouth. She makes herself drag her gaze away. "What are you studying?" She wishes she could kick herself. Acting like a floozy in this bar. Has to be the atmosphere. She doesn't normally think about this stuff. She doesn't just look at an attractive man and think about his mouth on her skin.

"Dammit!" The thought almost makes her quake inside. She spills soda on her suit jacket.

"You're having a bad day, aren't you, Desirae?"

His smile is intoxicating, if a bit crooked; although his teeth are perfectly straight and brilliant white. His eyes sparkle. Rae reaches out to tuck his too long hair behind his ear and barely catches herself.

"I am. I'm having a really bad day." She clears her throat. "Started in court earlier and apparently, it's not over yet."

"In court. You're a lawyer?"

"I'm a corporate attorney, yes."

"That's sexy," he says softly.

To get her mind out of the gutter, Rae looks down at her jacket to see how bad the soda spot is. Of course. Big and noticeable, besides.

"Just take your jacket off."

She does. She shrugs out of it and then realizes too late that she's wearing the silk shell, with thin spaghetti straps, and if Chip can't see the lines of her bra under the thin silk material, he can surely see the straps of her bra under the spaghetti straps.

"Shoot!" She reaches back for the jacket again, but Chip stops her with a hand over her wrist.

"I kind of like that look," he tells her.

"What're you studying, Chip?" she asks again. She is

hot. Well, okay, honestly, she's been hot and bothered since crushing her body against the solid wall of Chip's chest, but she has to admit now that she's hot. It's warm in the tavern. It's not like her to act this way, and she is a bit self-conscious sitting in a public place in what feels like under-wear. But then, everything else about this day has been bizarre, so she decides it's not going to hurt her to sit like this and finish her burger and then go home.

"Education."

"And do you live here?"

"I have an apartment on campus. I'm from Decatur."

"Mm-hmm." She nods and continues to eat. "And do you have brothers and sisters?" She cringes at how stupid she sounds. She always manages to talk too much when she's nervous, and sitting here with this gorgeous kid's—*he's just a kid, Rae!*—eyes trouncing up and down and all over her, she's definitely nervous. She wipes her hands on a napkin, not because of the food, but because her palms are sweating.

"Two sisters," he answers. "Both older. One lives in Boston and one lives in Key West."

She laughs and continues to wolf down the burger and fries. An uncomfortable quiet settles around them at the table. At least it's uncomfortable for Rae. Chip looks relaxed though, kicked back at the table with his arms folded across his chest.

An old boyfriend used to say that there was a lag in conversation at twenty after the hour, every hour. The thought makes her check her watch. It's almost quarter 'til seven!

"Oh, no!" She takes another quick drink of her soda, dabs at her mouth with her napkin, and then reaches behind her to put her jacket on. How is she supposed to go to this meeting at the hospital? She's in a rush, her hair is a mess, and she's got soda on her suit jacket. Oh. And a broken nail. All she needs now is a runner in her nylons.

"What's wrong?" Chip sits forward, ready to do battle for her.

"I have a meeting I need to get to." She stands up and reaches for her cell. "Give me your address, so I can mail you a check."

"I don't want a check." He stands. "Where's your meeting?"

"At Blessing Hospital—Blessing at Fourteenth. Really, Chip, I owe you for the meal—"

"I enjoyed talking to you." He follows her as she steps toward the door. "*Where's* Blessing Hospital? I thought it was on Eleventh Street."

"Used to be. It's just a few blocks down Broadway."

"That's St. Mary's," he tells her as they step outside together.

"It used to be St. Mary's," she corrects him. "The hospitals consolidated in 1992. Now they're both Blessing."

"Ninety-two?" He laughs and shakes his head. "Whatever. My uncle is a doctor there. That's why I came down here to go to school."

Rae stares at him silently. She glances toward the street. Older Camaros. Older pick-up trucks. Station wagons. Where are the Trackers and Sebrings? She looks back at the window of the bar they just left. An old-fashioned Pabst Blue Ribbon marquee flickers, as if it is about to go out permanently. Her eyebrows jump when she sees *Hi Hat Tavern* in neon in the windows.

Hi Hat Tavern?

"Chip, what year is it?" she asks him. Chip studies her closely, probably wondering if she's on drugs or if she's escaped from the mental floor of the hospital just down the street.

"1980."

1980.

Rae squints and looks away from Chip's inquisitive eyes.

"Really? It's 1980?" Her voice is small and frightened. "Seriously?"

"Really." Chip touches her shoulder. "Rae, are you alright?"

Rae stares silently at the sidewalk. 1980. How is she standing on Broadway in 1980, when this morning she woke up in 2000? When just two hours ago she'd been in 2000?

Charlie.

Chapter 2

Oh no. She'd been at Charlie's just before she'd come here to the tavern. How had she gotten here? Rae runs her fingers through her hair and tries to remember something before coming to the tavern.

She can't. Nothing. There's Charlie's. And then wandering down the sidewalk on Broadway, feeling the vertigo.

Charlie's been working on a time machine for years. He's never had any luck, so Rae's never paid much attention to his ramblings about it. By day he's a medical researcher, searching for cures for diseases. But in all of his free time, he chases that crazy time travel dream.

Looks like he finally got it right. Somehow her visit to Charlie has catapulted her back almost twenty years in time.

Now how in the world can she get back?

"Rae?" Chip touches her shoulder and leans forward to look at her. She looks away before he can see the panic in her eyes. "Do you need a ride somewhere?"

Rae licks her lips and answers with a slow, distracted

nod. "Yeah. Yeah, I do." She laughs softly at the absurdity of her predicament. She needs a ride somewhere, because she highly doubts that her 1999 Honda Civic is parked anywhere in 1980.

But where does she need to go? Because Charlie's house isn't Charlie's house yet.

"Okay." Chip lays his hand on her lower back and steers her around the building to the parking lot in back. He probably does think she's crazy, but she doesn't have time to worry about that now.

Think, Rae, you've got to think. 1980. Where was Charlie living in 1980?

First things first. How old was Charlie in 1980? Rae winces when she realizes she is going to have to convince a fourteen-year-old Charlie that he does indeed create a time machine in the future and that she has traveled back from 2000. Luckily she will have to deal with Charlie and not herself. In fact, she thinks she's heard Charlie ramble about how you should never encounter yourself when you're time traveling.

"Where can I take you?" Chip asks her as he unlocks the door of a beat up Camaro. Rae stops walking and studies the car closely. In another lifetime, it had probably been gold, but the paint is badly chipped and faded from too much sunlight. There is a dent in the passenger side back quarter panel. Rust eats at the panel, down low behind the back tire.

She guesses from the style that it might be a '79 model. Charlie had been a car buff until he'd gotten into college and finally gotten serious about studying. His first car had been a '67 Camaro.

"Rae?"

Rae turns her head to look at him, afraid she's

offended him spending so much time examining the rattle-trap car.

"Sixteen fifty-eight York."

Chip raises an eyebrow in appreciation and nods down at the open car door. With one last look around, Rae dips and slides into the seat. He's been nice enough so far, but alarm bells are going off in her head. Never get in a car with a stranger. Okay, so she'd done it more than once when she was in college. But somehow this is different. She's an adult now. Adult women do not get in cars with just anyone. Not in 2000 anyway. She could picture the headline in tomorrow's paper already: Unidentified woman found stabbed to death in South Park. Except she wouldn't exactly be unidentified, maybe, since she does have a purse and her ID. If her ID were found, the authorities would know who she was; they just wouldn't get why her license said it had been issued in 1999.

"Is everything okay, Rae? You seem pretty upset about something."

Rae looks up at Chip and flashes him a toothy smile. "Oh, I'm fine." She nods and looks out the windshield again. Fine, indeed. Just get home. Home, as in Mom and Dad's home—Wow. She was going to see her parents again, both of whom are now deceased—and talk to Charlie and get this figured out.

The house looks locked up tight when Chip pulls into the driveway. It is obvious there is no one here. Of course, Rae thinks, with a frustrated sigh.

"Do you have a key?" Chip asks her. The sun has dropped a bit in the western sky. Rae glances at her watch, ten minutes after seven. What will she do if she can't get in? Where will she spend the night?

She holds her breath when she remembers that Chip asked her a question. Hotels. Credit cards. Even if no one in 1980 knows what a debit card is, everyone knows what a credit card is.

"Could you—" Rae presses her lips together and lifts an eyebrow beseechingly. "Would you mind waiting just a minute?"

"It's no problem," he answers.

"Thanks." She smiles at him. He really is nice to look at. And at the moment, he's the only thing familiar to her. Her gaze locks with his. *Dangerous*. She tears her eyes away, but they only continue their jaunt down his face. To his lips. They look soft and inviting, parted, as if he is going to say something. Or like maybe he wants to kiss her.

"I'll be right back!" She snaps out of her thoughts and feels heat climb into her cheeks. Still facing him, she reaches back to open her door. Chip laughs, *he actually laughs*, as she scrambles backwards out of the car and bumps her head. "Dammit."

She shuts the door, leans down to smile at him, though she's probably fifteen shades of red by now, and hurries away from the car. Remembering she is wearing heels and a long, slender skirt, she slows her steps. Wouldn't do to trip or get her heel caught in a crack in the driveway and fall right in front of this kid.

Kiss her. Why on earth would she think this kid would want to kiss her? He probably thinks she is old enough to be his mother. He wasn't drinking at the tavern; he's probably not even legal drinking age. And here she is looking into his eyes and thinking about those lips on hers. On her neck. Lower.

"Rae!" she groans aloud and finally rounds the back of the house. Her parents had started putting a spare key on the back patio under a potted plant. She can't remember exactly how old she and Charlie had been when they'd started it, but maybe, just maybe she'll be lucky and she'll find the key and she can get inside and wait for Charlie to come home.

She spots the potted plant next to the swing where her mom used to sit every morning and sip her coffee. Out of Chip's sight now, she hurries to the plant and tips the pot just enough to see beneath it. Nothing. *Dammit.* She needs a closer look. With a look around, she quickly hikes her skirt up ridiculously high and squats down. Still nothing.

"Rae?"

Embarrassed again, Rae hurriedly stands so she can push her skirt back down over her thighs. She groans when she hears the rip. The slit on the side of her skirt now goes another four or five inches higher. Too much leg. At least she has nylon stockings on. Somehow it would seem even more indecent for her to be standing here with Chip staring at the bare skin of her thigh.

"This is my parents' house," she mumbles. "Obviously they aren't home."

"What are you doing out here?" he asks her. There is still a look of amusement on his face. She'd like to slap it off. And then maybe follow the slap with a kiss. Soft and gentle. To take away the sting.

She shakes her head, disgusted by her thoughts. "Looking for the key they usually hide. It's not here."

Chip nods. "Anywhere else I can take you?"

She longs to go home. To her apartment. But she can't. Her apartment complex doesn't exist yet. Right now, an old three-story industrial building occupies the block where her apartment complex will be built in fifteen years.

"No. Thanks." She folds her arms over her chest and shakes her head. The strap of her bag slips off her shoulder and the whole bag swings forward.

"Is this a purse?" Chip asks with a chuckle. "I've never

seen a woman carry something so big." He reaches to push the strap back on her shoulder and adds, "and heavy."

"No, it's a briefcase," she mumbles and then gestures toward the swing. "Thanks for the ride. I'll just hang out here and wait."

"You sure? I don't mind driving—"

"No, I'm sure." She sets her bag on the ground near the swing. "I'll be fine."

"It's kind of warm out here," he tells her. "You could go with me for awhile, and I could bring you back later."

It is warm. And the way he's looking at her is making her warmer. In fact his eyes keep sliding down from her eyes and then down over her mouth and then darting briefly to her breasts. She's feeling pretty hot at the moment, and it has nothing at all to do with the June weather.

June. June?

"Chip, what's the date?"

"June third."

She can't help it. She groans out loud and runs her fingers through her hair.

"What's wrong?"

Charlie always went to camp during the first week of June. He won't be back here until the weekend.

"What day of the week?"

"Tuesday."

She's got at least three more days of being stuck in 1980 before she can even talk to the man—boy—who sent her here.

"Rae, what's going on?"

"You wouldn't believe me if I told you," she tells him. "Trust me."

"Come with me."

She could stay here and wait for her parents to come

home. She's anxious to see them, even though she can't tell them who she is. Or she could go with Chip and have him bring her back here later.

"Where?" She feels the tip of her tongue touch the center of her upper lip and wonders who the hell has taken over her body. She's flirting with this kid, for heaven's sake. Flirting! He could be jailbait.

"Starlite."

She shakes her head and shrugs. In 1980, she would have been ten. She wouldn't have known much past Kmart, McDonald's, and school.

"It's a club."

"A nightclub?"

"Yeah." Chip grins and steps closer to her. "We could have a drink. And we could dance."

"Dance," she repeats. "You wanna dance with me?"

He steps even closer and looks down at her. "I do." He slides his arms around her waist and yanks her close. Their lower bodies touch. Heat shoots up through her belly, and before she can help herself, she gasps out loud. "We could do it here, but I think the neighbors might get jealous. We can go dance at the Starlite all night. And then I'll bring you back here."

His body is hard and muscular. One particular part of his body is particularly hard against her. Rae swallows hard. She needs to breathe, but breathing right now will mean moving against his body. Against *it*. Probably not a good idea. He's just a kid. *Remember that, Rae. He's just a kid.*

"Um. Sure." She lifts her hands to push him back a few steps. "Let's…let's get a drink and—and dance."

Chip picks up her bag for her and slings it over his shoulder.

"What's in here?" he asks her.

"File folders. Computer."

"A computer?" he asks incredulously. "How is there a computer in your bag?"

"It's a small, portable computer," she answers carefully. They walk back down the driveway to his car, Chip a few steps behind her.

"What do you do with a small portable computer?" He opens her door for her again and then stares down at her, waiting for her to answer his question.

"The Inter—" Rae catches herself. In 1980, there is no Internet. Chip is still looking at her expectantly. "Just some stuff for work."

He nods, but she can tell from the look on his face that he doubts her. She can't imagine what he would think if she were to tell him about the Internet. That she is from the future.

"Do you want me to put your bag in the trunk?"

"That'd be great."

"You'll need to get your ID out. They card."

Well, that's laughable, considering she's damned near thirty and this kid looks like he could still be in high school. She does as he suggests, though, and removes her driver's license from her wallet. Chip smiles again as he takes her bag and locks it away in the trunk.

"You surprise me," he says as he slides in behind the wheel.

"Why do I surprise you?"

"You don't seem like you'd be from around here."

He shrugs and starts the car. Rae has to admit that it might look like a crawling heap of rusted metal, but it purrs like a kitten when it idles.

"Is this a '79?" she asks him when he puts it in gear and backs out of the driveway. "And why don't I seem like I'd be from around here?"

Did he mean *here* as in this neighborhood? And if so,

why would he think she doesn't look as if she'd come from an affluent neighborhood? She's dressed to the nines. Or at least she was, before she'd more or less wilted outside the tavern, after stepping through Charlie's time zone. Before spilling soda on her jacket. Ripping her skirt.

Or did he mean *here* as in 1980? Because that one she can't fight. No way can she admit she's from the future. That would surely have him driving her straight to Blessing or whatever the damned hospital is called right now. He'd have a doctor greet her at the door with a strait jacket.

"Yeah. It's a '79." He fidgets with the radio and stops on "Escape, The Pina Colada Song."

"My brother is a car buff."

He's still looking at her. Driving down York. Eyes on her. All over her. "Why don't I? Seem to be from around here?" Her throat is dry. She'd kill for that drink right about now. The stronger, the better.

He shakes his head and looks back toward the road in front of them. Swerves to avoid a parked car but then glances back at her. She might be twenty years in the past, but she knows the look in his eyes. Any woman knows that look from any man, any era.

"Too classy," he answers with a tiny shrug. "You look like a city girl."

"A city girl?" she repeats. She mentally cringes. *Witty, Rae. Repeating him. Asking stupid questions. He's the kid here, not you!*

"Chicago. New York. Who do I know that carries a small, portable computer around with her in a briefcase?"

Rae smiles uncomfortably and looks away from his inquisitive eyes. She studies the scenery as he drives, and Rupert Holmes singing is the only sound in the car. Mostly, the town is familiar as he drives, familiar from her childhood. She sees Boags restaurant where now there is a

Walgreens, the old Modern Dairy where there is now a dry cleaning service. The old Quincy College campus which is now redone with a big parking lot—Lot B, the Visitors Lot —on the corner of Eighteenth and Oak.

"What's wrong?" Chip asks when she sits up and cranes her neck to watch her grade school building pass by. It makes her sad to see it now, but she can't tell Chip that.

"Nothing," she says quietly.

He watches her again instead of the road. Silently she raises her eyebrows. Wishes he'd pay attention to driving.

"Can I ask you something?"

"What?"

"Do you like pina coladas?"

Rae can't fight the smile, so she doesn't even try. "I do. And I even like being out in the rain. Sometimes."

Chip reaches toward her and strokes his fingertips over the back of her hand. Suddenly, she worries that he might decide to continue the game, the song lyrics. Would he ask her if she likes making love at midnight? What would she say? Of course she likes making love at midnight. Who wouldn't, but is that any of Chip's business? And would saying that she does make him think she's coming on to him? She isn't. Dear God, she is not coming on to this kid. He's so young. Probably young and innocent. She gets stuck on that thought. She wasn't so innocent when she was younger, so maybe she shouldn't assume Chip is. After all, this is the disco era. This is the time when guys like Chip drive around in conversion vans with ratty old shag carpet and big speakers piping out Barry White so they can get some action.

Okay, so maybe Chip isn't so innocent. She can't really know that without asking him, and she can't ask him without leading him to the wrong conclusion. So she'll drop that line of thinking. There's still Paul. She is seeing

Paul Bailey in the year 2000. Therefore she can not have any fantasies about this kid in 1980.

Except that Paul's kiss doesn't light her on fire the way this kid's eyes do. His *eyes.* The way he looks at her makes her hot. What would happen if he *touched* her?

"Chip?" Her voice comes out a little squeaky, like she's a cartoon or something. She glances at his fingers, still resting on the back of her hand. When he sees her looking at his hand, he quickly draws it away, and she pulls her own hand further into her lap. Into the safety zone. Only not really. Because if he reaches to touch her *there*, in her lap, he is dangerously close to an intimate touch.

One that she thinks maybe she would welcome. Oh hell, maybe one she would welcome with relish.

"Where's the club? Are we there yet?" Her voice still sounds all tight and squee-hawed. She feels the heat climbing up her body, so she fans herself and shakes her head. "I'm really thirsty. Ready for that drink."

Chip winks at her—he *winks* at her, for heaven's sake—what does he take her for? A ditzy blonde in a movie part? He's like a cheesy seventies or eighties actor in a cheesy movie, ready to take her out and twirl her around in a few cool disco moves and then press her up against the wall and slide her skirt up around her hips and lay his hand on her thigh. All that's missing is the mustache.

Rae glances down and realizes she does indeed have a long skirt on, and he could very well press her up against the wall and push the skirt up out of the way and slide his hand up her thigh. She frowns, trying to remember which panties she has on. Too bad she didn't get stuck in the past *last* weekend. She'd gone commando, just because her dryer wasn't working and she'd had no clean, dry panties, and she'd had to leave pronto to meet Paul at that art show.

Wonder what this boy would think if he slid his hand up her thigh, only to find—

"The club's right here," Chip says calmly. He taps the brakes, flicks on his turn signal and makes a left into a big parking lot. Big, *full* parking lot. The club is jumping, which amazes Rae because she'd had no idea such a place existed when she'd lived here in 1980. Then again, she'd only been ten.

"Great!" She yanks open the car door and all but falls out in her haste to put some distance between Chip and herself. A good bucket of ice water in the face or a swift kick in the butt would be even better, but beggars can't be choosers. "Really thirsty." She glances back at him and smiles.

Good grief. She's coming unglued. If Chip could read her mind, he'd think she was some sex-crazed plain Jane librarian who hadn't ever been with a man. Okay, so technically, that wasn't *so* off the mark. It had been several years, but she *had* been involved with one man. One relationship. She'd been in love. Not her fault the jerk had up and left her for a skinny little redhead with boobs the size of watermelons.

A bouncer stands outside the door. He's checking IDs. What if—*oh dear...*he'll be looking at her birth date. Looking at the year she was born. 1970. In 1980, she is only ten. How can she get in? And what will she do when he looks at the year the license was issued?

Chapter 3

WITH A TREMBLING HAND, SHE HANDS THE GUY HER license. He's a big, brawny bald guy. Scary-looking. Rae wants to scrunch down low and become invisible, but he only glances at the ID and then hands it back to her with a big smile. Now he looks like a big stuffed teddy bear, except for the fact that he's bald, so his head looks more like a bowling pin—

She needs to go to bed. She has no business being here with this kid when she's already half-delirious, and she hasn't even had a drop of alcohol. What on earth might she say if she takes a drink?

"Do you have a pocket?" Chip asks her as they walk into the club. She snaps out of her crazy dream world and looks at him. Really looks at him. Had she just a few minutes ago thought of him as a cheesy seventies disco guy who might take advantage of her? *Get real, Rae.* The kid looks like perfect little brother material. And he's been nothing but polite to her.

Except he's got those dreamy eyes and that nice, hard body.

"Do I have a pocket?" she repeats. "No. No, I don't." She pats her waist and hips, even though she knows she has no pockets. Why does he care if she has pockets?

"Want me to hold that for you?" He nods toward her license.

"Oh!" She laughs. "Oh. Um." What to do? Not like she can put it in her shoe for a while. She could always slide it down between her breasts, but the hard plastic might kind of hurt. Not to mention that she really doesn't have much cleavage so there really isn't much room to put it between her chest and the elastic of her bra. She looks back up at him and grins. He's the kid, and she's the one acting as if she's never been alone with a guy before.

"Sure," she answers finally. Throwing caution to the wind, she prays that he won't look at her license, and she hands it to him. "Just um…don't lemme forget it."

"Promise." He nods. "Let's get you that drink."

"Let's," she agrees. Chip walks beside her with his hand on her lower back. She thinks she can feel the outline of his fingers hot against her, but she knows she is being ridiculous.

"What do you want?" he hollers to her when they are standing at the bar. Music blares from speakers that must be six feet tall. There are four of them, all up by the sound stage, where a DJ is playing records. Real, vinyl records. Not CDs. Rae makes herself look at Chip. The dance floor is packed, and there are huge groups of people everywhere she looks. Chip has elbowed his way to the bar, dragging her with him, and bypassed several of these groups along the way. No one seems to care. Some of them are sipping on drinks, and some are sort of dancing and talking.

"What do I want?" she repeats. *Brilliant, Rae. Brilliant conversationalist, you are.* She is just about to suggest a piña colada when Chip grins and raises his eyebrows and says, "How about a piña colada?"

They laugh, and suddenly she is in his arms, laughing against his shoulder, and she sees a flash of that cheesy guy in her mind. But Chip does not grope her or kiss her or even whisper in her ear. It is a quiet, private laugh and then the moment is gone, and Chip is ordering them both piña coladas.

"You don't drink beer?" she asks him as he hands her one of the drinks. "Most guys I know would rather drink beer."

More inane chatter. *SHUT UP RAE.*

"I like beer." He shrugs. "I like piña coladas."

She nods as they turn and survey the club.

"And what about rain?" She surprises herself by asking.

"Depends on who I'm with," he answers. The smile on his face is genuine. Almost sweet. "Wanna dance?"

"I do." Another surprise. She does want to dance. With Chip. Right now. She squeals and laughs as he grabs her hand and pulls her toward the dance floor. Her drink sloshes over the plastic cup, but she doesn't care.

The music changes when they are three steps from the dance floor. From Kool and the Gang singing "Ladies Night" to the Atlanta Rhythm Section's "Imaginary Lover." Chip is a good dancer, but again, he is a far cry from the cheesy seventies kind of guy she'd imagined earlier in the car. He's got rhythm, but he's not so smooth that Rae slides right away from him. In fact, she likes dancing with him. They both hold their drinks while they dance, but they can't talk. The music is so loud Rae can feel the thump of the bass in her bones. It's okay, though, because she's not racking up points for scintillating conversation anyway. It feels good to just cut loose and dance and forget that she is stranded twenty years in the past.

Why 1980 and not the Regency period in England? Or medieval times? She's lucky, she supposes. How in heaven's name would she get back to her home if Charlie had dumped her back in Neanderthal time? Then again, if she'd been stranded in the Regency period, she might have met one of those sexy rogues that are always part of the title in the smutty romance novels she used to read when she was in college. But then she wouldn't be drinking a piña colada, either. She might be eating boiled calf liver or something.

"What's wrong?" Chip leans over to yell in her ear.

"Nothing. Why?" She shakes her head. Imagine trying to share this line of thought. Especially the part about time travel.

Rae is exhausted, several songs and two piña coladas later. This has been the most fun she's had in so long, she can't even remember the last time. Chip really is a good dancer, but mostly because he doesn't take himself too seriously. Sometimes when he dances, he kind of looks like a big goofy kid, and that reminds her to step back and rethink the fun and flirting.

He's popular, too. He doesn't drag her off to meet a hundred other people; he only has eyes for Rae, which is sort of exciting and unnerving at the same time. But other people—guys and girls alike—call to him between songs or wave to him on the dance floor. Chip answers each with a friendly smile and a wave, but he is always quick to turn back to Rae.

When it is nearing eleven, Rae can't keep herself from yawning any longer. She tries to drink her fourth piña colada, but she doesn't think she's going to get it down. She either needs to be at home in bed, or she needs to eat. The drinks and the dancing have gone to her head, and the cheeseburger she'd eaten hours ago is long gone.

"You're tired," Chip says when she tries to hide a yawn behind her hand. Rae looks at him, *really* looks at him, and smiles. She can't imagine Paul dressed in jeans and a casual shirt. She can't even imagine Paul without a tie. She can't imagine her hands yanking the tie off of him and then running up over his shoulders as she moves in to kiss him—

She *can* imagine all of the above *and more* with Chip. It's the *and more* that tells her she's definitely had too much to drink. Rae hasn't been intimate with a man in years, and as good as it sounds to her right now, she doesn't want the reason for intimacy to be too much alcohol. Too much fun.

She isn't drunk, though. Relaxed, yes. Intoxicated? No. Besides that, what would be wrong with a few kisses? Chip's lips look incredibly kissable right now as they smile at her. She wonders what the piña coladas would taste like on his lips. On his tongue.

"I am," she answers with a nod. "I'm very tired. I should probably ask you to take me back home now."

"Your wish is my command." He grins and takes their drinks. Rae watches him carry them to the nearest over-flowing garbage can. Her eyes are drawn to his denim-clad butt. She's been watching it all night while they dance. Imagining sliding her hands over it. Now she's hearing that sexy voice saying that her wish is his command, while he kisses her and his hands roam her body.

The world might stop spinning before this night is over. Sensible, serious Rae has never wanted a man like she wants Chip at this moment. Sure that karma is going to stick its foot out and trip her up—what in the world would she do if the world stopped spinning right now and she got stranded in 1980 forever?—she summons the energy to stand and nearly race out the door in front of him.

Darkness lays low over the still crowded parking lot. It hits her as he unlocks her car door for her that her miniature fantasy of him hiking her skirt up to her hips and touching her thigh as he leans in for a kiss has not happened. They are leaving the dance club, she's going to find Charlie, so she can get home—back to 2000—and she's lost her one chance at a decadent, steamy moment with a hot guy.

Kid, Rae!! He's just a kid.

"What're you thinking?" Chip asks. She gasps when he plays with the ends of her hair. She must look a sight. And yet, here's this gorgeous kid looking at her with smoldering eyes as if he wants to eat her for dinner.

"Just...um... that was fun." She clears her throat and smiles uncertainly. "I haven't done that in a long time."

Chip continues to stare at her for several, long moments. His gaze slides from hers, down over her face, and lingers on her lips. Her breath hitches when he leans closer to her and brushes his lips over hers. Rae almost jumps at the jolt his touch gives her. She even wonders if his kiss is that much stronger because she'd stumbled through some time portal earlier. Chip kisses her again, only this time she feels his tongue, warm and velvety soft, against her lip.

When she opens her mouth to protest, to tell him she can't do this, he steps closer to her and slides his arm around her waist. His tongue brushes against hers, and she tastes rum and coconut.

Rae is certain the world has stopped spinning when he breaks the kiss and steps away from her. She is cold where his body had been close to hers, and she is hungry for so much more.

"I've been wanting to do that since I first saw you."

"You have?"

She gives herself a mental kick. *More of the witty dialogue, Rae. Maybe you should just throw caution to the wind and have him make love to you over the hood of his car. Can't be any worse than your conversational skills.*

"There's something about you," he says softly. Before she can move, he leans toward her again and gives her another quick kiss and then he bounds around to his side of the car and flashes her a cute, boyish grin as he unlocks his door.

The evening is so calm and so mild that she hates to get in the car. She hates for this time with Chip to end, and she hates to waste what is left in the car. It would be so much more fun to walk with him under the stars and hold hands and pretend that they could be more than drive by flirts.

It isn't right, though. She's too old for him. And she needs to get back to the house, so she can talk to Charlie as soon as possible. Her life is twenty years in the present; Chip's life is here.

"Are you hungry?" Chip doesn't look at her when he asks her this. Instead, he seems to be paying an awful lot of attention to the road. Avoiding her eyes. She should tell him she's not hungry. She needs to do what is right for both of them.

But what if it's not what's right? Maybe for Chip, it would be best for her to walk away and go back to the year 2000 and let this night be a fun memory for him. He's a kid; he might even forget her by tomorrow. But Rae has to admit to herself that she likes Chip. Of course they've just met, but she *likes* him. He's funny and intelligent, and he likes to dance. He likes piña coladas. Plus he's got sexy eyes, a hot body, and his kisses set her on fire. How unfair is it for her to meet someone that could be the one, when she's meeting him twenty years in the past on a short, accidental trip?

"I am hungry." It's not that she feels she has to be honest with him, more that she doesn't want the night to end yet. How would it hurt for her to grab another bite to eat with him before he takes her back to York Street and hopefully, from there, back to the year 2000?

"How about Boag's?"

Boag's. Rae sinks her teeth into her lower lip. She and her family used to go to there on a regular basis. The waitresses had known her dad's name, and that had irked her mother to no end. They'd known that Dad liked his coffee black, and Mom took cream and sugar. They'd known that Charlie liked sausage links and Rae liked bacon.

Boag's had burned down in 1992. A month after her mom had passed away. Rae has always associated one loss with the other.

"Rae?" Chip finally turns to look at her.

Rae offers up a silent prayer that she will at least get to *see* her parents before she goes back to the future. Maybe she won't get to talk to them. She definitely can't say *hey, I'm Desirae, your daughter*. But if she could just see them one more time before she has to go back, she could carry the memory of them healthy and happy with her back to 2000.

"Sure." She raises her eyebrows in answer to Chip's question. "But I'm gonna owe you a ton of money before the night is through."

"Forget the money," he tells her. "But don't let me forget to give you your license back."

"You're a good dancer." Silence has fallen between them in the car. Not even the radio is on now. Rae remarks on his dancing, because part of her wishes she were still out on the floor dancing with him.

"My sisters." He shrugs. "They made me dance with them all the time."

"I have an older brother. He made me assist him in his crazy science experiments."

"And where is he now?"

Rae laughs softly. Who knows where Charlie is now, besides twenty years in the future? She wonders if he's realized yet that he's sent her back through time.

"He's into medical research. So I guess he put his interest in science to good use."

"My sister, Staci, got married and moved to Key West. I haven't seen her in over a year. And my sister, Lisa, moved to Boston. I don't see her much either."

Rae feels badly for him, but it warms her inside to know that he misses his sisters.

The town passes by in a quiet blur. Rae tries to pay attention, to absorb the details of the current past, but she can't. She's tired, and the alcohol is making her sleepy. What if she does a face plant in a plate of pancakes at Boag's? Nothing quite as sexy as maple syrup in your eyes.

Except maybe maple syrup in your hair.

There are three other cars in the parking lot. Boag's is open until 3 a.m. It was always a hotspot for a quick bite of grease to soak up any alcohol consumed at night. After a wedding reception. After a night at a dance club, apparently. It was always a good place to go after Sunday church, too. That's when her family was here most often, after church, for a heaping breakfast.

An older woman seats them in the back corner of the room. Rae gawks like a little kid, in awe of seeing this place again, after standing with her family and watching the building fall to the flames. Luckily, no one had been hurt in the fire.

They order breakfast to share: fried eggs, sausage links,

bacon, four pancakes, and two slices of toast. Chip drinks milk with his, which further reminds Rae that he is just a kid. He watches her suck soda through her straw and turns up his nose.

"I can't believe you drink Coke with breakfast."

"My mom never let me do it," she answers quietly. "But after she died, Dad didn't say much."

"When did your mother die?" Chip sounds surprised. Rae swallows hard, but the pancakes feel like a solid lump of glue in her stomach. She'd asked him to take her to her parents' house earlier. Well. Maybe that's not so strange. She'd still referred to the house as her parents' house, even right after her mom had passed away.

"Um…" She plays with her egg for a moment. "I was in high school."

"I'm sorry for your loss."

"Thank you." She nods. Her eyes burn with tears, but she will not cry on this kid. She has spilled her soda on herself, stumbled around like a drunk even before she had anything to drink, and probably bored him to death with her conversation. She refuses to cry on him, too. Instead, she makes herself smile and asks him where his sisters learned to dance.

He shrugs and mumbles something about TV shows like *The Pink Lady* and *Solid Gold*.

"Do you have any brothers?" She is determined to think of normal conversation, to keep her mind off her parents who are both gone now, and to keep her mind off how badly she wants to go around the table and dab her tongue in the corner of his mouth to get that tiny little drop of syrup for him.

"No." He studies her face again almost like he's trying to memorize it. "Rae, I don't want this night to end."

"Neither do I, Chip," she answers honestly. "It's been a

lot of fun."

"I wish I had a place of my own." This time she doesn't get the cheesy seventies vibe. This time, when he looks at her like that, she wishes he had a place of his own, too. Or that she could grab his hand and drag him back through the time portal or whatever it is, so he could be with her in the year 2000.

When the food is gone, and Rae feels like her skirt is going to burst open from eating so much, they leave the restaurant. Again, Chip unlocks her car door for her, but he doesn't kiss her. Rae slides into the car and feels the loss settle in around her. It's almost over. She's like Cinderella, and her carriage is about to turn back into a pumpkin. But unlike Cinderella, she will never see Chip—her prince? —again.

She's not sure when it happened, but when Chip parks in front of her parents' house, she realizes they are holding hands. Without a word, he kills the car's engine and gets out. Rae takes a moment to compose herself while he gets her bag from the trunk. And then all too soon, he opens her door and helps her out, and Rae knows she must say goodbye.

He walks her to the door, though, and Rae panics, because she didn't find the key earlier. What if her parents are on vacation? Had they ever gone anywhere without her and Charlie? Who's to say she and Charlie aren't with them? What if they are out of state, and she can't get in? What will she tell Chip? What if Chip leaves?

She'll break a window. If that's the only way into the house, it's what she'll do.

Chip sets her bag down on the small walkway to the back porch. Before she can say a word, he takes her hands in his and tugs her forward for another kiss. This time his lips are demanding and hungry. His fingers remain locked with hers, but Rae is so hot, she wouldn't be surprised if they were all over her, up and down her back and on her hips.

"I want to see you again," he whispers. Words every woman wants to hear from the right man. Words Rae would love to hear from Chip in a different time and place.

She kisses him and says no, she can't see him into his lips, hoping he will not really hear her.

"What?"

"Chip, I can't."

"What do you mean you can't? I thought you had fun tonight."

"I did." She nods. "I had more fun tonight than I've had in a long time." She squeezes his hand. "But I can't. See you again. I'm leaving tomorrow."

"Leaving for where? I'll wait, Rae. I'll be right here waiting."

His kisses drive her wild with need. His hands release hers and then suddenly, she feels his arms around her. His hands splayed on her hips. She is pressed up against him again.

"Chip, I can't," she whispers weakly. "I'm not coming back."

"Where are you going?"

Rae struggles to make her voice work. To find the words to push him away, but her mind is on his hands that have moved from her hips up her sides. His thumb is pressed gently against the side of her breast and all she can think is how it would feel for him to undress her and then clothe her again in his hands.

"I'm too old for you anyway." This time her voice is harsh. She desperately wants his hands on her body. His lips over hers. She wants his body over hers, pressing her into a mattress. Making love to her. She has *never* felt this burning desire for anyone, and the thought of going back to 2000 and Paul leaves her cold and sad.

"I'm twenty-three—"

"I'm too old for you," she repeats. "It wouldn't work anyway, Chip. I really am leaving tomorrow. I'm so sorry."

"Where do you have to go?" He almost looks broken. Rae refuses to believe this night could mean as much to him as it does to her. After all, he is a college kid, and he had a good time tonight and would have whether he'd spent the evening with her or someone named Debbie or Kelly.

"Nowhere you've ever been," she answers vaguely. "I'm so sorry, Chip. I really did have a good time. I'll never forget it."

He draws a ragged sigh and then nods. "Okay. If that's the way it has to be." He kisses her forehead. "Promise me one thing?"

"What?" She needs him to go. To leave. Before some bold side of her personality starts peeling off her clothes and pushes him down to straddle him on the old swing.

"Look me up." His voice is gruff, but he's smiling. "If you ever come back, look me up."

"I will, Chip—"

"Andrews. Chip Andrews." He steps back. "I'll be waiting for you."

She shakes her head. "Don't wait. Promise me that. Don't wait on me."

He stares at her for a moment, gives her a sad, wistful smile, and then turns to walk away. Rae stands completely still and listens to the sound of him starting the car and revving it once and then the sound fades away. And she is alone.

Damn you, Charlie. Set me up with the man of my dreams twenty years in my past.

Chapter 4

THE KEY IS STILL NOT UNDER THE FLOWERPOT, AND THE house is still dark. Is no one home, or are her parents in bed? What to do? Rae studies the dark house for a few moments. She can't just sit outside all night. What would the neighbors think in the morning if they walked outside to go to work and saw her sitting there on her mom's swing? Looking like something the cat dragged in, because Rae is sure she looks exactly like something that a cat would drag in.

But what's the alternative? Break in? Can she really break into her parents' house? And how? They'd hear her if she broke a window. She can't jimmy the door. She's an attorney, for heaven's sake. She has no idea *how* to jimmy a door, and what in the world would she do if the police showed up and arrested her for trying to break into a house?

Rae picks up her bag and throws the strap over her shoulder. With a quick glance around—no one is watching and the whole neighborhood is dark—she sneaks to the back door. *Sneaks.* Why is she sneaking? This is her parents' house, for heaven's sake. Just because they won't know who she is *now* doesn't mean she isn't welcome in their home.

She reaches out and tries the door handle, certain that alarms are going to go off and wake her parents, as well as the rest of the neighborhood. She reminds herself it is 1980, and her parents did not have an alarm system in 1980. Or ever, for that matter. The doorknob is locked, though, as she knew it would be. Frustrated, Rae hangs her head and closes her eyes.

The balmy night is quiet, save for the comforting chirp of the crickets. Funny. If Chip were here and they were sitting under the stars together, Rae would consider this a perfect night even though she is stranded twenty years in the past. But without Chip, the night has suddenly become too quiet and a little bit lonely.

She didn't think she'd had that much to drink, but now she has a headache. Maybe she should have stopped one drink sooner. But she'd been having so much fun dancing with Chip, and she hadn't really stopped to think about how she would handle the rest of this night.

And tomorrow. And maybe even the day after tomorrow, depending on how long it takes her to find Charlie, talk to him, and convince him to *believe* her.

The window. Rae back pedals off the back porch and raises her head, straining to see her bedroom window. Chances are her window is open. All she has to do is climb the tree behind the house and slip inside her open window. *All* she has to do is climb the tree? In her long pencil skirt? And if she makes any commotion at all, she'll wake herself up. And probably her parents, too.

She can't hike her skirt up, climb the tree, and carry her bag on her shoulder all at the same time. With a tired sigh, she hurries back to the porch and sets her bag close to the door. Climb the tree, slip inside her bedroom window, and then sneak back down through the house and out this very door to get her bag. She has to get the bag before her parents get up in the morning and find it.

Once she is standing at the base of the tree, it hits her just how ridiculous this is. How can she climb a tree with these heels on, for heaven's sake? And if she takes them off, she'll tear her feet up on the tree bark. Rae studies the tree, the thick, low branch that she and Charlie used to climb. In spots, it is worn smooth, but mostly, it is rough and it's going to kill her feet. But what choice does she have? She can't sit outside all night, because someone—if not her mom or dad, then a neighbor—will see her in the morning. They'd probably call the police about a homeless woman in the backyard. And then if she tried to explain her situation, they'd put her in a strait jacket and haul her on down to the crazy house.

Tree climbing, it is. Rae looks around again, kicks her heels off, and when she sees no one, she hikes her skirt up as high as she can. Which is pretty high, as slender as her hips are. Not that it matters, because no one of the opposite sex has seen or touched her hips—slender or fat—in years. She raises her arms and finds the grooves where she and Charlie used to hold on and pull themselves up onto the limb. With a big sigh and a big pull, she is squatting on the tree limb, skirt bunched up around her hips.

Each step hurts a little more, as the tree bark bites her bare feet. But it's not a big climb to the roof over the kitchen in the back of the house. If she can make it to the roof, she's home free. Unless there are no windows open.

Don't think about that, she tells herself.

She wonders what Chip is doing and immediately tells herself not to think about him, either. Off-limits. And yet as she moves slowly up the big branch, she can't stop thinking about his smile. About dancing with him. Slow-dancing with him, how nice it felt to be pressed up against him with his arms around her. The taste of the piña coladas on his lips. Her foot slips, and she sucks in a deep breath as she loses her balance and then catches herself. Heart racing, she takes two more big steps and then inches to the end of the limb and climbs up onto the roof.

She swears when the skin on her knees scrapes on the shingles. And again, when she puts her palms flat on the shingles to push herself up and scrapes them, too. *Charlie.* This is all Charlie's fault, and as Rae tiptoes across the roof to Charlie's bedroom, she vows to get even with him when she gets back to the year 2000.

Better to try Charlie's window, since she shouldn't see herself back in time. Well. Probably it'd be okay for her *now* self to see her *past* self, but it might be a disaster if her *past* self would see her *now* self. But it doesn't matter. She's not going to get in by Charlie's window, because it is closed and his drapes are closed, too. She considers tapping on it to get his attention, in case he is at home, but it won't work. Tapping on the screen isn't going to be loud enough to wake him. Charlie could sleep through a hurricane.

Feeling particularly desperate and a little bit childish, Rae crosses her fingers as she makes her way carefully across the roof to her own window. She almost cries with relief when she sees that it is open. Now she just has to remove the screen, which she'd done hundreds of times when she was a teenager, sneaking in and out at night. She pokes her finger around at the bottom of the screen and finds the small tear. Mindful of her younger self sleeping on the other side of the window, she pokes her fingers through the hole in the screen and slides them along until she can feel the little plastic release.

The plastic catches, and Rae breaks her fingernail. She

yanks her hand back to check the damage and cuts her finger in the process.

"Dammit!" Forgetting about the broken nail, Rae presses her lips over the small cut on her finger. She winces at the metallic taste of blood in her mouth. No time to waste, she sticks her fingers back through the hole in the screen. This time she unlocks the screen and slips it out of the window frame. Her curtains are open, but she can't see much without sticking her head in through the window. Startled to see a ten-year-old version of herself asleep in the bed under the window, she jumps back and steps away. Okay. So she's sleeping in there. All Rae needs to do is climb in through that window, move gingerly over the bed —without waking herself—and then sneak out of her bedroom. *No problem.*

She's never been the kind of sleeper that Charlie is, but she sleeps soundly enough that she should be able to do this. And to think she could be with Chip right now. She could still be dancing. Maybe kissing him.

Focus, Rae. She takes a deep breath, and then as gracefully as she can, she climbs through the window one leg at a time. She sits on the window frame, feet on her mattress, and eases the rest of the way through the window. One foot and then the other down to the floor. She teeters over the bed for a moment and then pushes away from the window and stands up straight. For a moment, she stands completely still and stares down at herself, still asleep.

No time to miss her childhood or catalog the details of her old bedroom. Instead, she turns around and moves silently to the door. Thank heavens it's open, because it squeals horribly loud when opened or closed. Feeling like an intruder, Rae moves cautiously down the hall, past her parents' bedroom—she fights the desire to peek in at them —and stops just outside Charlie's bedroom.

No music. No TV. Charlie must not be home, because he'd never have everything turned off at this hour. He's a night owl. Sometimes, he'd be up 'til two in the morning watching TV or reading. *Reading*. Maybe he's here, and he's reading. But she had checked his window just minutes before, and she hadn't seen any lights on. First things first. Get the bag from outside and then come back to Charlie's room. If he's not here, she'll just have to hide until he comes back. Unless she could get lucky and accidentally stumble back through the time portal. She supposes she could go back and wander down Broadway and see if she finds the tear in time.

Or she could make that a last ditch attempt. And pray that Charlie is in his room when she comes back upstairs with her bag in tow. All the way down the steps—and she's careful to skip the second step down completely, because it creaks, and to walk all the way to the right on the seventh step down, because it creaks in the middle—she tells herself how important it is that she focus on the problem at hand. The small details of the house call to her. She is dying to turn on a lamp in the living room and just drink it all in: Mom's afghan that was always folded on the end of the couch, Dad's recliner where he always watched the evening news and *Happy Days* reruns. The framed school pictures of herself and Charlie on the mantle above the fireplace.

No time, she tells herself. She's got no time to waste, and besides, Rae had taken both of her parents' deaths so hard, she fears she could get so caught up in this *remember when* game that she might never get back to her life in the year 2000. As enticing as it sounds—wouldn't it be just a little bit fun to walk your childhood life, as an adult?—she knows she can't stay here. For one thing, she's pretty sure it'd be a really bad thing to let her ten-year-old self see her twenty-nine-year-old self. Nothing like sneaking around for days on end, hoping never to run into herself. Besides that, her life is in 2000. She likes that life. Just because she is dating Paul in her own present and she's never *met* Chip there doesn't mean it's an unfulfilling life. She loves her career. She's joined the ranks of a high-powered law firm. She may never make it to partner, but she doesn't really care. That's society's desire for her, not her own. She's happy with the status quo. Except maybe…

Rae slinks into the kitchen. Almost to her bag. She stubs her toe on the cabinet and hobbles around, one hand clamped over her mouth to hold in any swear words she might like to yell. She looks out the window and thinks about the way Chip had kissed her goodbye earlier. Yes, maybe she needs to make a change when she gets back to her life. No more Paul. There is no fire, and now that she's felt a fraction of that sort of heat, she can't settle for someone bland and comfortable like Paul, and she certainly doesn't want to lead him on.

Okay, she nods and reaches out to touch the doorknob. Get the bag. Get back up to Charlie's room. Hide in the closet until Charlie shows up and then get back home. And tell Paul she doesn't want to see him anymore.

And then what?

How about punching Charlie for this asinine scheme?

She unlocks the door and leans out to get her bag. Okay. Now back to Charlie's room—she hopes he is back soon, because the thought of hiding out in her fourteen-year-old brother's closet scares her—and hopefully back to her real life.

Rae turns back to the kitchen but reaches back to make sure the door is locked again. Her heart hammers extra hard when she hears footsteps upstairs. *Someone is up!*

She holds her breath and prays that whoever it is is just

up for a quick trip to the bathroom. If someone wants a drink or a late snack, she's toast. It seems to take an eternity, but finally she hears footsteps and the sound of someone settling back into bed. Nope. Definitely not a good idea to get stuck in 1980 and have to dodge everyone or offer a ridiculous explanation if she's caught.

On tiptoe, Rae inches her way back through the kitchen and into the living room. She could hide in comfort in the basement. Maybe even catch a few zzz's on the couch or even watch the news in the morning.

But first she has to go upstairs and make sure Charlie isn't home. She has got to talk to Charlie. Numero Uno priority. She is almost to the steps when something catches her eye. A tiny sliver of streetlight shines through the crack in the heavy brocade curtains on the living room picture window. The streetlight falls directly over a small pottery bowl she'd made when she was in second grade. Her mom had acted as if she was a brilliant artist, and she'd kept the bowl on display in the living room. Rae knows that her father had left it there, years later, when her mother died, but somehow when *he* died, the bowl disappeared.

Rae picks it up and studies it. It is bumpy, and the painted flowers on it are sloppy and unattractive. But it's not the artistry of the bowl that touches her. It's the memory of how her mom had praised her work. In that moment, she misses her mom so much her stomach hurts. The thought of Chip and the uncertainty of her future are gone, and all she thinks of is her parents. If only she could sneak into their bedroom and watch them sleep. Just for a moment or two.

Would they miss the bowl? If she took it now and slid it into her bag to take back to the future with her, would they notice? Well, of course her mom would. She hates that it disappears after her dad's death, though. She wishes she could have it as a keepsake.

Maybe she could have Charlie send her back again to take the bowl. After her mom has been gone for a while. Maybe then no one would notice. If it's that easy, she thinks as she climbs the steps—careful of the creaky ones —maybe she could just time jump whenever she feels like seeing her family. She could go to a thrift store in the year 2000 and buy some clothes from this era so she is dressed properly. Then she could pretend to be a stranger. Someone dropping in to sell encyclopedias or something.

The thought makes her unbearably sad, so she forces her mind to stop. Stop offering up possibilities and memories. She just has to get through this until she can talk to Charlie and convince him to *send her back*. Once back in her real life, surely, everything will feel normal again.

She doesn't look into her parents' room. Not even for a second. She goes right past their room and stops at Charlie's door. And sticks her head inside. Okay, so it's dark, and it's hard to tell if he's in his bed. She doesn't think so, but she needs to check. She starts the trek across his room and nearly screams when her foot gets caught up in a pile of clothes. Knowing Charlie, dirty clothes. It's frightening, really, to consider just how dirty those clothes are.

When she is standing over the bed, she can see that it is made. There is no one lying in it, but she leans over and pats it just the same. Pillows. Blankets. No Charlie. *Is* he at camp? She will not survive this, if he is at camp, and he'll be gone another several days. She'll go stark raving mad, sneaking around this house, trying to avoid bumping into anyone. Especially when there is a tiny part of her that *wants* to bump into someone.

With a sigh, Rae opens Charlie's closet door—thank goodness it doesn't squeal—and slips inside. In the dark, she squats and then settles to the floor. Immediately she smells something, though she must admit it's not unpleasant. Something rich and heady. Cologne? Charlie was wearing cologne at fourteen? Did he have a girlfriend, or was he just out to impress any girl?

The thought makes her smile, and she leans back against the wall to sleep, thoughts of Charlie looking for a girlfriend filling her head.

Chapter 5

CHARLIE DOES NOT COME HOME THE NEXT DAY. AS LONG AS Rae hears movement outside his room, she does not leave his closet. When she hears her parents discussing *people these days,* she pushes the closet door open just a smidge so she can hear the conversation. They are irritated with young kids. Making out wherever the mood strikes them. Leaving their belongings wherever they discard them. And this in her mother's voice—*what kind of woman would wear that kind of shoe anyway?*—and that's when Rae realizes though she'd collected her bag and computer the other night, she'd forgotten her shoes. She'd left her heels at the base of the tree she'd climbed to sneak into the house.

So now she's homeless, barefoot, hiding out (illegally?), starved, and dying for something more than the apples she's snitched from the kitchen when the house has gone quiet, and she's prayed that no one was home.

What to do? And where is Charlie?

The house is quiet now. She'd heard her younger self tell her parents goodbye, but she has no idea where she's gone. Or where her parents are. Rae wants to take a shower. And she really would like to change her clothes, but she has nothing to change into. She could go buy something, but she isn't sure where they put her shoes. Maybe she should go take a look. Hiding out like this might be a bit more bearable if she could slip into some more comfortable clothes.

For that matter, she could get a hotel room. Why hadn't she thought of that earlier? A hotel room. A hot shower. A change of clothes. And something to eat. Well, she'd been so focused on finding Charlie, she hadn't thought beyond that. If she's not hanging around the house, she'll never know when Charlie is here, and Charlie is the key to getting back to the year 2000.

But if she can find her shoes, she could leave for a while. She could go to Kmart—the thought makes her shiver—she could go to the mall, she amends, (she can't remember if it exists in 1980) and buy herself a pair of jeans and a normal top and some tennis shoes. That'd be a good start. Get a hotel room long enough to take a long, hot shower and then maybe even stretch out and take a nap. And then come back and look for Charlie again.

There's a name for women who rent hotel rooms for the afternoon, and she certainly isn't that kind of woman. But if she is completely alone, how could anyone make that assumption about her? Besides, if Charlie doesn't come home soon, she will need to find an alternative place to stay. What in the world would she do if her mom decided to clean Charlie's closet out and yanked open the door only to find her hiding in here?

With that matter settled, Rae stands and groans when every bone in her body snaps and pops. *Time travel*, she thinks and shakes her head. Why *her* brother? This kind of stuff isn't supposed to happen in real life.

Her legs protest as she moves cautiously out of Charlie's room and makes her way down the hall to the steps. So far, so good. Seeing the house in daylight still takes her breath away. How many times since her dad died has she tried to conjure up the living room or the kitchen? And how disconcerting for her now to see that in her memory, she's always had something just a little off.

The heels she'd worn the day she fell into this year are sitting on the kitchen floor by the garbage can. She's so happy to see them, she almost cries. What a sorry state she is in if these heels have become her ticket to momentary freedom. She steps into them and winces, her feet still sore from climbing the tree.

Money. She can use a credit card to pick up another outfit, but what about food? Do grocery stores take credit cards in 1980? She doesn't want to take the risk. No scenes. She wants to blend right in with everyone else. She kicks off the shoes and quickly runs back up the steps. Charlie owes her. If it weren't for Charlie, she wouldn't be in this predicament. And she can always pay him back when she gets back to her present.

Good thing she knows where he keeps his cash stashed. Back into the closet she goes. Charlie had always done odd jobs around the neighborhood, and he'd always been a saver. But Rae is still surprised when she sees the bills hidden in his Nike shoebox. She grabs forty dollars, whispers an apology to her brother, and then hurries back downstairs. As scared as she is about being caught by her family, it feels good to have a plan. To be doing something, rather than just waiting for Charlie to come home and rescue her.

Rae remembers walking to the mall from her house when she was a kid, just not how old she was when she'd done it. Didn't seem like it should be a long walk, but today, after two nights of sleeping in a sitting up position in her brother's closet, existing only on apples and crackers, and teetering on these damned heels, it's a long walk. The bag on her shoulder is heavy and uncomfortable, and more than once she thinks about pitching it. The laptop and her cellphone are doing nothing for her right now, but the fact that she'll need them when she gets home is the only thing that keeps her from tossing the whole bag into the nearest trash can.

The mall in 1980 is quite different than the mall where she shops now. Rather than waste time looking in stores like Foxmoor—after all, she is twenty-nine-years old, and she still *looks* it, no matter that in reality she is ten and Foxmoor is one of her favorite stores in 1980—she goes straight to JC Penney. It's warm out, but it's not horribly hot, so she buys two pair of blue jeans, a white t-shirt and a yellow t-shirt, underwear, two bras—all plain white, like her mother would wear—and socks and a pair of simple white Keds. Again, just like her mother would wear. She's not out to impress anyone. She just wants to be comfortable until she can get home.

Feeling like an idiot, she puts on a pair of socks and the Keds when she leaves the mall. She tosses her heels in the garbage can and only wonders for a moment what her parents will say when they see that the shoes are gone from their kitchen. Hopefully each will think the other got rid of them. Her next stop is the Krogers in the strip mall next to the shopping mall. The Krogers has just closed in the year 2000, and it makes her feel a little funny walking into the building and seeing some of the young people who will probably work there long enough that they will lose their jobs when the store closes. She buys fresh grapes and cheese and then decides maybe she should save some of her money—okay, *Charlie's* money—to go out. She needs a meal. Real food. Served hot. New plan, she decides. Get a hotel room, do the hot shower, and then go out for a dinner and then back to the hotel for that long nap. And finally back to the house to see if Charlie is back yet.

"I wouldn't have pegged you for the health food type."

The familiar voice behind her in the checkout lane raises goose bumps down her arms. *Chip.* Though she's thought about him a lot, and okay—let's be honest—*fantasized* about him while she was stuck in Charlie's closet, she hasn't really thought about running into him again. He's a college student, for heaven's sake. She shouldn't have to worry about running into him when she's out buying Keds or grapes or looking for a hotel room.

"Chip." She looks up at him over her shoulder and smiles at him. She's happy to see him, but the look on his face tells her he certainly doesn't feel the same way. He gives her a small, tight smile.

"Rae." He nods. Rae winces when his eyes do a small sweep of her body and take in the fact that she's wearing Keds with the same suit she'd been wearing two days ago when she'd first run into him. She looks like the female executives at work who put on their tennis shoes with their skirts and nylons to go walking at lunchtime.

But what does she look like to Chip? Still in the suit she was wearing the other night, her hair is a mess, she has no makeup on, and she hasn't had a real shower—she's only been able to freshen up in the bathroom at her parents' house—she must look a sight to him. Homeless. She really must look homeless. And strictly speaking, maybe she *is* currently homeless.

She's carrying her shopping bag from Penney's, and of course, Chip notices that. What must he be thinking? He has to think she is either a true head case, or else he is able to overlook her disheveled appearance—yes, she's vain enough to hope he is doing exactly that—and wonder why she lied to him about leaving town the other day.

When the checkout girl gives her a total, she pulls out some of the cash she'd borrowed from Charlie to pay her. She realizes as she hands the girl the money that she owes Chip for the burger the other night.

"Um. I found some cash," she says quietly. She turns toward him, intending to give him a ten dollar bill. "I hope a ten will cover it."

But he shakes his head and holds his hand up palm out. "It's okay." He sets his loaf of bread and jar of pickles on the conveyer belt and shrugs without looking at her. "I'm not much into health food," he tells her and for a moment, she is lost, "so it probably wouldn't have worked out anyway."

The song. He is still referring back to the piña colada song. It doesn't make her smile this time, though. In fact, it makes her sad.

"Chip, I—"

"Don't." He shakes his head again. "Just don't."

With a lump the size of a boiled egg in her throat, she nods again, picks up her small bag of groceries, and walks out of the store. Her vision blurs as she steps outside. She knows it's not something in the air. Seeing Chip again, no —*Chip's reaction to seeing her again*—makes her feel guilty and sad. Not a good combination. Not when she really did like him, and she really does have to go, and now he thinks she just flat out lied to him.

She's still standing there thinking when he walks out of the store behind her. She is on Thirtieth Street. She needs to head down about twenty-five blocks west to find a hotel. Maybe she should get a taxi.

Chip sighs and looks around the parking lot. "Do you need a ride?"

She wants to say yes. She wants to just go with him and forget this headache she's found herself in. But going with him now will only prolong the goodbye, and it didn't go so well the first time around.

"No, thanks," she answers softly. "I'm fine."

Chip hesitates, and Rae wants to give him a gentle little push to get him moving. She doesn't want him to witness her trudging across the parking lot. She's embarrassed enough already, and she's saddened that she'd had so much fun with Chip a few nights ago, and now he thinks she is a liar, and he doesn't want to be around her.

"Are you sure?"

Rae clears her throat and finally meets his eyes. He raises his eyebrows expectantly, but she smiles and shakes her head. "Thank you anyway."

Chip shrugs, as if to say *suit yourself*. She watches him walk away, waits until he gets into his Camaro and drives out of the parking lot before she begins her trek west on Broadway.

———

THE HOTEL ROOM IS SUITABLE. RAE IS SO TIRED FROM ALL the walking today that she thinks she'd be happy with a cot and a blanket, even if she had to sleep on that cot out under the stars. Just as long as she can stay hidden from her family, from anyone who knows her a little bit longer. She checks in after two in the afternoon and strips her suit off as she makes her way to the bathroom. As she runs the shower and lets the tiny room fill with steam, she throws the suit away and dumps the new clothes she'd bought out on the bed.

Standing in the lacey pink bra and panties she'd thought were sexy just days ago, she quickly yanks the tags off of her purchases. She can't wait to stand under the hot shower spray and then put on the new clean clothes, even if the bra and panties are standard issue. Tags torn off and the bathroom hot and steamy, Rae peels the rest of her clothing off.

Normally she hates hotel showers, and she is in and out as quickly as possible. However, there is nothing normal at this moment in her life, and the hot water feels much too good for her to want to hurry in and out. Instead, after she soaps her hair and body and rinses until her hair is squeaky clean, she lingers under the hot spray until it grows cold. She turns the water off and towels herself dry, slathers on lotion that she'd picked up at Kmart and shimmies into the bra and panties and then collapses onto the bed. Within minutes she is asleep.

When she wakes, it is after six and her stomach is growling. Time for that dinner she'd thought about earlier. She dresses in a pair of the blue jeans and the white shirt and then quickly pulls her hair back into a ponytail. Where can she go where she won't run into Chip? Really, it's a big enough town that she should be able to go just about anywhere and *not* run into him. As long as she stays away from the college bars.

She decides on the Coach House, a local sit down restaurant that she and Charlie used to beg their parents to take them to. They'd never had much luck though, so Rae isn't worried that she will see her family there. The long nap did her a world of good, and even though she'd walked all over town earlier today, she feels energized and ready for the walk to the restaurant.

Rae is relieved to see only a few cars in the parking lot. Her legs and feet hurt, so she is happy that she'll be able to sit down and relax over a nice dinner. As the door closes, a cool hush engulfs her. She almost shivers in the air-conditioning. The hostess leads her to a small table for two and leaves her with a menu and a promise that someone named Janet will be with her shortly.

The empty chair across from her mocks her. Might be kind of fun to sit here and have a real dinner with Chip. Real conversation, not piña colada talk. A wave of guilt rushes her. Why would she sit here and think about Chip? What about Paul for heaven's sake? She is dating Paul in the year 2000. Paul must be frantically worried about her by now. She's been gone two nights, and she's not available by phone. Charlie is probably worried sick about her, too.

Charlie she can take care of. Once she eats dinner, she will go back to her parents' house on York and hide out again and pray that Charlie will be home tonight. There really isn't much she can do about Paul. Not at the moment, anyway. True, after this adventure she's sure she and Paul really have no future together, but she needs to tell him that. Rae has never been the type of woman to lead a man on.

And *Chip*. Well, it might be fun to sit here and talk to Chip, and it might not. He's just a kid, and he's a college kid at that. Probably living from party to party. Nothing in common, really, just a strange night and a few piña coladas. It's good that he was with her the first night she was stuck here in 1980, but it's good that they've left it at that. Better for both of them.

Janet takes her order—fried chicken and a baked potato—and then brings her a glass of tea. The ice has already melted, but Rae drinks it anyway. It is refreshing and cold, and Rae's stomach growls at the thought of the dinner she's ordered. There are three other tables currently occupied. Although Rae doesn't know any of the people at the tables, she stays alert while she waits for her dinner and then while she's eating. She wonders if the people think she is rude for staring, and for a moment, she wishes she'd have brought a book or a magazine to leaf through. And yet, if she were reading or even just thumbing through a magazine, she would be less alert to other diners.

Just as she is about to finish her dinner, she hears a familiar voice at the door of the restaurant. Though she can't place it—it isn't Chip and it isn't anyone in her family —it's familiar, all the same. Forgetting that she *looks* different as a twenty-nine-year old woman than she did as a ten-year-old girl and forgetting that most people are not going to look at her and automatically suspect that she is Rae Warner, who has traveled back through time, Rae almost swallows her fork when her fourth grade teacher walks into the restaurant. Mrs. Mixer looks so different in a pair of jeans and a casual knit top, Rae finds it hard not to stare. There's some sort of voyeuristic thrill in seeing an adult as an equal, rather than someone in an authority position. Rae squirms in her seat when a tall, dark-haired man follows Mrs. Mixer to a table. Must be her husband. Rae had never seen him back when Mrs. Mixer was her teacher. He's nice-looking. The thought of Mrs. Mixer with a man awakens the curiosity in Rae. What's he like? What's *she* like? What does this woman like to do outside of the classroom?

Mrs. Mixer glances casually around the dining room. Almost caught, Rae drops her gaze and studies her plate. She has to get out of here. No, Mrs. Mixer isn't going to see her and ask her just what she's doing here without her parents. And yet, what if Mrs. Mixer looks at her and sees something just a little bit familiar? Wouldn't it be better just to avoid that situation completely? Besides, it's time to get going. Time to see if she can find Charlie.

When Janet brings her ticket, Rae jumps to her feet and steps on the back of the woman's shoe. "Sorry," she mumbles. Janet smiles uncertainly at her, and suddenly Rae panics and wonders if Janet might recognize her. What if Janet had waited on her family before and recognized Rae as little Desirae Warner?

Get a grip, Rae. Not going to happen. No one in 1980 is going to recognize you. Not even Charlie. You're going to have to do quite the song and dance to get Charlie to believe you are his sister.

Still, it's a relief for her to pay her bill and get outside. It's warm, not hot, and the evening sun feels good on her arms. The restaurant and her worries have left her a bit chilled. She's miserably stuffed—she shouldn't have eaten the last few bites—and the only thing that sounds like a good idea is another long nap. But she doesn't have time for that. She needs to get to her parents' house. Maybe once she gets there and hides away in Charlie's closet she can get some rest.

Chapter 6

IT STRIKES HER, AS SHE WALKS UNDER GORGEOUS TREES and across old-fashioned brick sidewalks, that Quincy is a beautiful town. She'd liked it here as a child, and that's why she'd chosen to come back after college. Most of her friends hadn't made that choice. Most of her current friends—the ones in the year 2000—are people she's met on her job. Loneliness settles in her chest as she nears her parents' house. She's been so busy in her year 2000 job that she's forgotten how she misses both parents and the friends she'd gone to grade school and high school with.

The front door is open. Rae's heart skips a beat when she sees her Mom on the front porch. She longs to go to her and talk, but what in the world could she say? She can't tell her mom who she is. And she can't just approach her, as a stranger, and strike up a conversation. Even in 1980, people in this neighborhood didn't do that. It will look funny, too, if Rae just stands on the corner watching the house.

The sun has baked the restaurant chill from her, and now Rae feels sweat on her lower back. She sighs. This is so hard. *Dammit, Charlie, what the hell do I do?* And then as if her mom understands her predicament, she gets up and goes inside the house. Okay, so maybe this is her chance. She can at least sneak around to the backyard and hide. But where? Dad keeps the garage locked unless he's in it. And if he's in the garage, she can't hide there anyway.

The tree. *The tree? Really?* Can she climb the tree and stay out of sight until later in the evening, when her parents retire for the night? Before she can make a move, her mom comes outside to sit on the porch again. Rae heaves a sigh of frustration.

Suddenly she is aware of a car idling at the curb. Hot and distracted by her frustration, she turns to look at the car intending to ask the driver what the hell he wants. Seeing the '79 Camaro and Chip behind the wheel sends a jolt straight to her heart.

She narrows her eyes at him and slinks over to lean in the passenger window.

"What are you doing here?" The words come out like a hiss, and Rae figures it's appropriate because she's suddenly mad as a snake. Chip had driven over here, intending to go to her parents' house, looking for her. How in the world would she explain that? To her parents—who are currently complete strangers to her—or to Chip?

"I was going to stop at your parents' house to talk to you," he answers simply. "But now I'm kind of wondering why you appear to be sneaking around—"

"You've got a lotta nerve!" She leans further into the window of the car. All the anxiety and worry from the last few days explode inside her. A little fight with someone like Chip might be kind of fun right now.

"I've got nerve?" He looks taken aback. "Whaddaya mean I got nerve? What're you doing loitering around the neighborhood?"

"Maybe I was taking a walk," she answers quickly.

"How come I didn't see you go inside the other night? You couldn't find a key, and no one was home so you couldn't get inside. You know what I think, Desirae?"

"No. What do you think?" She can't help herself. She wants to know what he's thinking. Maybe hearing someone else's thoughts will help her get some perspective. Except not really, because no one in 1980 is going to understand or believe that she is here from twenty years in the future.

"How about we go for a drive?"

"I can't go for a drive. I'm waiting on Charlie—"

"You were waiting on—" he lifts his hands here and makes quotation marks in the air—"*Charlie* the night I met you. And now you're still waiting on—" again with the finger quotes—"*Charlie.*"

Rae stares at him with a slight frown, wondering when the fake quotes thing became cool. She's pretty sure it wasn't 1980.

"I'm busy, Chip," she finally tells him. "You need to go."

"What? Are you busy casing the house? You got a partner, waiting in the wings? Waiting for those unsuspecting people to go somewhere, so you can hit the house—"

"Are you crazy?" she yelps. "Those people are my parents! And I am waiting on Charlie, my brother. I need to talk to Charlie."

"Why don't you go sit on the porch with your mom then? Wait with her? You could chat about the weather. Or about her day."

"Why do you care?" Rae asks calmly. "I mean, what's it to you if I wait here or there? What difference does it make to you?"

"I just don't wanna see those people get hurt, because some big city girl and her partner have plans to—"

"Again with the big city girl?" Rae shakes her head. "Chip. I get that you're angry with me for blowing you off the other night—"

"I'm not angry—"

"Well, you're something, because you aren't letting this go, and you should. It's past time for you to let this go." She purses her lips and studies his face. "We had fun, yes. A few dances, a few drinks. Okay. Good time. End of story."

"How about the kisses?"

"What about the kisses?" Rae has to look away from him when she says this. Because the kisses were pretty damned good. In fact, that last one had been a scorcher, and she'd dreamt about what kind of follow through Chip might have, and those kinds of thoughts are certainly going to get her nowhere.

A young girl is riding her bike up the sidewalk. Toward her. Rae's heart hammers in her chest when she realizes it is her ten-year-old self riding toward her. Afraid that her two selves seeing each other eye to eye might put some sort of rift in time, Rae glances at Chip and dives headfirst into his car.

"What the—"

"Drive."

"What?" Chip grabs her ponytail, but Rae refuses to look up.

"Just drive."

Chip pulls away from the curb with Rae still upside down in the front seat. She hears the whir of the ten-speed as her younger self passes the car. Chip drives down the block as Rae scrambles to right herself in the front seat.

"If I get a ticket for not having a seatbelt on, you're paying for it," she mutters as she manages to pull her legs into the car and finally push herself up to a sitting position. Her ponytail is crooked and loose.

"Why would you get a ticket for not having your seat-belt on?" Chip asks suspiciously.

Rae opens her mouth to explain, but remembering that the seatbelt law was passed in the late '80s, she closes it without a word and shakes her head. "Nevermind."

He glances at the street in front of him but looks back at her and stares long enough to make her uncomfortable.

"Where are you taking me?" she finally asks him. He drives in silence for what feels like a long time, but in truth is probably no more than a minute or two. What if he's a psycho? Were there psycho people in the '80s? Well, yeah. How about Charles Manson? He was way *before* the '80s. What if this isn't safe? Maybe she shouldn't have gone to that club with Chip or danced with him or had a drink with him. Or kissed him.

"Where are you taking me?" she repeats, already feeling the heat from the memory of the kiss.

"You told me to drive," he reminds her.

"Well, I didn't mean to drive forever. I just meant—" Rae catches herself. What can she say that won't sound suspicious? *Drive until we get away from that block? Drive, so that girl won't see me?*

"I think we need to have a little talk," Chip tells her.

"I really, really need to get back to my parents' house. I need to talk to Charlie."

"Who's Charlie?" he asks and pretends to be confused. But Rae knows he is trying to trip her up.

"Why are you driving west? Where are you going?"

"Who's Charlie?"

"My brother," she answers.

"So you said." He nods. Rae fights the urge to scream in frustration, not fear. "And who was the girl on the bike?"

Rae swallows hard and raises her eyebrows as if to say *you got me*. "What girl on the bike?"

"The one you dove in here to get away from."

"I don't know her," Rae answers softly.

"You're not a very good liar," he mumbles. "Can't believe you're the front man on your job."

"I'm not on any job," she insists. "I just need to talk to Charlie. That's all. I swear." With a sigh, she lays her head back against the seat and remembers that her ponytail is crooked. Lovely. She must look as sexy as a train wreck.

"I thought you were leaving."

"I am."

"Mm-hmm." He nods, keeps his eyes on the road and the traffic. The sun is setting, and the purple and pink tendrils unfurled over the horizon catch her eye. Why can't Chip live in 2000? Why can't Paul be a bit more exciting? Is she just destined to be an old maid? "So you were leaving. Except that I ran into you at the grocery store. Buying groceries. Which seems to indicate that you aren't leaving. And then I find you on the corner of the street where your so-called parents live. When exactly *are* you leaving, Rae? Next year?"

"I just need to talk to Charlie first." The fight has drained out of her. She wiggles the pony holder in her hair and gently pulls it loose. He watches her work her fingers through her hair and shake it out.

"Nothing personal," he says with a shrug. "Just a few drinks and a few kisses and you gotta talk to Charlie and then head out of town."

"Yeah." She nods and glances at him. "That's pretty much it."

Quinsippi Island? He turns the Camaro into the river-front park. She hasn't seen the island in years, even though she's lived here most of her life. It used to be a fun, well-loved park with a petting zoo and small amusement rides. Now, *well—in the year 2000—*it's not really anything. A park with a shelter house. A place to maybe drink or make out, though she doubts that. There's no petting zoo anymore, no amusement rides, not even a swing set or a merry-go-round.

"Chip?" She sits up straight and turns to look at him. "What're we doing here? I need to go—"

Before she can move, before she knows what hits her, he leans over and gently presses his lips to hers. She'd been poised to fight, but with just the touch of his lips on hers, she is ready to skip that and just make up. Chip dodges her when she tries to kiss him.

"Do college people really come down here to make out?" she asks disbelievingly. There are no other cars in sight.

"Are you always so insulting?"

"Insulting? How is that insulting? Assuming you want to make out with me? That's insulting?"

"You know what I want," he answers. "But I find it insulting that I am lumped in a group of *college people* that wants to make out. Did I come off that way the other night?"

"You did kiss—"

"I kissed you, yes. But did I come off as a partying college kid who just wanted to—"

"Well." Rae shakes her head. "*No,*" she admits.

"We need to talk."

Rae leans her head forward and rubs the back of her neck. "Look, Chip. I'm sorry. Any other time, I would like this. You're a nice guy. And you're fun to talk to. But it isn't going to work. I don't belong here. I have a life somewhere else, and I need to get back to it—"

"Where?"

"What?"

"Where's your other life?" he asks calmly. "Where? Chicago? Los Angeles?"

"No. It's not like that—"

"Then what's it like?"

Rae sighs and pulls her door open. She gets out of the car and stands facing the river. She can see the water. It could be a beautiful night if other circumstances were different.

"I'm seeing someone else—"

"Is it like you're from the future or something?"

Startled, she looks over her shoulder. She hadn't heard Chip get out of the car. He's standing right behind her now. And he'd asked her—

Oh God. He'd asked her if she's from the future.

"What?" She tries to laugh it off. "What did you say? Why would you say that?" She's sweating bullets now and wishing she could just talk to Charlie and get the hell back to the year 2000. What're the rules? What are the rules of time travel? She has no idea. No flipping idea if she's supposed to lie through her teeth or give up the truth. She's pretty sure that letting her ten-year-old self in on the secret would be disastrous. But what about other people? What if someone else figures it out?

She almost laughs at the thought of time coming to a screeching halt. The earth stopping. People frozen in time. All because of her. Because she messed up the first time travel mission she accidentally fell into.

And what would set time back into motion then? A sneeze? A direct order? Getting down on her knees and making a sacrifice to the sun? Hadn't Charlie seen how inept she would be with this stuff? This crap is for sci-fi movies, not real life.

"Seriously, Chip, why would you say that?"

"Maybe because your license," he whips it out of his pocket as if he's been holding it there all day, "says it was issued in the year 1999. And right now, it's 1980."

Rae freezes, stares at him with wide eyes. What should she say? What do you say to that? Do you admit it? *Admit it. Admit it and have Chip haul my butt off to the psych ward? Deny it. Okay, yeah. Deny it, Rae.* She'd been Snow White in her third grade school play. She hadn't won any acting awards, but maybe she could dig deep enough to pull this off.

"What? My license says it was issued in 1999?" She laughs as if it's the craziest thing she's ever heard. "Are you serious?"

"Oh, I'm serious."

"Oh my God." She continues to laugh and then shakes her head. "Guess somebody made a big mistake, huh?"

"Did they? Make a mistake?"

Chip is so calm and so smooth, it is maddening. Rae takes a quick breath, careful not to be too obvious about it. *Don't panic.* Oh, she's panicking, all right. This is bad. This is very bad. Why couldn't she have just found Charlie and talked to him that first night and had him send her back to the future? The thought makes her giggle. Not a laugh this time, but a giggle. She looks around, wondering if Michael J. Fox might appear out of nowhere to talk to her. Maybe she's dreaming. Maybe she's dreaming that she's in a movie, another sequel to the *Back to the Future* movies. Any minute now she'll wake up and everything will be fine.

And dull. No life. Zippo. She has no life in the year 2000. Oh sure, she's a successful attorney. Okay, *moderately* successful. She makes enough money to pay the rent on her cute little apartment. To make the payments on her '99 Honda Civic. To dress nice. Yeah, okay, Rae, she tells herself. You do okay on the career and money front.

But where is the excitement? The passion? The fun? Where is the fun that you had with Chip the other night?

One night? You're going to judge your life on one fun night with a college kid? You don't even know him, Rae!

"Well, of course it's a mistake, Chip!" Even to her own ears, her laugh sounds forced and fake. "How can my license have been printed in 1999, if we're standing here in 1980? I think time travel is just for science fiction movies."

"Is that what you think?" he asks her.

Okay, his calm questions are driving her crazy. He's got her completely on edge, and he's just toying with her. This isn't fair. When did he get the upper hand here? *Enough of this, Rae. Take control and fast forward to home. To Charlie.*

This isn't real. Even if she really *is* here from the future, this whole situation is *surreal*, and she desperately wants her life back to normal. Even if that means life without Chip.

"Look, I'm—"

Before she can say that she's sorry, Chip is looming over her and sliding his arms around her waist. Those lips again. No piña colada today, but the kiss is nice, just the same. More than nice. In fact, Rae squirms in his arms as she feels the flames of desire ignite inside her. Her hands betray her and begin to climb his arms and her fingers dig into his muscles. Soft, supple skin over taut muscles. She tangles her fingers in the curls at the nape of his neck and lays the other hand flat against his hard, chiseled jaw. The beginnings of a beard tickle her fingers.

Her fingers creep toward his lips, the lips that are still locked with hers. A jolt of electricity zaps her when suddenly his lips are gone from hers and he's sucking her finger into his mouth.

"Chip!" she gasps. She's ready. If he flung her down on the hood of his car, she probably wouldn't protest. They are pressed middle to middle, and Rae could swear Chip feels the same way. But instead of manhandling her—she has to admit that at this very moment, it sounds very sexy —and taking her on the hood of the Camaro, Chip simply kisses each of her fingers, as chaste as a father tucking in his little girl at night, and steps away from her.

"Let's get you back home so you can talk to Charlie."

He is still maddeningly calm. So calm that Rae can not read anything else in his voice. Sincerity? Sarcasm? Anger? She doesn't know what he is thinking. Her insides still quake like Mount St. Helen as Chip escorts her back to the passenger door of the Camaro.

Moving on rote memorization—she can't be bothered with *really* thinking about sliding into the car and pulling the car door shut, not when she's revved up so tight she feels that just one touch would launch her to the stars—she gets into the car and watches as Chip rounds the front of the car and gets in the driver's side.

Without a word to her, he starts the car and turns on the radio. Andy Gibb's voice jumps at her. "Shadow Dancing." Rae turns away from Chip when Andy's words surround them.

Chip puts the car in gear and zips back across the one-lane bridge. Back to the mainland. Back to reality. Except not really. None of this is reality. Rae stares blankly out the window as they drive. She is tired. Deep down bone tired. This might have been an adventure in the beginning. Maybe it still could be for the right person. But right now, she just wants to go home. To her apartment. To sit on her tiny little patio and soak up the sounds of the year 2000.

"So what's his name?" he asks her.

"What?" Startled, Rae turns to look at him. "What's whose name?"

"You said earlier that you were seeing someone. What's his name?"

"Paul," she answers quietly. "Paul Bailey." Again she turns toward the window. This time Chip leaves her alone. She watches the streets and the stoplights go by, but she doesn't really notice them. She doesn't stir until Chip pulls over and lets the car idle at the same corner where he'd picked her up not even an hour before.

"I hope you find Charlie," he says softly. He turns sideways in his seat to look at her. "And I wish you and Paul every happiness."

He sounds sincere, but Rae is still suspicious and confused. Turning in her seat to look at him, she pulls her ponytail holder from her wrist and then gathers her hair and puts it up in a messy tail.

"That's it, then?"

"What do you mean? That's what?"

"You come back and find me and kiss me like that, and that's it?"

"What else should there be?"

"I don't know," she admits. "But this feels weird."

"You gotta find Charlie. You gotta talk to Charlie and go back to Paul."

"What about you?"

Chip shrugs and shakes his head. "I'm not seeing anyone."

"No." Rae studies her hands in her lap. "I mean, what're you gonna do now? What do you do on summer nights like this? Surely you're not in school now."

"Actually, I am taking a summer class," he answers. "But right now, I'll probably go back to my apartment and read. Maybe catch a baseball game on TV."

"Do you go to the club much?" She hates asking. She hates sounding like a jealous little girl when she *does* ask.

But she wants to know. She wants to know if Chip is a regular with the club scene. If he's a player. Although she's not sure what will hurt the most. If he is a player and she is just another notch on his belt—although a couple of smoking hot kisses don't really count—or if he is a more serious guy and maybe she was a little bit special to him.

"Not really." He plays with his keys that still hang from the car ignition. "I go now and then with some friends. But it's really not my scene."

She raises her eyebrows, pretty sure it hurts more knowing that she might have been a little special to him.

"Look," she says quietly, "it's complicated. I had fun with you. I like you. I like you a lot, Chip. But—"

"No, it's okay," he interrupts her. "You have a life. You have someone else. I understand. I just hope that he knows how lucky he is to have you."

Does he know how lucky he is to have me? Does Paul really have me? No. Not really. But that still doesn't change the fact that her life is twenty years in the future, and Chip is here.

She nods and takes her license when he hands it to her. "Thanks."

"Take care, Desirae," he tells her. He leans toward her and brushes a tender kiss over her eyebrow. There is nothing more to say or do now, unless she wants to come clean and tell him she *is* a time traveler from the future. And still there would be nothing to gain from telling him the truth. Instead, she nods, offers him a smile, and then turns and makes what she hopes is a quick, graceful escape from the car.

Sadness wells up inside her as he drives away. She is lonely this time in 1980, and she's still uncertain when she will be able to talk to Charlie. True, she doesn't have the calendar of a social butterfly in the year 2000, but at least there she would be at home and comfortable with her surroundings. A few work friends. And Paul. Maybe she could try to pump some fun and adventure into her relationship with Paul. Maybe she could get him to take her dancing. Or maybe they could take a train ride to Chicago and see a ball game. Something. Maybe now that she's seen what she and Paul are missing in their relationship, she could fix it.

Charged, suddenly, with a sense of purpose, Rae takes a deep breath and wipes quickly at her eyes. Her mom is not on the porch anymore. She takes that as a good sign. She begins walking toward the house, praying silently that this will be the day she talks to Charlie.

———

CHARLIE ISN'T AT HOME. RAE ALMOST CRIES AFTER climbing the tree again, tiptoeing across the roof to her bedroom window, and sneaking inside without waking herself up, only to find Charlie's bed as empty as it was on the first night she'd snuck in. Instead of crying, she slips back out of Charlie's room and down the hall and stops at her parents' bedroom door. She's desperate to get back home, to the year 2000, so the first chance Charlie gives her, she will take. She might not even get to see her parents before it comes.

Heart hammering in her chest, Rae steps into the doorway. From where she stands, her parents are no more than prone bodies on the bed. With another step, she can make out the shape of her mom's arm, her hand cradled under her cheek and her dad's arm up over his head. She'd forgotten he slept that way, although she shouldn't have because Charlie is the same now.

They look peaceful. So trusting that no one could break into their home and threaten them. Not that she is a threat to them, but the possibility that someone could have come into their home and harmed them nearly brings Rae to her knees. Eyes burning, she takes the final step and stands at her mom's side of the bed. Her mom could open her eyes at any moment and see her there, but Rae has to take the gamble. Just these few moments will last forever when she gets back to the year 2000.

She tiptoes back out of their room and down the hall. She should go back to her hotel room, get a good night's sleep, and then try again tomorrow. But right now, the loneliness eats away at her, and she simply wants the familiar. Charlie's closet has become a safe place of sorts. She hopes, as she crawls in and settles against the wall, that Charlie is home soon because a girl could go crazy hiding out too long in her brother's closet.

Chapter 7

TWO BIG BLUE FISH BOWL EYES STARE DOWN AT HER. RAE had been dreaming about bowling with her grade school best friend Jodie, and then she'd heard a strange popping noise and opened her eyes only to find herself staring up into these fish bowl eyes. She rolls her eyes to get a better view of where she is and what this thing is that is looking down at her. There is a small dome light above her. Stuff hanging. Dress slacks. A suit jacket. Acid washed jeans.

Acid washed jeans? Why would someone have acid washed jeans? Hanging in a closet? Closet. *Charlie's closet.* She's lying on the floor of Charlie's closet.

The blue fish bowl eyes blink, and a big pink bubble appears above her head. *Charlie.* Charlie is here! Charlie is a train wreck with gum. The thought comes to Rae out of nowhere, and suddenly she remembers that Charlie could *never* keep a piece of gum in his mouth for five minutes at a time. No matter if he was trying to blow bubbles or just talk and chew gum at the same time, the gum always ended up out of his mouth, on the floor, or in his hair, or wherever.

The blue eyes blink again, and Rae suddenly sits straight up. And bashes her forehead against Charlie's.

"Ouch!" Both of them fall away from each other and rub their heads. Charlie chomps on his gum as he rubs the sore spot where Rae hit him. Rae cringes as the gum hits the floor, the very same spot her nose had been twenty seconds ago.

"You are such a slob!" she tells him as she scooches back into the corner to get away from him. "Why can't you chew gum like normal people?"

Charlie picks the gum up and examines it. If she'd have appeared in 1975, when Charlie was nine, he would probably have put it back in his mouth. Thankfully, he scrunches his nose up and scrambles backwards to toss it in the garbage can under his desk, not taking his eyes off Rae the whole time.

"Who are you?" he asks calmly. Locks of blond hair curl over his ears and around his neck. He's cute, in a scruffy dog kind of way. Rae is so glad to see someone that she knows after all week of sneaking around and *not knowing anyone*, she almost lurches forward to hug him. She stops before she can make a fool of herself.

"Are your parents here?" she asks instead of answering him.

Charlie's eyebrows shoot up to hide under the long curl that dips down over his forehead. He raises his hands in innocence and shakes his head.

"Look, if you're that nine hundred girl, that was Travis, not me."

"Nine hundred girl?" Rae frowns and shakes her head. "What—"

"Toke bet Travis ten bucks, man. If you need…something…you need to talk to Travis—"

"I'm looking for you, Charlie," she answers, still not following him.

His face, even the tips of his ears, turn scarlet red. "I didn't ask for any sex—"

Her own face flushes when she realizes what he is about to say. She had never known that Charlie and his buddies had called 1-900 numbers when they were kids. She'd been pretty naïve then; she hadn't even known that kind of thing happened when she was ten.

"No, no, no, no." She hurriedly shakes her head before he can continue. "I'm not a nine hundred girl. I'm…" She swallows hard and wonders what to say. Somehow *I'm your little sister* doesn't seem like a winner.

"Homeless?" Charlie's mouth drops open. He glances at the door of his room as if he expects someone to come in.

"Yeah. Kind of," she answers. "I need your help, Charlie."

"My help. You're homeless, and you need my help." He nods. "I don't have much money, but maybe—"

"I don't need your money." Rae rushes to assure him. She'd never known Charlie was so easy, gullible really. She could be just about anybody, hiding out here in his closet, waiting to take advantage of him. Then again, her big brother is still a little bit like that in the year 2000. Like a big, overgrown kid. Compassionate. Goofy and distracted. And okay, sometimes fun.

"Why do you need my help then?" He narrows his eyes at her. Rae is almost glad to finally see some suspicion in his eyes. It makes her feel better for him, but it might prove all that much harder to convince him she is who she says she is.

"Are your parents home?"

Again, a suspicious look.

"No," he finally answers. "Just my little sister and me are here. Can I call someone for you? Who are you, anyway?"

Rae cuts loose with a big sigh. "I'm your little sister, Charlie, and I really need your help."

Finally he looks at her as if he sees her for the crazy, mental woman she must be for hiding in his closet and claiming to be his little sister.

"I'm callin' the cops," he announces.

"Charlie, wait!" she calls after him. She flinches, wondering if her ten-year-old self heard her. The last thing she needs is to run into herself back here in 1980 and put some sort of rift in the universe. Then again, as long as it didn't mess with anyone else's future, maybe it wouldn't matter. Not like she's got some hugely successful life going in the year 2000. But she'd hate to drive herself to the loony bin.

"Lady, I don't know who you are, but you don't belong in my closet and you sure aren't my little sister—"

Rae crawls out of the closet on all fours. She blows her hair up out of her eyes and then climbs to her feet. Her whole body aches from the night spent on Charlie's closet floor, particularly the spot just below her right shoulder blade. A glance back at the closet explains the pain. A Nike court shoe lay in the middle of the floor. Apparently Rae had slept with it lodged just under her shoulder blade.

"I am your sister. I can prove it."

"My sister is downstairs watching TV. And she's about twenty years younger than you." Charlie gives Rae a head to toe once over. "How did you get in here?"

"The window in my room," she answers. "I used to leave it unlocked a lot when I snuck out when I was in high school. I climbed the tree in the back, hoping I'd started leaving the window open before I started sneaking out."

"You climbed the tree in the back?" he asks, clearly surprised by her answer.

"What else was I gonna do? Ring the doorbell and tell Mom that I needed to wait here for you to get home from camp?"

"How'd you know I was at camp?"

"You always went to camp when you were a kid." She rolls her eyes and stretches her arms up over her head. "From the time you turned ten 'til you were fifteen. I thought it was weird that a fifteen-year-old would *want* to go to camp. Then again, you ate Fruit Loops out of the box while you watched *Bugs Bunny and the Roadrunner* when you were in high school. And you slept with a light on until you were seven—"

"Desirae wouldn't remember that. She was only three—"

"But Mom and Dad talked about it all the time."

"Okay, so someone we both know has told you things about me." Charlie stops talking and stares at her suspiciously again. "Went to camp 'til I was fifteen. I'm only fourteen. You're making stuff up hoping I'll believe you. Look, I don't know who you are, but you better get out of here—"

"When you were eleven, and I was seven, we pretended we were in a band. *Barbara Cooper* from *One Day at a Time* was our lead singer, because at that time you had a crush on her. You were the drummer, because even though you were the least coordinated kid ever, you thought you were gonna be the next John Bonham. Except he dies in 1980, so nevermind. I played bass guitar."

"Why did our band break up?" Charlie mumbles. He sounds more like he is wondering to himself than testing her.

"Maybe because Barbara was fictional, and we got

tired of not being able to hear her singing? Or maybe because you broke your wrist in a bike crash, and you couldn't hold a drumstick in your left hand."

"How about because you broke my drum set?" he answers and rolls his eyes. "You were jealous of that drum set from the word go—"

"Well, you were playing real drums, and I was playing air guitar. It gets kinda boring after awhile, Charlie."

"You're not my sister," Charlie says firmly, as if he is just remembering her outrageous claim. "So who are you?"

"What was your favorite thing to do when you were a kid?" she asks him. "Wait. Don't answer that. I will. When you were really little, you liked picking up bugs. To study them. You liked frogs and snakes. Then, when you were ten, you liked the planets. You were always talking about the stars and the galaxy. Not like *Superman* saving the galaxy, but the planets that made up the galaxy. You read all these books about the stars and the planets, and you used to quote them like other kids in your class talked baseball and football statistics. You always liked reading class, but when you were in fifth grade, science became your first love. Because you were old enough to enter the science fair. You begged Dad to help you make—"

"A time machine." Charlie nods. "I remember. But this still doesn't prove anything. Anyone I know could tell you all of this."

"Instead of a time machine, the first year you did a model of the universe. It was awesome. You got an A on it. You were mad, because you didn't get an A plus. Sixth grade, you wanted to make a time machine. Instead, you made an erupting volcano. Seventh grade, a huge magnet and in eighth grade, you made a little robot thing you named Jackal."

"I still have him—"

"Even in high school, you were obsessed with time travel. Dad would always get mad at you. He wanted you to study medicine. Or geology. To find a cure for cancer or to treat people with cancer or to study the earth and be able to predict earthquakes. He said time travel was malarkey that only belonged in science fiction or gushy romance novels. You guys went for three weeks without speaking, when you were a sophomore because Dad wouldn't support you."

"I'm going to be a freshman—" Charlie breaks his sentence off and stares at her, as if what she hasn't told him is sinking in. "You know what? If you just tell me what you want, I'll get it for you and you can get out of here. No one will ever have to know you broke in—"

"I didn't break in."

"You said you climbed the tree and came in through my sister's window—"

"And do you know how mad Mom and Dad would be if they found out someone *had* broke in and you let that person go? Promise me that if I were really some bad guy who broke in you would call the police—"

"You said you could prove who you are."

Last night, Rae had put her license and her money in her pocket and left her bag and computer at the hotel. She slips her fingers into the back pocket of her jeans and pulls the small piece of plastic out.

Please believe me, she thinks as her shaking hand offers it to Charlie.

"I need your help getting back to the year 2000," she says quietly. Charlie snorts and looks at her license.

"As I said, you can go now and I won't call the police. If you don't leave, I'm going to call and say you're harassing me and my sister."

"My sister and me," she corrects him automatically. "My life is on hold. I have been stuck here since Tuesday. I have people in my life who are probably wondering where I am, you included. I have a job; I had a meeting Tuesday night that I missed, all because when I was leaving your apartment, I stumbled through some damned time portal *you* created. I need your help."

"Why don't you go home and sleep it off and then if you still think you're lost twenty years in the past, I'll call and get you the kind of help you really need."

Rae stares silently at her brother. She's never heard him talk to anyone this way. A mix of hurt and surprise and frustration churns inside her.

"Charlie?"

The hairs on her arms and the back of her neck stand on end when she hears herself call to Charlie from downstairs. Charlie edges around his room until he's blocking her way to the door.

"I'm going downstairs with my sister. I suggest you leave the way you came and find someone else to scam."

The realization that he is trying to protect her—the younger her—makes Rae feel a tiny bit better for a few moments. But the frustration, the *desperation*, of her current predicament quickly surfaces again.

"I'm not scamming you, Charlie," she says quietly. She mumbles the name of the hotel where she's staying, but by this time, she's sure Charlie is not listening anymore. He steps back and watches her, obviously serious about making her climb back out the window and down the tree.

Chapter 8

"So what does Paul do?"

Rae stops looking around the McDonald's for just a minute to look at Chip. It isn't that she doesn't want to talk to him. If she's going to be stuck in 1980, and if she's going to keep running into Chip, she should talk to him. *Right? Enjoy his company.* It's just that she's so distracted by this McDonald's of her past: the framed pictures of Ronald McDonald and gang on the walls, the framed black and white photographs and newspaper articles about important people in Quincy in the 70s and 80s, even the way the tables and seats are connected and the way they are arranged in a row down the center of two different sections of booths. She misses this.

"Um," she clears her throat and stares blankly at the three fries in her fingers that were en route to her mouth, "he's an attorney, too."

Chip takes a long pull from his strawberry shake. Chip had ordered a Big Mac, fries, and the milkshake. Rae had seriously wanted to order a Happy Meal. What would it hurt to stretch the whole *going back to your childhood* theme?

Well, for starters, Chip already thinks she's nuts. No need to add to his notions. Instead, she'd ordered the makings of a Happy Meal: cheeseburger, fries, and a Coke. She could do without the little paper box with the fun and games and vividly colored pictures of *Ronald* and *Hamburglar* and *Grimace*. And the toy. She didn't need the toy.

"Is he at your firm?"

Rae feels sorry for kids today. A Happy Meal isn't the same as it used to be. For one thing, it's served in a bag. A flat white recyclable bag. No bright colors. No Ronald McDonald and gang. And the choices now are boring. Sure, kids can choose chicken McNuggets, but they also offer apple slices and white milk. Hello? Doesn't McDonald's get that the burger, fries, and soda are the excitement about McDonald's? Then again, when she was a kid, her family didn't eat out often, so a trip to McDonald's was a big deal. For kids these days, it seems like the norm.

"What?" Rae pops the fries into her mouth and goes back to soaking up the atmosphere. The brown and gold interior, the brown seats, the black iron on everything. She focuses on Chip, who is again sucking on his milkshake.

"Rae?"

Rae is alarmed to realize she's staring at Chip's mouth and imagining it on her body. She's even more alarmed to realize her body is responding to her thoughts. Her breasts suddenly feel full and tight, and her nipples bead inside her plain Jane white matronly bra. Why hadn't she found something a little sexier? Just in case.

Seriously?

"No. Paul works at a different firm."

She has to look away when she says firm. Because she's not thinking about Paul and where he works. She's thinking about Chip's hard, firm body pressed up against hers. Blindly, she fumbles for her Coke and gulps it down, but it doesn't put out the fire inside her.

"What's he like?"

"Who?"

Rae looks back at Chip when she hears him laugh out loud. *Damn. He asked you something else about Paul.*

"What's Paul like?"

Finished with her burger, Rae crumples up the yellow wax paper and puts it on the brown tray on the table adjoining theirs.

"He's..." Well, she can't say boring. If she wants Chip to back off, she definitely can't say Paul is boring. Besides, maybe it isn't Paul. Maybe it's her. Or the combination of the two of them. He's a nice enough guy. He just isn't like Chip. "He's a good man."

A good man? Good God, Rae. That one sounded like it came straight out of a Christian romance novel.

Chip raises his eyebrows, obviously amused by her discomfort.

"Paul's a nice guy." She tries again. "We haven't been seeing each other long."

She didn't owe Chip any explanations. Well, actually, maybe she did. She certainly hadn't acted like a woman who was seeing someone the first night she was here. Perhaps she'd given Chip the wrong signals, and it's her fault that she's in this predicament now.

"How long?" Chip pushes. His Big Mac is long gone; he'd inhaled it in about three bites. He sits back and drains the milkshake and then sets the empty cup on the table.

Rae remembers the taste of the piña coladas on his lips. What would a strawberry milkshake taste like on his tongue? Which would she like better? The piña coladas or the strawberry shake?

"Um..." She gives herself a mental shake. "We've gone out a few times."

Chip nods and continues to stare at her. "And who is Charlie, again?"

"My brother."

"And you need to see Charlie before you get out of town."

The last is spoken like a statement, not a question. Rae simply nods in response.

"Is there anything I can do to help you?"

Rae stares at Chip blankly. She's certain he could do any number of things to relieve the building pressure in her body. To quench a need she's never felt so strongly before. But she can't say that to him! Instead ,she flashes him a smile and stands on shaky legs.

"Can you excuse me for a minute?"

"Yeah." Chip nods and looks around. He smiles at her as she walks past him to hurry to the ladies' room. Once there, she waits in line for a few moments and tunes out the conversations around her. There are two young girls talking about going swimming tomorrow. Rae steals a good, long look at them to make sure they aren't friends of her younger self. Once she decides she doesn't know them, she feels her body sag in relief. She steps sideways to get out of the way of two middle-aged women who are talking about a woman named Donna and how she always makes a huge to-do over nothing. Rae laughs to herself. Some things never change. Two women will always talk about a third, even a fourth woman, when they are alone. Rae figures that most likely, when Donna is around them, they smile and talk to her as if she is a best friend.

Finally, the restroom is empty. Rae takes several deep, calming breaths. She bends over the sink and splashes cold water on her face. Stands up straight and catches her reflection in the mirror. She's gotten some sun here in 1980. From walking everywhere, no doubt. The walking might be helping to get her in shape, too. Well, minus the crappy food she's been eating. She wonders if the suntan and the exercise will stay with her when she gets back to the year 2000. *If* she gets back.

Again, she wonders what would happen if she just stayed here. She takes a deep breath, tells herself she can't possibly stay in 1980, and then pats her face and her neck with a damp paper towel. Chip is waiting. He was nice enough to give her a ride here. She shouldn't tie him up for the rest of the night. Determined, once again, to get back to her parents' house and find Charlie, make him believe her, Rae leaves the restroom and finds that Chip has cleared their table off. He stands when he sees her and follows her out the door.

"So what're you doing tonight?" he asks as they walk to his car.

Rae glances at him. "Um. What? What am I doing tonight?"

She's uncertain what to say. She's made it clear that she's determined to find Charlie, and Chip's made it clear that he doesn't believe her. What else *is* there to say?

"Wanna go to a movie?" Chip asks from the driver's side of the Camaro. "We could drive by the theater and see what's on."

Rae narrows her eyes at him, wondering what he's doing. Ignoring her quest to find Charlie, obviously. But why? Because he seriously doesn't believe her? Or because she hasn't been able to get Charlie's help yet, and maybe he wants to spend time with her while she's still here?

Doesn't matter. Rae's not sure she could sit through a movie. Not right now. It's one thing to grab a bite to eat with him. She has to eat. But to go to a theater and sit in the dark and be entertained, all the while knowing she is stuck in the wrong year, and she needs to get home? That seems a little irresponsible. Rae's streak of rebellion started and ended the night she'd gone dancing with Chip. She really can't afford to waste the time now. Besides, chances are she's already seen whatever movie is showing.

"Um." She smiles again. She can't go to a movie. But *why* can't she? What can she say as an excuse? The whole *I need to find Charlie and leave* thing isn't working, and Chip is a good guy, and he's just given her a ride again, and he'd insisted on buying her supper at McDonald's, and she feels indebted to him again. It would be rude to say no, wouldn't it?

"C'mon. Let's just go see what's on."

Rae realizes she's nodding, and then suddenly Chip ducks into the driver's seat and vanishes from her sight. She takes a deep breath and then yanks her door open and gets in his car. Okay, so she can go to a movie tonight to repay Chip for his kindness. And then tomorrow, he'll be busy and she can go back to the house and find Charlie again. She just has to figure out a way to make Charlie believe her.

Chip drives to the theater downtown. The Adams Cinema. Rae catches her breath when she sees the old, two-story building. In the year 2000, it is empty. After spending the last few years of its life as a discount movie theater, it had closed in 1999. Rae had seen plenty of movies at the Adams when she was a kid. Both with her family and her friends. How exciting to be able to see it again!

"*Urban Cowboy*." Chip slows the car to a crawl so he can read the sign as he drives by the theater. "Whatcha think?"

"Yes," she agrees quickly. Chip gives her a quick look and arches an eyebrow at her. He probably thinks she's got the hots for John Travolta, when in truth, she's just excited about seeing the inside of the theater again. John Travolta is just an added bonus. She can't deny that even at the age of ten, she thought he was cute. Rae doesn't think he's aged all that well, but she can't tell Chip that.

"Okay." Chip turns the corner and cruises on past the theater. "The sign said it comes on at seven-thirty. Is that okay with you?"

"Sure."

Rae glances at the watch on her wrist. It is only four-thirty now. What can they possibly do to pass three hours? She turns her head to look out her window when she feels the blush climb her neck and flood her cheeks. She'd love to do that for three hours. The hours she's spent in Charlie's closet have left her plenty of time to fantasize about exactly what she'd do to Chip's body if she had the time and the opportunity. Oh. And the guts. Rae has never had guts when it comes to *any* man. One that is as good-looking and sexy as Chip? No way. The automatic klutz would turn on, and she'd do something horribly stupid to embarrass herself before they ever got inside her hotel room.

"Do you need some time to yourself? Have something you need to do?"

Rae almost laughs out loud. This is probably where other women would curse dead batteries, but Rae doesn't own any sex toys. Not in the year 2000 and certainly not in 1980. She could use a nap, though. And maybe a shower. Actually, maybe she should go shopping again. Another trip to JC Penney. Not necessarily to buy something dressy or sexy for a date. Not necessarily to buy anything lacy and scrappy and barely there. But she's been wearing the same two pairs of jeans and t-shirts for the past several days. She'd hit the Laundromat the day before yesterday, but still. It would probably be a good idea to buy another outfit or two. She still has plenty of the cash she'd lifted from Charlie's stash; she fully intends to pay him back. It won't be a problem, as long as she is able to get back to 2000.

"Actually, yes, if you don't mind," Rae says to Chip.

"Okay. I'll pick you up around seven? A little after?"

"That sounds great." It does sound great. A couple hours should be plenty of time to get to JC Penney, purchase a few new things, and get back to the hotel for a shower. Probably not enough time for a nap, but let's be serious. She's not going to get any sleep thinking about going to a movie with Chip. The whole idea excites her now. Hanging out with Chip instead of hiding away in Charlie's closet, begging him to listen to her when he finds her again. Seeing a movie in the Adams Cinema. The theater hasn't been closed that long in the year 2000, but she hasn't seen a movie there in years. Going tonight she will see it as it was when she was a child, and she can't wait for that. Wait until she tells Charlie. The year *2000* Charlie.

"Where are you staying?" he asks as he turns left onto Maine Street.

"Um, actually, I'm back the other way," she answers demurely. "At the Ramada Inn."

"Oh." Chip nods and makes a quick right turn at the next corner. Rae watches the scenery out her window again as he drives. She loves the old buildings here downtown. In 1980, there are still some that look well-kept. By the year 2000, a lot of them look ramshackle, like a sneeze might blow them over. But some of them have been completely remodeled by 2000 and look nice. Rae supposes every town changes through the years. It's only natural. But going back in time really drives it home, how much places and people change. The thought makes her sad, and she's determined not to be sad. Not now. Not when she has a date tonight. Okay, not a *date* date. But she's going to the Adams Cinema. After last year, when the theater shut down she assumed she'd never set foot inside the place again.

When Chip drops her off, she decides there's no way she has time to go to the mall and get back and shower. Not if she's walking. Maybe she should have had Chip drop her off at Penney's. But then he'd have felt obligated to wait there for her, and Rae can't justify that. She can't demand all of Chip's attention and spare time. There are a few women's clothing stores on this end of town. Rae grabs some cash from her room and sets off on a walk, hoping she can find something suitable within walking distance.

Chapter 9

IN THE MORNING, RAE'S THOUGHTS TURN TO CHIP AS SHE gets ready to trek back to her parents' house to find Charlie. She hangs the pink blouse she'd worn last night, the one she'd found at State Street Store, in the closet. Straightens the hotel bed she's been sleeping in. Showers and dresses in the blue jeans and white t-shirt she'd bought at Penney's on that first day she'd gone shopping. Thinks about the movie with Chip last night. It had been fun. Just fun. Even without the kisses and the flames that ignite inside her when Chip kisses her, it was a fun night. The movie was okay, hadn't been that much different from the first time she'd seen it. But the atmosphere had been incredible, and Rae had seen a couple at the movie that had been friends of her parents. There'd been enough people milling about in the lobby of the theater that Rae hadn't felt the need to hide. Besides, she'd decided there was really no threat of anyone looking at her and knowing she was Rae Warner, visiting 1980 from the year 2000. Sure, she'll still be careful around her parents and her younger self, but other than that, she's sure it's not going to be a problem.

Driving Chip's car had been a thrill. The growl of the engine as she'd stepped on the gas had been so exciting. And knowing that Chip was watching her while she drove, watching the happiness and excitement play out on her face had been an added buzz. She'd love to drive it again. She'd love to get it out on the highway and put the pedal down. But she knows that isn't likely to happen. For one thing, she really needs to stop seeing Chip. Last night, she'd been so silly as to wonder if she might be falling in love with him. This morning she knows she is just lonely here in a place where she can't be herself. Chip is a good kid, and he's been a good friend to help her pass the time. But she knows she has to stop it from going any further. She's leading Chip on, and what will happen to him when she finally gets back to her own time? Poof, she'll be gone, and Chip won't even have a clue where she went.

Besides, even if she does see Chip again—he'd said he was coming by her parents' house today, didn't he?—she isn't going to ask to drive his car again.

It's just after eight, but when she leaves the hotel lobby and steps outside, a wave of warm, steamy air rolls over her. She's lost track of the days, but she knows it is getting to be mid-June, and the summer heat and humidity are barreling in to settle for the rest of the summer. She probably should've bought a couple of pairs of shorts, because the jeans she has on are already terribly uncomfortable. The thighs feel tight and hot, and even the loose legs down on her shins feel sticky and gross. She'd kill for a pair of shorts and some flip-flops right now. Then again, she's got a long walk ahead of her yet again, and the Keds she has on are much better for walking than flip-flops would be. She snorts and shakes her head as she crosses Fourth Street and then York and heads toward Maine. *Keds are better for walking than flip-flops. God, Rae, you are so old. Live a little. Wear flip-flops.* She'd never known before how much of a stick-in-the-mud she was, but it seems that in 1980 (this time around) she's seeing herself in a new light. She doesn't like what she sees. It's one thing to be a successful attorney during work hours, but it wouldn't hurt to wear flip-flops and eat ice cream and dance now and then, would it?

Wouldn't hurt to have a fling with a good-looking guy, would it?

Well, no, maybe it wouldn't hurt her, but it might hurt Chip.

The lie niggles at her in the back of her mind, and when she ignores it, it settles in her gut and makes her feel a little sick.

Funny how she'd noticed the difference in cars and the buildings when she'd first realized she was in 1980. Like when a business remodels or a building is demolished. It doesn't take long for a person to completely forget what used to be in the vacant spot. Doesn't take much for a person to forget what a remodeled building looked like before the renovations started. Already, Rae is now so comfortable with her 1980 surroundings, she finds herself trying to visualize the WCU Building and the Granite Bank Gallery in the year 2000.

She wonders where Chip is right now. He'd said he had a class today, but she doubts he'd be there yet. Not if he won't be free until after one. Unless he has other obligations, which is possible. Did he think about her last night? Dream about her? She'd dreamt of him, but not like she thought she would. Nothing hot and sexy. She'd dreamt that she and Chip were sitting side by side on the roof of the kitchen, bare feet dangling, debating the case of Led Zeppelin versus Lynyrd Skynyrd. Maybe some women would have preferred the hot, sexy dream—Rae wouldn't have minded that one, of course—but she'd been so content to sit there by Chip and talk to him. When she awoke, she'd believed the conversation had happened, because the dream had felt so real.

Her stomach growls as she walks down Maine. She'd shoved some cash in her pocket before she'd left. She'll grab something at the McDonald's on 13th and Broadway, she decides. A bit out of the way, but not so much. Before she even crosses Maine Street to head a few blocks north, she remembers there is no McDonald's on 13th and Broadway yet. Plan B. A donut? She could go to Dixie Cream at 24th and Broadway and grab a glazed donut or two. A cup of coffee. Too bad she can't just show up at her parents' house and hit her mom up for some breakfast. Save her some money, anyway. Or rather, it would save Charlie some money.

Speaking of Charlie's money, she needs to get this situation ironed out because she's going to run out of Charlie's money, and she can't just march back into his room and take more. Even if she pays him back in 2000, it just feels wrong to keep taking the money now. Not to mention that it's really a waste. If she could just get Charlie to believe her, she could get back to 2000 and sleep in her own bed in her apartment, and not owe anyone for anything.

She wonders what Chip thinks about her staying at the Ramada. If her parents live on York. He probably thinks it's weird that she isn't staying with them. She would think so if their roles were reversed.

A smile touches her lips as she thinks about Chip in those dress pants and the plaid shirt yesterday. In 1980, he was pretty fashionable. She wishes she could take him to 2000 and put him in a business suit. White shirt and tie. Or jeans and a tight-fitting t-shirt. Or boxers. Or briefs.

Rae gives herself a mental shake.

At Dixie Cream, she orders two glazed donuts, thinks better of it and orders two more donuts—jelly-filled with chocolate icing—and a big cup of coffee. Maybe she can reach Charlie through his stomach. She doctors her coffee with a little cream and sugar, makes sure the wax paper bag is folded over good, and turns to leave. She nearly runs smack into her uncle. Uncle Walt. He'd passed away in 1982. Only fifty-six, but he'd had a massive heart attack, and he'd been gone before the paramedics had even arrived at his house. Rae stares at him for a moment, wishing she could say something. Wishing she could warn him. Talk him out of the donuts today. The hell of it is that he doesn't look to be a pound overweight. Just in horribly bad shape or terribly unlucky, she figures. He won't listen to some strange woman warning him about a heart attack, anyway.

He notices that she's still staring, and he turns to really study her. Rae's hands sweat, but she can't even wipe them on her jeans because of the coffee cup and the donut bag. She should move, walk out, but she can't make her feet go anywhere. Instead, she's taking inventory. The brown hair, shot through with threads of silver. The kind green eyes. The loose-fitting carpenter shorts, and the tape measure clipped to the tool belt around his waist. The way the skin around his eyes and lips crinkles when he smiles at her. That was Uncle Walt. A smile for everybody, friend or stranger.

"Morning," he says to her as he walks by and heads to the counter to order. Rae stands frozen a moment longer and then finally finds she is able to shuffle her feet and move through the doorway. She takes a deep breath, but she comes up with more steam, nothing fresh. At least she's left the smell of donuts, coffee, and cigarettes behind. She cuts through the alley behind Dixie Cream and heads back across Maine to York. Prays that this time Uncle Walt will not die in 1982. Knows that it's a useless prayer, because God can't change the past for one person. Seeing Uncle Walt makes her think about Aunt Ellen. And her cousins. By the time Rae reaches the corner across the street from her parents' home, a heavy sadness fills her.

A person might think visiting the past and seeing loved ones who've been gone for so long would be a good thing. But it's not. Rae decides that staying in 1980 a moment longer is going to break her heart.

For once, luck throws her a rope. Charlie is outside. Mowing the front yard. Mowing became his chore when he turned twelve. Rae quickly crosses the street and hurries down the block. Charlie doesn't look up until she's standing right in front of the house. When he does see her, he's not happy. Even though the mower is running, she can hear him sigh with frustration. He cuts the engine and walks a little closer to her. He's careful, though, to keep a bit of distance between them.

"You again?"

"Are Mom and Dad home?"

"No. Mom's working a blood drive today at the hospital, and Dad's at work."

"What about..." She almost says me, but that's too weird, even for her. "What about your sister?"

"She's at her friend's house," he answers. Sweaty ringlets cover his head now. Most guys might hate curly hair, but Rae thinks Charlie's never noticed that he *has* curly hair. She watches him lift his t-shirt and wipe the sweat from his face.

"So can we talk for a minute? Please?"

Charlie sighs again and shakes his head. "I gotta finish this. And then—"

"I really, really need your help." Her voice falls to a whisper. "I've managed to stay away from Mom and Dad, but I just ran into Uncle Walt, and it's so hard to see him after he's been gone for so long. It sucks to fall back in time twenty years, Charlie. It's lonely, and it hurts, and I just wanna go home." She realizes she's rattling, and too late, she realizes she's said something about Uncle Walt dying. Charlie stares at her silently, but from the look on his face, she can tell he's hung up on that part. "I brought donuts."

She knows she has him when he jerks his gaze to the white bag in her hand. A smile tilts the corners of his lips.

"Just for a minute."

"Absolutely," she agrees and follows him down the driveway to the back door of the house.

When she follows him inside, she feels the house settle in around her. The smell of detergent coming from the laundry room to the right of the kitchen. The lingering smell of the coffee her parents drank for breakfast. Memories build inside her until she almost can't breathe. Charlie turns his back to her to grab the milk from the refrigerator, so she takes advantage of the moment to take a deep breath. Maybe that was a mistake, breathing in more memories, but she exhales slowly and then sits at the table in the same seat that had been hers when she was a kid. Charlie grabs a glass from the cabinet and then turns to the table and stops. Stares at her like he's seen a ghost. Maybe he's noticed that she's in *her* seat? Maybe something in the way the light touches her just now makes him see that she really could be his little sister, visiting from the future?

The moment slips by quickly, and Charlie reluctantly joins her at the table. Rae sips her coffee and watches him splash milk into his glass.

"Messy Marvin," Rae mumbles. Charlie looks up

quickly and gives her a suspicious glare. Rae barely stops herself from throwing her hands up in defense, escaping a coffee spill. She presses her lips together as she thinks *Messy Mary*. That's why Charlie is staring at her just now. She'd used her mom's nickname for Charlie without thinking. *Oh well*. It's not like she's trying to hide from Charlie who she really is.

"So?" Charlie apparently decides to forget that Rae called him something only his mom ever called him, something maybe only a relative—a close relative—like Rae would know. He drops his gaze from her face to the white bag she'd set on the table.

"Oh. Sorry." She smiles and pushes the bag toward him. "Jelly-filled. Your favorite."

He glances at her again, but this time he returns his attention to the bag of donuts immediately. She watches his long, delicate fingers open the bag and reach inside. He pulls out the first of the jelly-filleds and lifts it to his mouth.

"Let me just tell you it's not a good idea to eat five of them on a hangover, though."

"A hangover?" Charlie repeats around a mouthful.

Rae nods. "On your twenty-sixth birthday, you really tie one on. Like shots of tequila or something. I'm not sure what got into you. You were with a few of your college friends." Rae shudders at the memory. "When I left the bar, they had you propped up between two bar stools, still slammin' 'em down." She takes a drink of her coffee and reaches for the donut bag. "Whatever possessed you to do the shots in the first place is beyond me, because it's so out of character for you. But then to stuff five jelly-filled donuts down the next day…"

As Charlie stares at her, he stops chewing. Rae decides she's said too much. She takes a bite of her own donut and chews methodically and then washes it down with a sip of coffee.

"Did you hit your head or something?" Charlie finally breaks the silence.

"What?" Rae reaches up quickly to touch her head. She doesn't feel any bumps or blood, and she doesn't remember hitting her head on anything since she's been back in 1980. Her feet are still sore from climbing the tree barefoot and from hot-footing it all over town for the past couple of weeks, but her head is fine. "Why?"

Charlie shakes his head and stuffs another huge bite of donut into his mouth. "Most people don't go around spouting off about things that happen in the future."

"Haven't you ever seen the movie *Back to the Future*?"

"What?"

"Hmm." Rae raises her eyebrows and offers Charlie a lame smile. "Sorry. That comes out in the mid-eighties."

Charlie takes a drink of milk and then reaches out to fiddle with the donut bag. Rae assumes he wants another donut, but he's afraid to take a second.

"There's another for you."

But he continues to fidget and then finally he looks at her with serious eyes. "What you said about Uncle Walt…"

Rae purses her lips. She simply nods, not really wanting to go into detail.

"When?" he finally asks.

"Two years from now."

Charlie takes the second donut and stares at it for a moment. "What about Mom and Dad?"

"Can you help me?" she asks. No way is she going to tell him about when or how their parents pass away. It's one thing to talk about a particularly heinous hangover he once had or even to slip about their uncle. But she can't tell him about their parents. "I'm not trying to hustle anybody.

I don't wanna hurt anyone. I just need to get back to my life, Charlie."

"Where are you from?"

"The year 2000."

"No, I meant, like, what city?"

So, now they're back to him not believing her?

"Here, Charlie. I live here. You live here. I have an apartment on the west side. I'm a corporate lawyer...well, I was. I have the feeling my job's gonna be gone, since I've been AWOL for at least...ten days."

Charlie chews his donut and watches her, but he says nothing.

"You live in an old house on Vermont. Behind Barney's."

"Who's Barney?" Charlie asks with a frown. Of course he wouldn't be familiar with the bar. Not when he's fourteen.

"It's a bar. Around Eighteenth and Broadway. The Hi Hat Tavern? You live in a house behind it. On Vermont. It's an old house, but it's really cool. Red brick. You have a really cool man cave going. Cool TV and gaming system. Nice stereo. Then again, you don't use much of it, because you're still the same dreamy, flighty scientist type you've always been."

At this, he perks up and shows a bit of interest.

"Time travel isn't real."

"I used to believe that." She nods.

"Am I married?"

Rae sits back. His question takes her by surprise. Does he care? Really?

"No."

"Well, that's something, anyway," he says more to himself than in answer to her. "Wait. What about prom? Do I take a date to prom?"

"You do." She nods. Figures telling him that much won't hurt.

"Who?"

"Uh-huh. Not telling."

"Is she pretty? You can at least tell me that much."

Rae remembers Charlie and his prom date. Taking pictures on the front porch. Charlie in the tux and Wendy, his date, in a blush pink formal dress.

"Yes."

He considers this and finally nods.

"So do you believe me?"

"Not really." He gulps the last of his milk. "I mean, would you? If I were you, and you were me, would you believe me?"

Rae blinks. The question gives her a headache.

"Probably not."

Charlie shrugs.

"Look. You have always been fascinated by time travel. You collect the weirdest stuff. From garage sales and estates sales. Old electronic equipment. You'd just brought home something from an estate sale in Barry or something. And you were all excited about it. You told me you were this close to making it work. To really making time travel work. And I left your house to get to a meeting at the hospital, and the next thing I know I'm in 1980."

"Barry? The only times I've ever been to Barry is for the apple festival."

Rae actually laughs. She'd loved going to the Barry Apple Festival every fall.

"Well, in the year 2000, you went to some sale or auction or something."

"Old electronics?" he repeats, obviously thinking it over.

Rae nods. "You have a room full of computer components."

"Computer components? How do I possibly get my hands on computer components?"

"They're everywhere. Computers…" Rae's words trail off as she realizes she has proof to show Charlie that she is from the future.

"What?"

"Computers. I have my computer with me. I can show it to you. So you'll believe me. And maybe somehow it can help you get me home."

"You have your computer with you? Here?" Charlie scoots his chair back and looks under the table.

"It's at the hotel," she answers absently.

"So in the year 2000, people lug around computers? For what?"

"They're laptops," she tells him with a frown. "Very small, very compact. People use them for business stuff. For organizations. They use spreadsheet programs for busi-nesses. Databases. You name it. Most people probably use them for research, because you can access the Internet with them."

"Internet?" Charlie shakes his head. "What's that?"

Rae sighs. "I'll show you. Well, I can't show you, exactly, because there is no Internet now. But…I can show you my laptop. I'll get it and bring it back here later."

"No."

"No?" Rae repeats, stunned that he still doesn't believe her. That he still won't help her. "No?"

"You can't come back here today. We're going out of town."

"What?"

"Mom and Dad will be back around lunch time."

Charlie glances at the wall clock above the sink. It's nearly ten-thirty. "We're going to Wisconsin for a long weekend."

Rae opens her mouth to say something, but she finds she can't. Wisconsin. They're going to the Wisconsin Dells. For the weekend. She remembers the trip well. It had been a blast.

"I could bring it really fast. And you could help me before you go?"

"No. If you're telling the truth, it sounds complicated, and it might take a while to figure it out. Mom and Dad will catch you here."

Rae lays her head on the table and groans in frustration.

"We'll be back Monday."

"I know. I'm gonna get so sunburned, I end up sick. And you. Watch out at the hotel pool. You're gonna cut your foot. You have to get stitches."

When she lifts her head to look at him again, he's studying her suspiciously.

"Look, I gotta be honest," she mumbles. "I am stranded here from the year 2000. I have no cash on me. I have debit cards and credit cards—"

"What's a debit card?"

Rae shakes her head and continues, "I've been staying at the Ramada for six or seven nights now. I borrowed from your shoebox stash, and I swear I'll pay you back in 2000 when I get home. But the longer I'm here, the more of your cash I need and the more I owe you."

Charlie drums his fingertips on the table and then shrugs. "Stay here. While we're gone."

"I can't."

"No, seriously. Stay in the basement. They won't know. Be out of here Sunday night."

Rae thinks about the coming weekend. Stuck in the Ramada again, all weekend. Bored. Tired. Hungry.

"Are you sure?"

Charlie nods. "Leave on Sunday. Come back on Monday morning, bring your lap computer or whatever you said it is, and I'll see what I can figure out."

Rae's body turns to jelly as relief sags through her. "Really? You will?"

"Yes."

"Thank you!" She almost reaches over to touch Charlie's hand, but she decides he might not be comfortable with that, so instead she stands up and grabs her empty coffee cup and the donut bag. "Thank you so much!"

"I can't promise anything," Charlie warns her.

"I know." She nods her agreement and walks to the back door intending to get out of his hair. To disappear before her parents show up.

"Rae!" Charlie calls as she pulls the back door open. It's the first time he's used her name since she's been back here. The sound of it in a familiar voice stirs that sadness inside her again. She misses the year 2000 Charlie.

"What?"

"Do I get laid? After prom?"

"Eeww!" Rae shivers and laughs and then shakes her head. "How the heck would I know?"

Chapter 10

Rae isn't sure what to do with the rest of her morning, but she leaves her parents' house and heads back to the hotel on foot. It's close to eleven when she arrives at the hotel, and she has until one to meet Chip back over on the corner by the house. Actually, now that she knows her parents are leaving town and Charlie has invited her to stay in the house, she could just turn around and go back. But she's tired. A bit warm from walking. Maybe just a quick nap before she meets Chip. She sets the alarm on the clock by the bed, pulls the bedspread back, and stretches out with her head on the pillow. Yep, a nap might be just what she needs. It occurs to her that she has a long walk back to her parents' neighborhood if she leaves the hotel for good. She'll be carrying her laptop again, and though it's not so heavy to carry, after several blocks in this heat, it will feel like it weighs a ton.

She wishes she could call Chip and have him pick her up at the hotel, but she doesn't have a number where she can reach him. Besides, he's probably in class right now, and it's not like he carries a cell phone she could call.

Nope. She'll just have to walk. Again. At least she had a good talk with Charlie this morning. Things are looking up. She might be going home in a couple of days if Charlie can help her. But what if he can't? She hadn't thought of that possibility before now. What if Charlie really doesn't know what to do and can't figure something out? She supposes she'd live if she got stuck in 1980 permanently, but she would prefer to get back to the year 2000. Wouldn't she?

When she goes back to the year 2000, she'll have to say goodbye to Chip. Permanently. She's not crazy about that thought; she has to admit to herself she'd like to get to know him better. But seriously, she can't stay twenty years in the past and be involved with a kid who's younger than she is. A kid who's still in college. And what about her job? She can't practice law in 1980. She can't do anything in 1980, because her life, her documentation, her license, her money—everything—is in 2000. In 1980, she is only ten, and nothing she's accomplished in her adult life has happened yet.

Her eyes drift closed, and she thinks about Chip. The movie last night. Driving his car. She wonders what they will do today when they meet on the corner near her parents' house. Maybe he'll let her drive his car again. Maybe he'll kiss her again. She'd definitely like for him to kiss her again.

———

IT'S AT LEAST A HUNDRED DEGREES HOTTER WHEN SHE SEES Chip pull around the corner on York. She has wilted; her jeans are thick and heavy and stuck to her skin. Her t-shirt is wet with sweat; her hair, which she has pulled back in a pony-tail, is flat and lifeless against her head. The laptop did indeed get heavy on the walk to the corner, but when she'd arrived on the corner, she'd set her bag down on the ground by her feet. She's tried not to think about what the neighbors might be thinking if they see her. Especially if they see her get into Chip's car and then later, come back to her parents' house and go inside. What if they jump to the same conclusion Chip had the other day? What if they think she and Chip are working together to rob her parents' house? As Chip slows the Camaro at the curb, she tries to remember the neighbors from when she was a kid. Are they nosy? Do they work? Is there anyone even around to see her skulking about on the corner, or is she working herself into a panic over nothing?

"Hey." Chip smiles at her when she yanks the car door open, drops her bag to the floor of the passenger side, and gets in.

"Hi."

"Have you been outside all day?"

Rae presses her lips together and raises her eyebrows. *You look so bad he actually had to comment. How embarrassing.*

"Just walked over here from the hotel."

Chip flinches. "Why didn't you just tell me to pick you up there?"

She shrugs and reaches up to brush her limp bangs off her forehead. *Ugh. If you look this bad, you have to smell worse.*

The car still idles in park while Chip continues to smile at her.

"What?"

"You look cute."

"Cute?"

He shrugs. "Yeah. Cute. Like a little kid who's been outside playing all day."

She gives him a slow nod and then turns away to look out the windshield.

"That's great, Chip," she mumbles.

"Have you had lunch?"

"I...um." She'd had to pay the hotel a big chunk of Charlie's cash when she'd checked out. She still has some, but her own little stash is definitely dwindling. She hadn't eaten, though. She'd napped in the cool, dark room for as long as she could, and then she'd walked here to meet Chip. "No."

"Where do you wanna go?"

Rae considers Quincy in 1980. Where could they go for lunch? Pizza, maybe? Cassano's?

"Cassano's?"

Chip grins and nods. "Okay, yeah." He puts the car in drive and eases around the corner to head back toward Broadway.

"So how was class?" Rae desperately wishes for a shower. Clean clothes. Maybe she can get a ride to JC Penney and grab a few more things and then wash the few things she's purchased here in 1980 at her parents' house. The thought of a shower and fresh, clean clothes lifts her spirits.

"It was good," Chip answers vaguely. "I don't mind classes, but I don't like being in a classroom in the summer."

Rae nods her understanding. She'd taken summer classes, and she'd hated it, too. But, she muses, maybe summer classes prepare a person for the professional world. Because she certainly can't call in to her job—miss meetings or court appearances—because it's a nice summer day, and she'd prefer to pass the afternoon hours poolside or working in the yard.

"Hey," she says with what she decides is too much enthusiasm. She turns in her seat to look at Chip while she talks. "Thanks for letting me drive your car last night. That was cool."

"You liked that?" Chip glances at her. He slows to a stop at the traffic light at Twenty-Fourth & Broadway.

"I did," she answers. "Very cool. The movie was cool, too."

From the corner of her eye, she sees a book on the seat behind Chip. Not a text book. A book book. A mass market paperback. She twists further around and leans between the seats.

"*The Amityville Horror*?" She reaches with her left hand to grab the book and wraps her fingers around Chip's arm with her other hand, so she doesn't lose her balance and fall completely into the back of the car. Her left hand manages to snag the book from the backseat, but her brain is stuck on the hard muscle under her right hand. Chip's bicep feels like rock under her fingers. Except that his skin is kind of soft and warm. Rae wonders if she kissed him there, would he taste salty from sweat? "You read…" As the words tumble out of her mouth, she realizes they sound insulting. Why should she assume that Chip doesn't like to read? Just because he's a guy? Plenty of guys read. Well, she *guesses* plenty of guys read. Charlie does. Then again, Chip and Charlie don't seem to be much alike at all. She certainly can't imagine Charlie dancing at a club and kissing a strange woman and letting a stranger drive his car. "Horror?" She coughs to try to hide her almost insult. "You like horror?"

"Sure. Why not?" Chip nods. "Do you?"

"Yeah," Rae answers. "Yeah, I do."

"What's your favorite?"

"Mmm…probably *House of Leaves*," she finally says, and then she rushes on when she realizes she'd just read it earlier in the year 2000. "Who else do you read?"

"John Saul."

"Me, too!"

"Favorite?"

Again, she considers the earliest John Saul books she'd read, because most of her favorites have definitely not been written yet.

"*Punish the Sinners.*"

"Okay." Chip chews on his lower lip. "I liked the last one the best. Um...*Comes the Blind Fury.*"

"What about Robin Cook?"

"*Coma.*" Chip rolls his eyes as if to say there's no contest. "Did you read *Lovestory*?"

"*Lovestory*?"

Rae draws back and looks at him in surprise. Of course she's read *Lovestory*, but she's shocked that he has and this time, she doesn't even try to hide it.

"Yeah," she answers with a nod. "Seriously? You read *Lovestory*?"

"Well. Yeah." Chip seems confused about the fact that he had read *Lovestory* and a little pained to admit it. "My girlfriend read it and insisted I read it."

"Did you like it?"

Chip sighs as he drives. Rae hopes he is considering the book and not bored with their conversation. This really nice hot guy just got even sexier. Rae is a sucker for books, and any guy that enjoys reading and talking about books is a dream. A guy that enjoys reading, talking about books, and has a body and a smile like Chip's is a walking fantasy.

"Yeah, I did. I mean...I guess I'd prefer to read Robin Cook or whatever. But I did like *Lovestory*."

"I had a little music box that looked like crystal. It played the theme from *Lovestory*. My dad gave it to me one year for Valentine's Day." Rae wonders whatever happened to the music box. She'd love to have it now if she could find it.

"I got one for my girlfriend after we read the book," Chip answers with a goofy-looking smile. "I mean, it wasn't real crystal, of course, but she liked it."

Rae tries to picture Chip with a girlfriend. It's not a stretch of the imagination, and yet, she doesn't like it. The thought of Chip holding hands with someone else. Kissing someone else goodnight. *Seriously, Rae? You're jealous of a teenager?*

"What's her name?"

"Jenny."

Rae flinches. "What happened to her?"

Chip laughs softly. "Her family moved away after we'd been dating for about a year. They went to Alabama."

"Oh." Rae imagines that it was hard for Chip and Jenny to be separated after a year of dating, but this is better news than what happens to Jenny in the book *Lovestory*. "Did you love her?"

"Yeah. But..." Chip pulls into Cassano's and parks his car. "I was fifteen when we started dating. Kinda young, I guess, to really fall in love."

Rae purses her lips. Young, maybe, but love is love. It can happen at fifteen, just the same way it can happen at twenty-five or fifty. Just a different set of complications for fifteen-year-olds than for adults.

"At least that's what her dad said."

At this, Rae laughs. "That's what dads of young girls are supposed to say."

Chip grins and nods. "Good point."

The restaurant, another old haunt from Rae's child-hood, is dim and cool after being outside in the soupy mix of heat and humidity. Cassano's is still open in the year 2000, though it has relocated again. Rae hesitates just inside the building, soaking it all in. These are the things that make her wish she could stay here in 1980. Well, the childhood memories and Chip. Every moment with Chip makes her wish that much more that she could just stay here.

There are a few tables occupied, but at this time of day, Cassano's is not hopping. The hostess leads Chip and Rae to a booth. The tall, wooden booths offer privacy, but Rae refuses to think of it as romantic.

"Do you ever hear from her?" As soon as they give their drink orders to their waitress, Rae returns to their earlier conversation. She's not sure why. It's depressing to imagine Chip in love with someone else.

"Jenny?" Chip looks up from his menu. It seems like her name brightens his smile a little, but maybe Rae's imagining that. "No. She was a year and a half older than me. I think she loved me, too, when she was here. But..." Chip shrugs. "I never heard from her again after she moved."

"So you were dating a seventeen-year-old?"

Chip grins. The waitress returns with their drinks and jots their order down. A large ham and sausage pizza with extra cheese. Rae hopes Chip is hungry. She can and will eat a lot, but a large is so big. Cassano's cuts their pizzas into small squares, rather than big triangles. Once, when they were younger, she and Charlie had bragged that they'd eaten twenty pieces each. Twenty pieces of their pizza probably equaled four slices from Pizza Hut.

"She was sixteen when we started dating."

"So you like older women."

Dangerous, Rae. You're heading into dangerous territory.

"Older women don't scare me," he answers with a smile.

"I don't imagine there's much that does scare you, Chip Andrews."

Chip laughs out loud and sits back against the booth. "*The Amityville Horror* scared me."

"Well, hello." Rae lifts her hands, palms up and laughs. "I kinda think it would scare the daylights out of anyone."

Chip reaches for her hand, and suddenly Rae's not afraid of a movie or a demon or anything. Only this moment. Because Chip holds her hand, and he rubs his thumb over the back of it and just looks at her. Really looks at her. Like he's trying to memorize her. She certainly wishes she could memorize him.

"Where did you come from, Rae?"

"What?"

"Where did you come from? You are so beautiful, and you just appeared in my life one day out of nowhere. You keep warning me that you have to leave, but you're here. And I like you. I like you a lot, and I just keep waiting for you to just disappear."

Rae takes a deep breath and lets it out slowly. A pang of guilt slices through her center. She should never have agreed to keep seeing him. Because one of these days, hopefully this weekend, she *is* going to just disappear, and Chip will never see her again.

She will never see Chip again. Unless...No. Charlie isn't going to just let her run back and forth from 2000 to 1980 and back whenever the mood strikes. *Who knows?* There might even be time cops or something like in that Jean Claude Van Damme movie, *Timecop*. What if she was to become a frequent time traveler and then she got arrested and locked up somewhere or something?

"I don't wanna disappear," she whispers when she finally has her voice back. "I don't wanna leave you."

Chapter 11

THE DRIVE BACK TO HER PARENTS' HOUSE IS CHARGED WITH new electricity, intensity that fills Rae with dread. Somewhere over that pizza and soda lunch, things had gone from fun and spontaneous to deep and scary. Rae isn't ready to say she's in love with Chip. She's always been much too cautious to be the kind of woman to fall in love so quickly, so easily. Yet, she knows that if she is around Chip much longer, the danger of falling for him is very real.

She's certainly never been brazen or bold with men, but she feels certain that Chip feels something for her, too. If she were staying in 1980, maybe they could go with this. Try it on for size. Walk on in and test the water. But she isn't, and this can go nowhere, and now things feel very strained between them. She'd have liked to put this off until—well, forever—and just enjoyed the last couple of days she has with Chip. As friends.

"Is this really your parents' house?" Chip asks as he pulls his Camaro to the curb in the front. Rae knows she needs to answer him, but at the moment, she's more concerned with what the neighbors will think of this strange car parked here in the middle of the day. She glances to her right, at the front porch, relieved to see the front door is locked up tight. Should she have Chip park in the driveway? Back by the garage? But, wait. It shouldn't matter. It's not like Chip will be parked here all weekend. Maybe for a while each day, but she hasn't planned to spend every waking moment with him. Or every sleeping moment.

As if. *Sleeping.* Whoever created that euphemism for sex clearly didn't get it much. Rae almost laughs out loud. Actually, she doesn't get it much, and she could have made up that euphemism herself. Then again, before Chip, she honestly rarely thought about sex.

"Rae?"

"Hmm?" She looks back at Chip and remembers he'd asked her a question. Oh yeah. Was this really her parents' house? She isn't offended by his question. Her behavior, since getting stuck here weeks—*really?* weeks ago—has been more than a little suspicious.

"Is this really your parents' house?"

"Yes, it really is."

"Are you...estranged...from your parents?"

She laughs softly, but she shakes her head no.

Chip continues, "Because I don't get why you're staying at the Ramada Inn, and you only seem to come here when there's no one home."

Rae takes a deep breath and stares silently at Chip for a moment. Why not just tell him? What's going to happen? She'd told Charlie, and okay, it had been a hard sell. But nothing had happened. No time travel chopper with time travel cops had swooped in and ripped her away from the kitchen table this morning. So maybe Chip won't believe her. Maybe Chip will think she's nuts. But there's an off chance he'll believe her.

Right?

"Why don't you come in for a while?" she suggests. "I have something I want to show you."

Chip purses his lips and thinks about it for a moment, which makes Rae wonder if she should have invited him in. Maybe he *isn't* that interested? Maybe he senses that she is trouble. Dangerous. Well, only if he's holding on to her when she goes through the time portal. He might consider that dangerous.

Finally, he tugs his keys from the ignition and opens his car door. But once they are out of the car, once Rae has grabbed her bag from the backseat, and now that she's standing on the sidewalk waiting for him, he hesitates again.

"What's wrong?" she asks.

Chip frowns and stuffs his hands in his pockets. "Are you sure it's okay? For me to come in?"

Rae almost chuckles, but somehow she can't. She likes that he's worried about what is proper. And besides, in 1980, she's just a little kid and it wouldn't be at all kosher for Chip Andrews to be in their house with her *or* Charlie.

"Yes," she answers firmly. "I'm sure. Come in. Let me show you something."

With one last glance around, Chip nods almost imperceptibly and follows her up the driveway. Rae panics for a moment when they reach the back of the house. She still does not have a key. What if she has to climb that damned tree again to get in through a window? No way will Chip believe anything she says if she has to get into the house that way. Heart pounding so hard she thinks Chip must be able to see it in her chest, she makes her way to the back door and reaches for the knob. She keeps her face turned away from him as the doorknob turns and the door opens. She can't let Chip see how relieved she is.

"Are your parents at work?" he asks as she strides purposefully into the room. Her first thought is to sit with him at the kitchen table, just as she had earlier today with Charlie. But she can't do that. There are windows all the way around the table, and another over the kitchen sink. If they sit here to talk, surely a neighbor will see them. Nineteen-eighty might be before the age of cell phones, but neighbors watched out for each other back then and there are landlines and surely, her dad had left a contact number for the hotel where they'd be staying with one of their neighbors.

"They left today for a little mini-vacation," Rae explains. She could take him upstairs to her bedroom, but that thought totally squicks her out. Maybe it would go a ways in making him see that she really is Rae Warner, just twenty years back in time. But she can't possibly take this kid to her bedroom, when in this time she is ten. Besides, if they are up there after dark and a neighbor sees a light on, she has the same problem.

Gonna have to be the basement. Which is okay. The basement is finished. There's a comfortable place to sit. Couch. Recliner. TV. Mini-bar. Full bathroom. Okay, so the basement is basically a miniature apartment. She could hide out down there forever, except that her family *does use* the basement. Not as much in the summer time, granted, but *still*. Whatever. For right now, it will do.

"C'mere," she says as she pulls the door to the basement steps open. "Come with me."

"Rae, are you sure this is cool? I feel like I'm trespassing."

"No, it's fine," she assures him. She flips the light on and leads him downstairs. Once in the basement, Rae is overcome with memories again. She stands for a moment and simply breathes in the moments of her childhood that she's long forgotten: playing Monopoly with her dad and Charlie while her mom read her *Ladies' Home Journal*. Playing video games with Charlie and her cousins. She glances toward the TV; sure enough, the Atari game console is still stored on a shelf immediately to the left of the TV. Even her dad's black leather recliner kindles the deep-burning desire to go home. Or rather, stay here, now that she is home.

Chip clears his throat, and Rae realizes her behavior isn't doing anything to reassure him that she is who she says she is. With one last look around and one last flash of feel good memory, Rae moves toward the couch. She perches gingerly on the edge of the seat and looks up at Chip. He flashes her an uneasy smile and shoves his hands into his front pockets. Wondering what he will think once he hears her story, *the real story*, Rae slides the strap of her bag from her shoulder and then slowly unzips it. Chip wanders over to sit by her, though he leaves a generous amount of space between them, as if one of her parents might come downstairs and catch them sitting too close together.

That's another memory altogether, and Rae feels her face blush furiously before she can push it away.

Chip watches her with interest as she eases her laptop from the bag, lays the bag to the side, and sets the laptop on the coffee table in front of the couch.

"What is that?" he asks with a curious frown. Without a word, Rae opens the laptop and powers it up. She glances at Chip and then reaches back into the bag for her cell phone.

"This," she finally says, after setting her phone on the coffee table beside her laptop, "is my computer. It's a laptop. Does everything a regular desk-top computer does, only it's portable."

Chip's frown deepens. He reaches out to touch the laptop, but his hand stops half way there.

Too late, Rae realizes that most families don't have access to anything resembling a desktop computer yet. And if they do have a computer, it looks nothing like the desktop she'd had in college.

Chip stares at her for a moment, and then he looks back at the laptop, obviously confused. "What do you do with it? What's a desktop computer?"

Rae takes a deep breath and mentally pictures herself taking the plunge from the high-dive at the country club pool where she'd spent so many of her summer days when she was a kid.

"Remember how my license said that it was issued in 1999? You asked me about it that day down by the river?"

Chip nods.

"It was issued in 1999."

"What?"

"I'm from the future, Chip, and I've been trying to get Charlie, my brother, to help me get back."

Chip stares at her blankly. "You're from the future," he repeats with a straight face. "How is that possible?"

"I have no idea, but it's possible, because here I am. The day I met you, I woke up in the year 2000 and ended up thrown back into 1980 by dinnertime."

"I thought when you time-traveled, you'd actually go… you know…way back in time. I mean, twenty years?" He frowns at Rae and then shakes his head.

"I don't know," Rae answers with a shrug. "I've never done this before. All I know is I need to get back to the year 2000."

Why did she need to get back to the year 2000? Surely,

she'd lost her job by now. Paul had probably assumed she wasn't into him and therefore wasn't returning phone calls, and he'd probably moved on. *Charlie.* Okay, yeah, she needed to get back to 2000 just to assure Charlie she was okay, if for no other reason.

"You know this is really weird, right?"

Rae, who had been studying the screen of her laptop, looks up at Chip and snorts. "You're telling me? For weeks I've been trying to get Charlie's help, all the while dodging my parents and anyone else that might see me and wonder who I am. I almost ran into my uncle yesterday."

"And Charlie's—? How old?"

"Fourteen."

"Rae, how's a fourteen-year-old going to help get you back to the year 2000?"

Rae feels a small smile play at the corner of her lips. Is Chip just humoring her, or does he believe her?

"Charlie had an obsession with time travel. When we were younger…" Rae frowns as she hears herself say the words. "Well…now, I guess. He was fascinated by the idea. Read any stories he could find on time travel. Obsessed over how to do it. My dad used to get so mad at him. Charlie's brilliant, but Dad wanted him to focus on something that was possible. He grew up to be a research scientist, but he kept playing with the time travel idea. In his spare time."

"And so, apparently, he found a way to do it?"

Rae stands up and walks around the coffee table to pace the floor. "Apparently. I'm pretty sure I was at his place just before I was walking around and ended up in the bar."

"Where we met?" Chip raises his eyebrows.

Rae nods.

"You did seem pretty out of it that night."

"Thanks."

Chip grins and shrugs innocently. "You did."

"I keep trying to remember what was at Charlie's house. He's always got stuff…everywhere. Clutter. He goes to garage sales and antique sales and estate sales, and he buys the weirdest stuff. He's convinced that he'll find the secret to time travel."

"So, no telephone booth in the corner of his porch, huh?" Chip falls back against the couch and sighs. "Nothing quite so obvious?"

"Actually, he does have an old telephone booth in his basement. But, trust me, that's not what got me here. He's had it for years, and he's tried a million times and more to make it take him somewhere. No magic there."

"Wouldn't really be magic, though, would it?" Chip frowns. "Science fiction, maybe, but not magic."

"Whatever. It's not what brought me here."

"So what was new around his place that last day you were there?"

Rae closes her eyes and tries to remember being at Charlie's place. The kitchen table overflowing with books and papers and Charlie's notes. The table in the dining room, covered with gadgets like remote controls for TVs and walkie-talkies and even yo-yos. What was there the last time that hadn't been before? Rae doesn't have a clue, and she doubts that Charlie knows, either. How could he, with so much stuff piled on every surface? Rae had asked him once how he even ate a decent meal in his house, because there was no flat surface to use as a table. He'd told her he ate standing up, usually a TV dinner, and Rae had been saddened that her brother lived that way.

"Do you believe me?" Rae turns to look at Chip. She leans back in her dad's recliner and watches about a hundred emotions paint Chip's face. Finally everything falls away, and Chip just stares at her with a blank look. He shrugs.

"If anyone had asked me this morning if I believed in time travel, I'd have said no." He laughs and shakes his head. "But. There's been something…mysterious…about you from the first time I met you. Something that didn't quite click. This makes…sense."

Rae chuckles. "Never thought you'd hear yourself saying that, didya?"

"So you don't remember whatever Charlie used to send you back here?"

"No." Rae shakes her head. "I don't. I'll keep thinking about it, but at the moment, I'm drawing a blank."

"You said your family is on a mini-vacation?"

"I talked to Charlie this morning. He said they're going to Wisconsin Dells for the weekend. They'll be back on Sunday night or Monday."

Chip purses his lips and blows his cheeks out to make a childish face. Rae watches him stand and pace the floor. He stops in front of a wall of pictures and studies them.

"This is you?" He points to her fourth grade picture, hanging just under Charlie's eighth grade picture, next to a giant circular clock with all the numbers made to look as if they've fallen to the bottom. The middle of the clock says *It's the perfect time for a drink*. Her parents entertain here in the basement quite often in the winter.

"Yep. Fourth grade."

"And you were—what? Ten?"

Rae nods.

"Like…in 1980…how old are you?"

"Ten."

"Wow." Chip drops his hand from the picture and stuffs it in his front pocket. "That kinda makes me feel like a dirty old man."

"Well, I'm older than you now, so don't sweat it."

Chip glances at her and flashes an impish grin. "Let's go somewhere. Do something."

"Okay." Rae nods. It's not as if she can sit here in the basement and figure this out anyway. In the back of her mind, she wonders what will happen when Charlie comes back and together, they still can't figure out how to get her back to the year 2000. But there's no point in dwelling on that until the time comes. Might as well get out and enjoy a summer day with Chip. "What should we do?"

"Let's go to my uncle's. He's got a pond behind the house. We could...go fishing."

The Nitty Gritty Dirt Band song "Fishing in the Dark" flashes through Rae's brain, but she shuts it off quickly. It wasn't released until the later 80s, so there's no way Chip's ever heard it. And anyway, it's not night time, and Chip is clearly uncomfortable with the idea of her being only a little girl in 1980, so he's obviously not suggesting they go skinny-dipping or messing around out by his uncle's pond.

"Okay." She agrees. "But I'm not touching any worms,"

She feels a flush rushing up through her chest and her neck, so she turns quickly so Chip doesn't see her blush. It's not like he's thinking of the Nitty Gritty Dirt Band or anything sexual for that matter. Apparently, Rae has acquired a dirty mind while stuck twenty years in the past. She scrambles to put her laptop and phone back in the bag. Just in case. Her parents *should* be gone through late Monday morning, if she remembers this trip right. But, who knows? Better safe than sorry. She zips the bag and hides it in the closet under the stairs.

"I feel bad now. Knowing that you've been staying at a hotel, trying to find food and stuff. Here, I thought you were seriously thinking about breaking in here."

Rae glances at Chip and giggles. He follows her up the steps.

"The first night, after you left, I had to climb that tree in the back. Sneak in my window. To find Charlie. And he wasn't even here."

"You climbed the tree? The one in the back?"

"Mmm-hmm."

"But you were wearing…"

They stand in the kitchen now. Chip flutters his hands around his hips and then a little lower to indicate that Rae had been wearing a skirt.

"Yeah. A skirt and heels."

"How'd you climb a tree? In that?"

"Kicked the heels off and hiked the skirt up around my hips."

"Oh God." Chip groans. "I'm thinking really sexy things right now."

"Yeah? Nothing wrong with that."

"You're ten."

"That me is ten. I'm not her now." She reminds him.

"Let's go. There's a tackle box and fishing poles in the shed at my uncle's."

Amused by the struggle going on in Chip's head and apparently his jeans, too, Rae follows him outside and leaves the back door unlocked. She wishes she had a key, but Charlie hadn't offered one. He'd left the door open for her, so she leaves it unlocked now and walks side by side with Chip down the driveway.

"What kind of fish does your uncle have in his pond?"

"I dunno," Chip mumbles as he yanks the driver's door open. "I'd be good with goldfish right about now."

"Goldfish?"

"Damn," he mutters. "I let a little kid drive my car."

"I turn thirty in September. I'm older than you."

"It's weird." He starts the car and drops the gearshift into drive. "Man, I bought you a drink. I bought liquor for a minor."

"Chip, I'm not a minor."

"I could use a drink. Right now."

Rae grins at him. "Piña colada?"

He laughs and shakes his head. "Stop it. We're gonna go catch fish. And then we're gonna clean 'em and cook 'em and eat 'em."

This time, Rae laughs. "That's sexy."

"And we're not gonna say that word."

"What word? *Sexy*?"

"Stop it!"

Rae sighs. The tension has ebbed, but now Chip's hung up on the age difference. The time travel age difference that really shouldn't matter.

Should it?

Chapter 12

Rae does not consider herself much of a fisherman, and when they are an hour into fishing and the fish are not biting, she is bored. Chip's uncle has a nice brick ranch house, and she finds herself daydreaming about going inside and taking a tour. The long yard is immaculate, and even the shed is kind of a fancy little building with terribly bright white siding on it. If the yard and shed are this nice, probably the interior of the house is pretty nice, too.

That and air-conditioned.

Rae can feel sweat rolling down her back and between her breasts. She's taken her shoes and socks off, and she's parked her fishing pole in a holder on the dock where apparently Chip and his uncle sit often for this very reason. She lets her legs dangle off the dock, but it's no use. The dock is up too high to even skim the water with her bare feet.

Within minutes of being out here with Chip, she'd pulled her hair up in a ponytail.

It's still hot. She can't help but think that if she were in the year 2000, she'd be in her very air-conditioned office.

No matter that she'd be working. At least she wouldn't be melting.

Chip glances at her a few times before he sets his pole in another of the small, rounded holders attached to the dock.

"Want something cold to drink?" he asks.

"Sure."

"I'll go see what Uncle Jeff's got in the shed."

"In the shed?" she repeats, because what could possibly be cold to drink in the shed?

"Stocked fridge," he answers.

She nods and wishes he'd said he was going to the house to find something for them to drink. She'd have been on her feet in two seconds, ready to follow him. Within five minutes, Chip is back with two cans of Coke. Rae takes the one he offers her, pops the top, and gulps down half of it before rolling the can back and forth over her forehead.

"Wanna go for a swim?" he asks. He'd watched her roll the can over her forehead and then down over her neck, but now he's not looking at her. He's staring at something out on the water. Rae glances out there to see what he's looking at, but when she sees nothing, she takes another drink of soda—this one smaller—and laughs softly.

"Don't have a suit." She shrugs and wishes she'd have picked one up, even though in her real life, the one she lives in in 2000, she hates swimsuit shopping, and she probably has not worn a suit in well over two years. At least, she hasn't worn one in public. Now and then she'll sit out in the sun at her apartment, but then, it doesn't matter how awful a swimsuit looks on you when there's no one around to see it, does it?

Chip glances at her. "Do we need suits?"

Rae raises her eyebrows, but when Chip doesn't laugh

and doesn't say anything else, she wonders if he is serious. Is he really suggesting that they skinny-dip?

"I don't need trunks," he says quietly.

Rae squints and again searches for whatever it was out on the water a few seconds ago that had Chip so intrigued. "Are you suggesting we go skinny-dipping?"

"Why not?" Chip shrugs. "Wouldn't be the first time."

Rae purses her lips. Should she tell him it would indeed be the first time to skinny-dip for her? Probably not, but apparently, she's wearing the confession all over her face, because suddenly Chip pokes her and when she looks at him, he's wearing a big grin, and she feels her cheeks burning.

"Okay," he says with a nod. "You're right. We probably shouldn't do that."

Rae nods her agreement. What could they do? Well, they could go back to her parents' house. Maybe watch a movie? But the thought of watching a VHS tape on a VCR, the thought of watching an old movie, doesn't excite her. Truthfully, the thought of skinny-dipping here in this pond with Chip excites her. Now that Chip's suggested it, she can't stop thinking about it. It would definitely feel good to just jump in the water. Rae can almost feel it, how good it would be to just plunge in headfirst.

She imagines Chip's hard body in the water. His arms and shoulders naked with beads of water on them. His wet hair slicked back a bit, and the sun biting his nose, touching his cheeks. But it's broad daylight. What if someone sees them? She glances around. The pond itself is almost completely closed in by big trees. Except for the dock and Chip's uncle's backyard. And Chip had told her his aunt and uncle never get home from work until well after six. She thinks he'd told her where they work, but at the moment, she can't remember. She can't be bothered to try.

What would it hurt? Just to jump in and cool off? Then they could go back to her parents' house. Find dinner. Or maybe Chip had plans for tonight, and she could just hang out at the house or something.

"So," she starts in a small voice that she hates, "how often do you skinny-dip?"

"Now and then," he answers easily. "But not lately."

She nods, but she says nothing else. She can't very well seem too anxious, can she?

"Why?" Chip finally asks when the silence has dragged on for a few too many moments. "Do you want to?"

Rae presses her lips together and shrugs nonchalantly. Or at least, what she hopes is nonchalantly.

"It's pretty hot."

Chip agrees with a nod. Rae flinches when he climbs back to his feet. She watches him reel in the fishing lines.

"What are you doing?"

"Putting these away."

"Why?"

"I don't wanna go swimming with fishing hooks out there, do you?"

Rae feels a blush creep over her face again. "No."

He disappears for a moment. Rae figures he's putting the fishing poles and the tackle box back in the shed. She looks up when she hears him coming back across the dock. He's already got his shirt stripped off, and his hands fumble with the zipper on his pants. Rae looks away quickly. She hears his pants hit the wooden planks and then she hears a splash as Chip jumps into the water from the end of the dock.

Suddenly, the temperature seems to have kicked up about fifteen degrees. Rae is unbearably hot, and she fears the water will do nothing to cool her off now. She takes a quick peek out over the water, and there he is, his naked shoulders visible above the water line, a big grin on his face. Her mouth goes dry when she imagines his body below the water line. Maybe, she tells herself, maybe he's wearing boxers or something. But when Chip ducks his head back under the water, she takes a quick look at his pants on the dock and sees his boxers there, too.

Chip is completely naked in the water.

Hotter still, Rae feels sweat rolling down her neck.

"You comin' in?" he calls.

"Um." She swallows hard. "How's the water?"

"Nice," he answers. "You'll feel much better. Betcha."

"Okay," she says softly. "Okay."

"Go ahead," he says. "I'll turn my back."

She stands as he turns to give her some privacy. Of course nothing is going to happen. She'd freaked him out earlier with her time travel tale, and now Chip is hung up on the fact that in 1980, she is only ten. Even though right now she's a grown woman, and she's burning up with grown woman needs.

She slides her pants down over her hips and steps out of them. Still in her panties, she pulls her shirt over her head. Considers jumping into the water in her panties and bra. But the thought of putting her dry clothes on over her wet underwear makes her skin crawl. She takes another look at Chip. He's at the other edge of the water, back to her, looking up at the trees.

"Is it deep?" she asks, hands reaching back to unhook her bra.

"Yeah. Jump. You'll be fine."

Jump. You'll be fine. Loaded words.

Rae flicks the hook of her bra and lets the band of white material fall to the dock. Next she hooks her thumbs in her panties and pushes them down. She glances at Chip as she steps out of them, but true to his word, he's still not looking. Well. Okay. Even if this is just skinny-dipping, it *will* feel good to cool off. But she's still just a little disappointed as she jumps from the end of the dock into the water.

It's cold but in a refreshing way. Not painfully cold, the way a swimming pool can be too early in the season. She breaks the surface of the water and reaches back to pull the elastic holder from her hair.

"Nice?" Chip asks as she slips it around her wrist.

"Feels great," she agrees.

"Never thought of it, but I guess we could have gone to the pool."

Rae smiles sheepishly. "I don't have a suit."

"Mmm." He nods. "I used to swim here all the time when I was younger."

"In trunks?"

"Oh yes," he answers with a laugh. "My sisters and I used to swim here a lot."

"So then…when did you skinny-dip?"

Chip grins. Rae watches him swim a few feet away. She can see the shape of his muscular back and the curve of his butt just under the water. Probably she should look away, but she doesn't.

"The first time I was fourteen. And last time was just a year ago."

"Fourteen?"

"You've never done this?" he asks her with a suspicious frown.

"Um, no." She smiles. "I actually didn't swim much at all when I was younger."

"You look like a good swimmer," he tells her, which makes her laugh, because so far, she hasn't moved from where she'd ended up when she jumped in. She's only treading water.

"Do I?"

He grins and nods and looks away. "How about a race?"

"A race? Seriously?" She looks around. She has no problem with swimming in a pond; she's not one of those girls who doesn't like critters in the water with her. But she doesn't really want to *race* in the pond. That seems more like a big pool adventure. She looks back over her shoulder to say something to him, but he's disappeared. He's swimming underwater. She begins to swim just a bit, because part of her wonders if he's going to swim close to her and grab her. Not that that would be all bad.

But still her heart's pounding a bit too hard.

Suddenly he pops out of the water. Much closer to her now. In fact, he's not even a foot away from her. Much to her disappointment, he doesn't touch her, though. Her heart is still beating in her throat, and it kind of hurts. Does he want to race her, because he's thinking of her as a kid?

Chip reaches out slowly and rubs his thumb over her eyebrow.

"You had…something…" he mumbles. She smiles, but the nerves that now hum in her stomach chase the smile away quickly.

"So." Chip takes a deep breath and cocks his head. "You're from the future."

"Sounds like a bad movie, doesn't it?" Rae is uncomfortable with how close they are physically and how distant they are in every other way. She looks up and meets his eyes, but she quickly looks away.

"Bad movie, but a gorgeous actress," he answers softly.

She looks up again and sees Chip move even closer. His

hands reach toward her and then his fingers slide under her chin and over her face, and he leans in and touches his lips to hers. The kiss is so soft, it barely registers as a kiss.

"So we're skinny-dipping, and I'm coming on to you." He bites his lip. "Sounds like a bad movie, doesn't it?"

"Bad movie, but a gorgeous actor," she says quietly.

"Are you gonna think I'm a jerk if I tell you I want to touch you? That I want to put my hands all over you?"

"No."

"I mean…" Chip drops his hands and moves back from her. "It's not like you took your clothes off, and now I think this is what has to happen next."

It feels like tiny electric volts are shooting through Rae's arms, and her fingertips tingle. Her nipples tighten, and it has nothing to do with the cold water.

"If it makes you feel any better, I've wanted to put my hands all over you since we danced that night. When we danced and drank piña coladas."

Rae smiles.

"So," she takes a deep breath, "what are you waiting for?"

"It just seems like it'll be sleazy if I do it here. Now."

Rae considers his words. She's pretty much wanted his hands all over her since they danced. Actually, she's been thinking about his body since she slammed up against it in the bar. She had decided she'd try her hand—and every-thing else—at casual sex for him. Now she's gotten to know him, and she likes him, and it doesn't seem so casual anymore. At least not to her, and that makes it huge and a little scary.

But she still wants his hands all over her. Now.

When Chip still doesn't move, she reaches for him. Feathers her fingers around the back of his neck and leans into him. She follows his lead, and this kiss is just as soft and gentle as his was. Within seconds, he moves closer to her and Rae feels his arms slide around her waist, his palms flat against her hips and then her back. Better, but not enough.

He pulls her in against him, and her breasts flatten against his chest and their legs bump and slide as they tread water. Nice, but still not enough. Rae needs his hands in other places. Now. If it's possible, she's hotter now in the water than she'd been fully clothed on the dock.

Certainly, if she's never skinny-dipped before, she's not made love in a lake or a pool before. While it seems like it could be interesting, it hinders what she needs most right now. She breaks the kiss and then watches Chip's eyes open. Drops of water cling to his lashes. With his whole body naked before her, she is fixated on his eyes. They are more intense now, brown with flecks of gold. His hair falls in wet ringlets down his neck. What kind of universe gives her this in a time zone where she doesn't belong? How can she possibly go back home now?

Desperate to move things along, desperate for the magic she is sure Chip's body will bring, Rae locks her legs around his waist and pulls him closer. She feels him then. Long and hard against her leg. Pressing into her middle. Better still, but still not enough.

"Are you sure?" His voice is tight and small. Rae watches the way his mouth bobs just at the water level. Above the water, he licks his lips, and Rae thinks there are better places for his tongue, his mouth to be.

"I'm sure," she whispers.

Arms still around her, he swims on his side to the edge of the water. Rather than leave the water completely, he stops where they can stand. Rae lowers her legs and finds that her knees are weak. Eyes on hers, Chip traces his fingertips over her bare shoulder and then down her chest, careful to treat each of her nipples with extra attention, and then he continues around the curves of her breasts and down over her stomach. Still standing in water past their knees, he kneels in front of her and caresses the back of her legs, careful to brush the back of her knees with extra attention, and then his hands disappear and she feels his fingers stroke over her feet and her toes. She needs to sit, but she can't move.

Mostly, her sex life has been very vanilla, and she's used to the missionary position, and while she's been *satisfied* with what she's had, she thinks there might be more to Chip. More to making love to Chip. Her heart hammers in her chest, but she wants to let him lead. She wants him to take her on his terms, and so she stands on trembling legs as he slowly stands before her again. His hands slide back over her waist and her hips and cup her bare butt and pull her hard against him. He ducks his head and scrapes his teeth gently over the curve of first one breast and then the other.

Rae's knees buckle, but his hands, still on her backside, hold her up. Needing more of an anchor and needing to fill her hands with Chip, she reaches for him. She slides her hands up over his shoulders and holds on as suddenly, his fingers are moving and sliding between her legs.

Rae groans as her knees buckle again.

"Stay with me," he whispers against her breast, and then he drags his open mouth up and over her chest. He plants a kiss in the hollow of her throat, and his fingers flicker gently over her core, and her blood is slow and thick in her veins like a drug. He licks his way up her neck, and then he nips at her chin and her lips, and his mouth covers hers, and she feels like this kiss is his mouth making love to hers.

He applies more pressure at her center, rubs slowly and steadily, and Rae moans and leans heavily against him.

"Like this?" he whispers, and he moves a bit faster and then faster still when she shivers against him. "Do you like this, Rae?"

She only manages to breathe, and even that is choppy, but she is blind now as she rides his hand. She wants to touch him. She wants to take him in her hand, but she can't let go of his shoulders. She will shatter and fall into the water and drown, and so she holds on until suddenly, riding him hard, his fingers caressing and rubbing and then sliding into her, she does break apart. She whispers his name on a sob, and then he kisses her again and swallows the tiny moans, the purrs that come from deep in her throat. Still he touches her and still, Rae rides him, and her body quivers. She has never been pushed like this. No lover has ever pushed her past an orgasm; the minute she's done —*if it happens*—any other man (and there have only been two) has climbed on top of her and driven into her, anxious for their turn.

Chip doesn't let her go. He only moves to dip his head again and draw her nipple into his mouth. He scrapes her with his teeth, and then his lips tug at her as his fingers drive her over the edge again. She laughs and cries and says his name again and then finally, he draws his hand away, and she rests her head on his shoulder.

"Are you okay?" His voice is low and thick in her ear.

She nods against him. Her body feels heavy, languid like she could curl up against him and sleep for days. But then she feels his erection now, pressed against her middle, and she slides her fingers down over his chest and cups him in her hand.

He groans and covers her hand with his. Still standing in water up to their knees, Chip's hands cup her bottom again, and she lifts her legs around his waist. And then she feels him as he sits her over his erection and pushes into her gently. He watches her eyes as her body stretches to welcome him.

"Good?" he asks.

"Good," she breathes. He fills her completely. It's good, but again, it's not enough. She straightens her body, trying to move on him. He grins.

"I know." He nods.

She needs him to move. She wants to feel him rub against her, to feel the pressure moving inside her.

As he walks to the side of the pond, she leans into him and presses her open mouth to his jaw. Nips at his jawline and then finds his lips, open and waiting for her. And then they are out of the water, and Chip squats, still holding her, still with her legs wrapped around his waist; he sits in the grass, and Rae straddles him and she moves. She's never made love like this, well—*obviously*, she's never made love in the middle of the afternoon, at the edge of a pond—but she's never been in control. She loves the way Chip's eyes and his hands move over her breasts and her stomach as she moves over him.

She watches his eyes glaze as he fights to hold on. To make it last longer. And then finally, he digs his hands into her hips and sits up half way to meet her. She leans in, and he takes her mouth in a kiss that Rae believes touches her soul. When he flips her to lie on her back and drives into her one last time, he groans out loud and calls out to God and then he chants her name over and over, and Rae knows she's in trouble.

She can't do casual sex.

Chip Andrews is the first man she's ever fallen head over heels for, and she can't have him. Not beyond this. Not beyond the now.

"Oh God," he says on a deep breath. "God. If I'd have known what you were hiding, I think I'd have started this a long time ago."

She smiles weakly. Thinks briefly about the two other men she's been with and wonders where Chip learned to satisfy a woman like this. She decides she probably doesn't want to know, any more than she wants to tell him she would never have guessed it was in her to behave this way.

"That was incredible." He sounds sleepy.

It was incredible, she thinks. She turns on her side and lays her head on his chest. How unfortunate they'd wasted so much time together. Rae closes her eyes before she can think too far into the future. Where she will return and Chip will not.

"Hey Future," he says after a few quiet moments. Rae lifts her head. His eyes are closed, but he has a lazy grin on his face.

"Hmm?"

"Whenever we figure out how you go back?" His arm around her, he runs his fingers down her side. Before she can answer him, before she can say she doesn't want to go back, he continues, "I'm going with you."

Chapter 13

RAE STARES AT HIM SILENTLY. IT SEEMS LIKE THE WORLD should just stop after an announcement like that. She should tell him no. That he can't go back with her to the year 2000. It's not possible. And yet, she is lying with him, and they've just made love, and Rae can think only that she wants to be with him again. All day. All night. Tomorrow.

Forever.

She can't say that, though. She can't say that and turn around and tell him he can't go back to her life with her. Water still beads his skin, and rather than answer him, because she can't talk—not now—she traces her fingers over his chest and then molds the palm of her hand over his shoulder. His eyes, though drowsy and dreamy, watch her with hunger, and when she leans closer to kiss him, he meets her half way.

His lips are warm; his skin under her hands is hot, even, and Rae remembers they are naked, lying at the edge of his uncle's pond, and the midday sun is beating down on them. They'll sunburn, and making love will hurt, but still she kisses him and ignores everything else.

"Is this okay?" she finally whispers. She doesn't know why she whispers, because there is no one around. Since they've been here at the pond, she's heard only birds chirping and an occasional dog barking. There's no one around, and she has to admit, skinny-dipping and making love in the open like this is a delicious experience and not one she wants to hurry through.

"This is so incredible." Chip's teeth tug at her earlobe, and then he moves and drops soft, sweet kisses into her hair and then across her forehead, and he nibbles on her other ear. His lips and his tongue feel good on her skin, but Rae is hungry for him, and she opens her mouth and licks his neck, flicks the tip of her tongue in the hollow at his throat. She wishes for a moment that they were at the ocean, and that when she kisses him, she could taste salt on his skin, and she thinks they should go some day. On a romantic getaway weekend, where they can sip piña coladas and relax on pretty white sand and make love in a cottage on the beach.

Because they can't, because this moment is all they can have, Rae slides her hands down and around his waist as she wiggles into place beneath him again so that she can feel his weight between her thighs. Her sighs of pleasure, and his heavy breathing fill the afternoon sunshine.

His lips find hers again, and he lingers there. Slow and gentle. Deep and hungry. He drinks her in as if he is parched, and she is water. Rae has never been kissed this way in her life. Never been kissed as if she is vital to a man's survival. She's never known the pleasure of lying with a man in the afternoon for the sole purpose of enjoyment. Fulfillment.

When Chip breaks the kisses and lifts his head to look

at her, she is punch-drunk, and her heart feels like a butterfly in her chest, struggling to fly.

"When we danced…" he says and he lowers his face to hers again to press kisses to her forehead. She closes her eyes and feels his touch on her eyelids. "I wanted to kiss you. I wanted to put my arms around you."

"I wanted you to," she whispers.

"I wanted to slide your skirt up over your thighs."

A little giggle escapes her, and she opens her eyes to find him watching her with a smirk on his face.

"Why's that funny?"

Rae lifts her right hand and strokes her fingertips over his cheekbone.

"I had visions of you dragging me off to a dark corner and sliding my skirt up over my hips and pressing your knee between my thighs."

"Yeah?" The smirk spreads into a grin. "Why didn't you say so?"

It's ridiculous, because she's lying here naked under his naked body, and they've just been as intimate as two people can be, but she blushes anyway. She is embarrassed not for what they've done, but for all that she's never experienced before being with him.

She shakes her head and hopes he will let it go.

"What?" He leans forward again and licks the center of her upper lip. Pokes at her until she parts her lips, and then he kisses her again. A long, searching kiss, and Rae feels his tongue sweep her heart and her soul.

When he pulls away from her, he's watching her again, waiting for her to answer him.

"I'm not very…" She begins, but she can only shake her head in dismissal and press her lips together.

"Experienced," he finishes for her.

She looks up at him, wide-eyed now. How can he tell

that? Had she done something wrong? Did she touch something he didn't want her to? Had she been too eager? Had she rushed it? She'd never come so quickly, so fast and hard as she had when he stroked his fingers over her center earlier before they'd made love. Was that something she should be able to control?

"What?" she asks quickly. "What does that mean?"

"Hmm?"

"Why do you say that? That I'm not very experienced?"

"You're pretty uptight, Rae—"

"What?"

She's uptight? She's lying here at the side of a pond, soaking lazily in the aftermath of what she'd thought was earth-shattering sex, and—

"Since we met," he told her. "You've been very jumpy. Nervous."

She stares at him anxiously. Waits for him to tell her what she'd done wrong now. What nervous mistake she'd made when he'd touched her. Personally, she liked it this way much better. She'd never been intimate with Paul; they'd only had a couple of dates. But the other men she'd been involved with—*all two of them*—hadn't particularly been skillful lovers. Her first hadn't bothered to notice if she'd enjoyed sex. The second had labored over her for long minutes and when he'd climaxed and she hadn't, he'd worked for what felt like an eternity to pleasure her. She'd finally experienced an orgasm, but compared to what she'd just felt with Chip, it was weak and left her exhausted and desperate to sleep alone.

"Since we—?" she repeats when she realizes Chip's intense eyes are still watching her closely. "Since we met?"

"Mm-hmm." He nods. "What'd you think I meant? You were jumpy at the bar. When I drove you to your parents' house. Remember? You hit your head trying to scramble out of my car so fast."

She laughs softly, but she lifts her head to press her forehead to his chest.

"Don't try to hide from me."

"I thought you meant…"

"What?"

"Nevermind."

"You thought I meant what?" He coaxes her to lie back again. Plays with her hair for a moment and then frames her lips with his fingers.

"That I did something wrong."

"Wrong?" He arches his eyebrows in disbelief. "Was there something wrong with this?"

She shakes her head no. "It was so fast."

He grins. Nods. "It was. But that's my fault." He tilts his head, chin to his chest and looks an eyeful at her breasts. "I've been thinking about this too long. Couldn't control myself."

"I'm not complaining."

"We can do it again."

He trails his fingers down over her neck and the curve of her breast and then rubs a slow, soft circle around her nipple.

"Can we?"

"I told you I'm going back with you," he reminds her. "We're gonna be busy for the next fifteen or twenty years making love."

"Chip—" She starts to protest, but he's moved his fingers from her breast and skimmed them low over her belly. She loves the feel of his body pressed into hers, but she only moans in protest when he shifts to her side. His fingers play over her inner thighs and back up over her belly. Her body is melting now, and it has nothing to do with the sun high above them. Flames of desire lick her inner thighs and that soft skin at the back of her knees, and her body feels drunk again as Chip finally strokes his thumb over her core. He flicks at her lazily, and though her eyes are closed, she feels him watching her.

She wants his lips on hers, though she doesn't move. Feels too good to just lie here and feel his fingers stoking the fire. Too hard to concentrate on anything, even to feel anything else. He moves, and his lips close over her nipple and suck at her. She lifts a hand that must weigh fifty pounds to tangle her fingers in his hair. Waves of pleasure tease just out of reach, and she sighs in frustration.

He draws his hand away from her, and she opens her eyes, ready to protest. But he's only shifting so that he can put his lips on her other breast. She lifts her hips in the air as he slides his fingers over her again. He teases her, changes the pressure of his fingers from gentle to harder and back to gentle again. She watches him for a moment, the way he curls his tongue around the under curve of her breast. It is incredibly sexy to watch him, to see his hand on her further down their bodies, but selfishly, she closes her eyes to concentrate on his touch.

She feels it again. The tightening of her body, the way she breathes harder. But she feels self-conscious about it now since they talked about it. Before she can grab the feeling and ride it, it slides away from her. Desperate to pull it back, to feel the waves of pleasure smother her again, she reaches her hands out. One finds Chip's shoulder, his hair. The other touches the cool grass and mud where they lie.

"Let go." He presses his words into her breasts, and then closes his lips around her nipple yet again. The consistent tug there adds to that building pressure she so desperately needs to explode. "Come for me, Rae."

"I can't," she moans, and she wants to sob. She feels her body fight it off again, and she's frustrated.

"You can." He nods and blows his warm breath over her breast where he's licked her skin. "Just relax."

"It's okay—"

"I like this," he tells her. "I like touching you like this."

She sighs again, and this time when she feels the pressure, feels her body tightening, she moves her hips just slightly, and she squeezes Chip's shoulder. Closes her other fist around a handful of grass and concentrates on that feeling.

"That's it," he tells her when she breathes harder and says his name on a whisper. And then on a moan. And finally, she forgets where they are and as the waves of pleasure crash over her, she says it louder and louder, and Chip still strokes her even after she explodes, and her body quivers again at his touch.

He slides his body over hers again and while the aftershocks of her orgasm are still rolling over her, he gently pushes inside her again, and she circles her legs—again, her body is heavy with satisfaction—around his waist and moves with him, thrust for thrust. This time, they move slowly and enjoy every stroke, and Rae decides she has never made love like this. Like it means *love*. Like Chip loves her as much as she loves him.

She does. She loves him. She loves him, and this has been the best few weeks of her life, and it saddens her that she will have to give this up. When she goes back to 2000, Chip cannot go.

Desperate to put that thought out of her mind, she throws herself into their lovemaking. Their kisses. The joy and pleasure they give each other, and she refuses to think it is how they will say goodbye.

Chapter 14

THE REST OF THE AFTERNOON, INTO THE EVENING, RAE IS bothered by a sense of loss so deep it steals her breath away. Each time it happens, each time she remembers she will have to leave and Chip will have to stay, she gasps for air, and her eyes burn with tears, and she has to fight panic. She tries to hide it from Chip, because he will argue with her. He'll say he's going back with her, and Rae knows that he can't, and she doesn't want to waste whatever time they have left arguing and unhappy.

They dress and leave the pond well before Chip's aunt and uncle come home. Though she hates to leave their private slice of paradise, and she regrets it more with each item of clothing Chip dons, she is relieved to be gone before his family members find them lounging naked by the pond. They are easy together now that they've made love, and they touch with affection and longing. They hold hands when they walk, and Chip drives with his left hand, his right resting on Rae's thigh.

She finds herself dangerously close to saying those words. Words she's never been tempted to say to a man in her life. But probably, saying them will only make leaving harder. Saying them will hurt them both, and so each time she finds them in her mouth, on the tip of her tongue, she struggles to hold them inside.

They grab drinks and dinner at The Abbey, a restaurant and bar a block away from the college. In 2000, it is a university, but Rae doesn't want to spend the rest of the evening filling Chip in on the changes to Quincy in the years between his now and hers. She's not entirely sure she wants to be here at The Abbey, when they could be alone somewhere. And yet, she decides, this is important, too. Food, sustenance, yes but spending time together like this. If she were to stay, they would likely go out on dates, so this feels normal and fun, and she watches Chip across the wooden booth as she sips her piña colada.

He talks about his sisters again, and Rae finds herself wishing she could meet them. Wishing she could introduce Chip to Charlie. She supposes she could, but she doubts Charlie in 1980 would be particularly impressed with him. Maybe in her present day, Charlie would like him. Maybe Charlie would be happy she'd found love for just a fleeting moment.

Chip plans to be a teacher, and she can't tell him that he can't come back to 2000 with her, because he won't have finished his education. That he'd lose that dream if he were to go with her. She loves him too much for him to sacrifice his goals for her. He asks her about her job, if she's considered her future and if she wants children, and only because they can't be together, she changes the subject. The thought of being with him, whether it's in 1980 or 2000, of waking up with him every morning and marrying him and having a family with him makes her wistful and sad, and she can't hide that, so she talks about major league baseball and the St. Louis Cardinals and barely keeps it to herself that they win the World Series in 1982.

Maybe it's good that she is the time traveler. What if someone else who knew Charlie took advantage of him and manipulated time in order to gamble? Think of the sporting events a person could win a fortune betting on if he knew the outcome. Think of the stock market. Rae wonders if she should share her concerns with Charlie if she ever gets back to 2000.

The Abbey is a dark bar with polished wooden booths and rough wooden floors. Two levels, the second just a small sidestep off the first, though windows run the length of the narrow section. She and Chip sit in that smaller sidestep, and now and then she glances to her right and watches the older model cars make their way down Eighteenth Street.

After dinner and two drinks each, Chip drives them back to her parents' house. He'd offered her the keys, but after the afternoon in the sun and the drinks and dinner, she is drowsy and somewhat tipsy, and she tells him no, it's probably not a good idea for her to drive. She tells Chip to park in the driveway, but he hesitates and decides it's not a good idea, and instead he parks at the curb. He's right, and yet, even parked at the curb, the neighbors will wonder who the Camaro belongs to. They hold hands as they walk down the driveway, and Rae prays that dusk hides them from nosy, curious eyes.

"So." He props his shoulder against the house as she reaches for the doorknob. "You climbed that tree. In your skirt."

Rae looks over her shoulder at the tree in question and then nods and looks back at him with a grin.

"Charlie and I used to climb that tree all the time. For

fun when we were kids. And then when I was in high school, I would sneak out my window and climb down."

Daylight bleeds from the sky, and even this close to him, his face is in shadows. She sees the arch in his eyebrow, though, and she assumes he is amused by her sneaking out when she is clearly not a rule-breaker now. The fact that she has indeed broken into this house isn't as important as the fact that she's twitchy and nervous and would make a horrible thief if she ever opted for a career change.

"What?" She ducks her head and opens the door. They move inside the house, into the dark kitchen. She closes and locks the door behind them.

"What'd you do when you snuck out?"

"I met my friends," she answers indignantly.

"And you did what? Snuck off to McDonald's for milkshakes?"

Embarrassed to be teased for what is essentially the truth—they'd never snuck off to McDonald's, but Rae figures he would laugh at their pathetic attempt at rebellion: sipping from someone's parents' supply of vodka or whisky, watching R-rated movies wherever someone's parents were not at home—she ignores him and forgets to look around the kitchen to absorb more details for when she goes back home, and she opens the basement door and leads him down the steps.

She'd wanted to undress and lie in his arms. Make love. Just be together. But now she is sore about the teasing, and besides it feels a little weird to her to think about doing it here in her parents' basement. Not that Chip's apartment would be much better. She doesn't relish the idea of having sex in his room while his roommate or mates listen from the next room. But time is running out, and she's desperately afraid to let another minute go by without touching him.

She shouldn't have left the hotel. They could have had a quiet, private room with a bed where they could have made love and slept in each other's arms.

"What should we do?" he asks when they are standing in the basement. Rae turns to him, and he smiles, and the hardness inside when he'd made fun of her and her friends melts away.

"I dunno."

He raises his eyebrows. Looks around. There's a couch, yes. And the floor, although Rae did have a rather tepid make out session on the floor when she was seventeen, and she remembers it being hard and unforgiving, and now that she's older, maybe she wouldn't be able to move tomorrow.

Chip slides his hands into his pockets and looks around. His gaze stops on the TV. He looks back at her and nods his head at the TV in question. She shrugs and nods, and then she opens the cabinet under the TV, and they sit together on the floor and sort through the VHS movies stored there. They decide on *Halloween*, though Rae figures it will give her nightmares.

"There're six more of these," she mumbles as they snuggle together on the couch. After the afternoon in the sun, after days of walking the streets of Quincy in the high humidity, Rae is suddenly chilled. Chip tucks his arm around her and pulls her closer to his side.

"Six more what?"

"*Halloween* movies," she answers.

"You're kidding me."

"So not kidding."

"I figured there'd be a sequel, but six?"

She rests her head on his chest and closes her eyes.

"The third one has nothing to do with the Michael Myers story line. The rest do."

"Hmm."

"I won't tell you how they end."

"Good."

The movie starts, and Rae finds that she's as creeped out by it now as she was the first time she saw it when she was a kid. The part where they show the kids walking out on the sidewalk from inside the house, as if they are showing Michael Myers' viewpoint, fills her with dread. She remembers that scene from when she was a kid. She hated it then, too.

Half way through the film, she is restless, and she climbs to her feet.

"What're you doing?" He looks up at her and reaches for her.

"Just gonna…" She shrugs and nods her head back and forth. "I just wanna look around the house. So I remember everything."

"Can I ask you something?"

"What?"

He takes her fingers in his and rubs them gently.

"What do you think your brother can do here to help you? You said he has all kinds of gadgets in the year 2000. There's nothing here for him to…use…to build anything."

"There's nothing to build," she answers simply. "For all the…" She almost says junk, but she catches herself, because she feels a soft spot for Charlie, she misses the grown up Charlie, and instead she says, "stuff he has, there's no machine. There's no visible time portal."

"You're trusting a kid to do something huge—"

"I have to be ready," she says quietly.

Chip watches her for a moment and then he nods and draws her hand to his lips to kiss her fingers. She smiles, but behind the smile, she's a wreck again, because if she is stranded here in 1980 with Chip, she will be abandoning Charlie, and he needs her. Not to mention, he might go to his grave believing something terrible has happened to her. That she's become one of those stories on the news about a twenty-something-not-thirty yet woman who's gone missing. And if Charlie can find a way to get her back home, she will lose Chip, and she won't find someone like him again. True love comes once in a lifetime, and Chip is her only.

He seems content to watch the movie as she meanders through the living area. She picks up a miniature beer mug her dad brought home from a trip to the Anheuser-Busch brewery in St. Louis. Rubs the dust away and puts it back. Leans over the bar to study the deck of cards someone left out. Could have been her parents, could have been her or Charlie. They used to play War and Slap Jack on rainy summer days.

The movie plays, but Rae almost doesn't hear it anymore. She is lost in the memories, and when she turns to look at the couch and sees only Chip sitting there, she is confused. In her mind, the basement is full of relatives and her parents' friends. Chip doesn't notice when she slips out of the living room and wanders into the room where she and Charlie had played most of the time. When they were very young, it was their toy room, but when Charlie turned ten, he'd started calling it the *game* room.

She eyes the ping pong table thoughtfully. If she could find the paddles and the balls, she and Chip could play a game or two. At fourteen, Charlie was already really good, and though she wasn't bad, he mopped the floor with her on a regular basis. Nowadays, she is as good as he, and when they do have an opportunity to play, it's always a competitive game. It hits her, then, that she and Charlie have not played ping pong in a few years, and saddened by this, she crosses the room to search for the paddles and balls. She'd rather play now with Chip than be sad remembering how much fun she and Charlie had had playing when they were younger.

In the long walk-in closet across the room, she finds the big old cardboard boxes her parents had kept her and Charlie's toys in. She stands by the first and paws through the top layer of toys—mostly action figures—half-heartedly, and then moves on past the next two boxes. Ignoring a stuffed dog she'd loved when she was little, it's probably musty and dirty, she inches past the last of the toys and stands in front of the big bookcase where she and Charlie's board games are stacked neatly. If she can't find ping pong paddles, she and Chip could play Bonkers or Clue or Checkers.

She'd rather go out and tear his clothes off him and kiss him until his lips are swollen and blue, but she stands where she is and studies the games. When her dad passed away a few years ago, she and Charlie had spent days on end going through the boxes and the toys and the games. They'd had to blow layers of dust and dead bugs off of game boxes and books. Right now, it's pretty clean, although when she looks down, she sees a dead cricket, upside down near the corner of the bookcase.

She sees what she thinks is a ping pong paddle, and she starts to reach for it. Hopes she can find at least one ball, because the paddles won't do much good without one. But as she reaches for it, her fingers detour, and she touches a red handheld game that looks somewhat like a cordless phone. She picks it up.

Merlin.

She'd forgotten about Merlin. Charlie must have

disposed of it, because she sure hasn't laid eyes on it in years.

"Rae?"

She looks up when she hears Chip call for her.

"I'm in here," she yells back. She'll go out in a second, tell him what she's looking for. But she wants to check out Merlin first. She feels a sloppy grin on her face; she and her friends used to play with Merlin all the time. She feels a rush of innocence and happiness as she turns it over in her hands, wonders if the batteries are good. When she finds the black on and off switch on the side, she flicks it and chooses game 3, Echo, which is like Simon, another electronic game she'd liked when she was a kid.

The musical tones sound in the closet, and Chip calls to her again. Head ducked over the game, Rae pushes the buttons to play back the sound. She steps out of the closet and finds herself in darkness.

"Chip?" she mumbles uncertainly. Why had he turned the lights out? She grins when she gets the Echo sequence correct and then looks up for Chip.

Except she is not in her parents' basement anymore.

There's cement under her feet, and the humid night breeze lifts her hair from her shoulders as she walks. Cars zip by her, dangerously close and fast. Rae's head is pounding, and the dinner—more likely the piña coladas—she'd had with Chip make her stomach sour, like she could vomit. She stops walking and turns to her left. Lifts her head and looks around, swallows hard when she recognizes Broadway. She is across the street from Ben Franklin. She turns in a circle and finds that she stands in front of Barney's, the tavern she'd thought she'd stepped inside several days ago now to grab a burger and a Coke before her meeting at the hospital.

The burger and Coke that Chip had bought for her.

Chip.

She looks around again, dizzy from the spinning and the heat and the fact that she's just crossed back through twenty years in a matter of seconds. Merlin the Electronic Wizard is still in her hands, but Chip is apparently still in the basement of her parents' house. Looking for her.

She has to get back. She has to find a way back to Chip. Desperately, she presses the buttons on the Merlin game, but it is dead in her hands. No sounds, no lights. Maybe Charlie can help her get back to 1980. She wasn't ready. She wasn't ready to leave him, to say goodbye. She has to go back if for no other reason than just one more kiss.

Chapter 15

She bangs her fist on Charlie's front door and yells his name and only wonders what time it is and what day it is when he finally pulls it open. He stares at her in shock for a few moments, and Rae gathers that she's been gone longer than a day. She has no idea how time passes in the present when a person disappears into the past. She hadn't known what to expect when she came home. Now that she's here, she decides she's not ready to find out.

There are no plainclothes policemen around, no detectives in nondescript gray or navy suits. No one is sitting with a phone and a giant tape recorder the way Rae has seen in movies when someone's been kidnapped and the police are trying to trace a call. She hasn't seen any billboards with her picture on them or any newspapers with headlines screaming that Rae Warner had been kidnapped. Nevermind that she's seen no billboards or newspapers *period*. Only the Ben Franklin building, the tavern, and now Charlie's house.

Charlie, however, is surprised to see her, so she knows he was at least a bit worried about her. Dressed in red and black athletic shorts and a black Nike t-shirt that appears at least a size too small and black athletic socks that he's stretched all the way up to his knees—she's told him about that. Women do not find socks worn at the knees paired with shorts attractive. Ever.—he lunges for her and grabs her hand and tugs her into the house.

Rae lifts her eyes to look over his shoulders, but he flings the door closed and falls against it and then scrambles to throw the deadbolt. She narrows her eyes at the closed door, at the back of her brother's head, and then looks to the window to the left of the door. The filmy curtain filters out the streetlight, and she can't see much of anything outside.

"Charlie?" she says quietly.

"Where have you been?" He turns to her, props his hands on his hips and stares at her as if he's their dad and about to lay into her for sneaking out at night. Except that her dad had never caught her sneaking out or in, and anyway, she'd have been back in before ten-thirty at the latest. Even when she was eighteen.

"What day is it?"

"Friday," he answers and shakes his head like it's a crazy question.

"No. I mean, what's the date?"

"Are you drunk? Did you hit your head?" He frowns. Moves to the window and pushes the curtain aside. "Did you drive here, and you're drunk?"

Her car must be outside. If only she could get in and drive back to 1980. To Chip.

"I'm not drunk. What's the date—"

"I can't believe you would do this. Just up and take off like this. What was I supposed to tell Paul—"

"What's the date?" she yells. She lifts her hands to get

his attention, startled to realize she is still holding Merlin the Electronic Wizard.

Charlie notices it in her hand. He looks from the game to her face and back to the game.

"Where'd you go?" he asks her again, but he's calm this time. "You've been gone for two days."

"So it's still June?" She raises her eyebrows. "Early June? And the year is 2000. Right?"

"Rae." Charlie steps toward her. He reaches for the Merlin game, but she pulls her hand back out of his reach. "C'mon. Let's get something to drink."

She follows him down the dark central hall in the house, past the cluttered dining room and to the kitchen. The table is covered with parts. As if he's in the middle of dismantling the engine of every car in the last Daytona 500 race. Screws and bolts and carburetors and clutches and screwdrivers are strewn over the tabletop and the counters. Rae decides his black socks are the least of his worries. He is a good-looking guy, and he's a good-hearted guy, but she doubts there is a woman on earth who would put up with this.

"Charlie." She keeps her distance from the table and the miscellaneous parts. Not because she worries about getting grease or rust on her 1980's fashions, but because she doesn't know where the time portal is. She doesn't know what she'd done the last time she was here. As much as she wants to return to 1980, what would happen if she jumped in and through the portal without the right directions or coordinates or whatever they're called and ended up in Spain in the year 1529? She'd be too late to catch Columbus for an autograph, and anyway, she needs 1980 Quincy and Chip Andrews.

Charlie pulls his refrigerator door open, and much to

Rae's disbelief—she'll never get over it, no matter how many times she sees it—the shelves are stocked full and arranged so neatly, it looks like the dairy department at the grocery store. To her knowledge, Charlie does not cook, which would explain why he's so skinny, except that he eats out a lot, which should by all rights make him fat. Rae takes a quick peek at her hips and imagines the pizza and burgers and beer she's indulged in with Chip and decides wherever she ends up, she has to start watching what she's eating.

He pulls a can of Diet Coke from the refrigerator and then reaches back in for a can of Grape Crush. Still waiting on the threshold of the kitchen, she watches him pop the tops and then bring her the Diet Coke.

"No. No." She shakes her head when he starts clearing junk from the kitchen chairs so they can sit.

"What? What do you mean no?"

"I'm not sitting in there."

"Seriously? Those jeans looks like they're out of Mom's closet." He shoots her a look of outrage and continues to sort through a pile of old newspapers. "Let me help you ruin them so you can buy a new pair."

When she was there, in 1980, it had never occurred to her to borrow something of her mother's. Possibly, her mom's clothes would fit her now. But it would have felt wrong to go through her closet and take something. What if she'd grabbed a pair of jeans her mom had planned to pack for Wisconsin? On the other hand, if she'd done that, she'd have another small piece of her mom with her right now. She thinks again of the pottery ashtray she'd made that her mom had loved. Maybe if she ever got back to 1980, she'd grab it. She'd already taken the Merlin. She'd take the ashtray and Chip.

She couldn't, though. The ashtray, maybe. Her dad might not recognize it as something she'd made or something they'd found at a yard sale. Might not notice if it suddenly was gone. However, Chip is an entirely different story. Though he's not with her here, Chip (presumably) exists somewhere in this year, and he most likely has a wife and children, and if Rae were to bring him here with her from 1980, he'd never meet his wife and his children would never be born. And who knows? His child might one day find the cure for cancer. Or solve the problem of peace in the Middle East.

"Let's sit outside," she suggests, still standing just outside the kitchen.

"What's wrong with you?" Charlie finally stands up straight and looks at her. She notices dark smudges of purple and blue under his eyes. He's not sleeping. She hopes that it is his over-stimulated brain that has been keeping him up nights and not worry over her.

"I need your help."

He nods and shrugs. Lifts his hands dramatically and then points them both down at the chair he's now cleared.

"No."

"What?" He frowns. Rubs his thumb over the bridge of his nose. He has a headache, and Rae assumes she is surely the cause of this much.

"The last time I walked through your kitchen, I walked outside into 1980."

"I'm sorry?" He shakes his head and pinches the bridge of his nose. The headache's a doozy. Rae winces as she watches him smooth his hand over his face and around the back of his neck. "You what? Did you say something about 1980?"

"I was here…" She almost says *two weeks ago*, but she isn't really sure anymore how much time has passed, in 1980 or here in 2000. Besides, maybe that's a detail that doesn't matter so much at the moment. "Remember?"

"Yeah. You were in a hurry. You had to be in court for that…" He waves his hand in the air and continues, "and you had that meeting with the person about the thing at the place."

When he stops moving and stares at her, Rae is wounded.

"What?" he yelps. "You're always so busy, Rae! There's always something else going on. You never slow down." He remembers his Grape Crush and reaches for it where he left it on a tiny corner of counter space. Rae squints, afraid to look, afraid he will bump the can wrong, and purple soda will spill everywhere. What if it ruined his time portal? His long fingers close around the soda, and he collects it and lifts it to his mouth for a long drink. "The hospital. You had a meeting at the hospital. It was the last time I saw you."

"And that was how long ago?" she asks quietly.

"What?"

"Nevermind." She shakes her head. "I walked out of here. Out of your house. And when I looked up again, I was walking down Broadway in 1980. Out in front of Merkel's."

"Are you mocking me?" Charlie narrows his eyes at her. If they were kids, he'd chase after her and probably give her a cow bite on the back of her leg. And then she'd swat at him, and her mom would catch her—never Charlie.

No." She takes a drink of her own soda and then reaches to check her ponytail. She feels her hair hanging loose; the elastic in her hair is loose. She must look a fright. "I'm not mocking you! Where do you think I've been lately?"

Charlie sighs. "I thought you'd ducked town to get away from Paul. That guy's a stick in the mud."

"You thought I'd—" Rae throws her hands up in frustration and remembers to level her soda can so she doesn't spill anything, and then she realizes she is still holding Merlin. She'd been playing the Echo game on Merlin and Chip had called out to her and whammie, someone had scooped her up and plopped her back down on Broadway in 2000.

"What is that?" Charlie asks as he steps over a pile of old car magazines. He reaches for Merlin and this time, she lets him take it. "Merlin? Where'd you get this?" He steps around her and wanders absently back down the hall to the front of his house. "Didn't we have one of these when we were kids?"

"Really, Charlie?" She groans and follows him into the living room. No car parts or grease, but a ventriloquist's dummy on the couch, arranged like it's watching TV. A mannequin in the corner of the room dressed in Chiefs apparel, which is bizarre because Charlie is not a football fan, much less a Kansas City Chiefs fan. Two baby dolls are on the floor in front of the couch, one of them appears to be missing a head and the other has the word *MILK* written in black magic marker, all in capitals on its leg. Rae isn't concerned about a time portal in this room, but spirits and possessions do come to mind. If she didn't know him better, she might think her brother was a mad toy doctor destroyer like Sid in the movie *Toy Story*.

"What is this?" she asks as she sits on her knee on the couch and bends something cardboard and then hears something crack.

Charlie flinches as she picks up a record album, the vinyl inside now apparently broken in two.

"Benny Goodman." She looks up at him and then back at the record. "Really?"

"Found it at that last estate sale I went to."

"You don't even have a record player to play it on," she tells him.

He perches on the arm of his recliner and nods his head to the corner of the room. Rae feels a stab of guilt when she sees an old wooden cabinet that does indeed seem to be a record player.

"Sorry."

"Eh." He lifts a shoulder lazily, and that easily, she's forgiven. She watches him turn the Merlin game on, but when he starts to press a button, she panics and calls out to him as she slides over the top of the coffee table. When they were kids, this coffee table lived in their mom's living room. Charlie took it when they had to sell the furniture.

"What?" He sees that she's still half on the coffee table. In a half crouch, her right foot and part of her lower leg still rests on the table, though it is anything but comfortable.

"Don't do that."

"Don't do what?"

She snatches Merlin from his hands and turns it off again.

"Focus, Charlie. I need your help."

"My help with what?" He sighs and rubs his eyes and then looks at her with the eyes of an old man.

"I left—"she almost says *the love of my life* in 1980, but if she can get Charlie to hear her, to listen, to believe her, she can't tell him she has to go back to 1980 for Chip. That's a big no-no, very frowned upon in the world of time travel. This much she's gathered from all of his ramblings about time travel through the years. Going back because she loves Chip and needs to be with him, no matter what year they choose to stay in, will alter the next twenty years somehow, and Chip's life could be radically different from how it is here and now. But, maybe she can talk Charlie into helping her go back in time to retrieve her cell phone and her laptop. Not even for herself so much as protecting her parents and their family. They won't understand what either item is or how to use it or how it came to be left there and that could alter something in the next twenty years for *any or all of them*. Not to mention the case files and memos and documents stored on her laptop. Those are confidential items, and if someone found them in 1980, it's possible *that* would affect the world of business here in 2000.

"You left what?"

"I left my cell and my laptop there—"

"You forgot your laptop? Where in the world did you leave it? How'd you get wherever you were, anyway? Hasn't your car been outside—"

How, indeed?

She stares at Merlin the Electronic Wizard and wonders if maybe she's holding at least part of the answer to that question in her hand.

Chapter 16

"I don't know how it happened," she says for what might possibly be the seventh time. "I don't know. This is your thing, not mine."

"My thing," Charlie repeats. "Why is it my thing?"

"Because you're the one who's always been interested in time travel!" she snaps. She's long since climbed off the coffee table, and now she's pacing the room. She would almost rather be in the kitchen, because the dummy and the mannequin give her the creeps and she feels the dummy—which Charlie apparently calls Noodie— watching her as she strides back and forth over the hardwood floor.

"Time travel." Charlie rolls his eyes. "C'mon, Rae. That was my thing when I was, like, ten."

"Really?" She looks back at him over her shoulder and nods. "You were ten? You wanna tell me what all the electronic stuff is you have piled everywhere? All the mechanical parts and the grease and stuff? If you're not trying to build a time machine, what exactly are you doing?"

Charlie twists his mouth and then gnaws on his lip for a moment.

"There's no way you just walked into 1980."

"I walked into Barney's," she tells him again. "Only it was the Hi Hat Tavern. Remember? By the Bottle Shop? And I ordered food. Tried to pay with a debit card. No one had ever heard of a debit card. I had no cell service. And when I used a pay phone to call you, a girl answered and said no one by the name of Charlie was there."

"So you dialed the wrong number."

"Why are you being so argumentative?" She shakes her head, frustrated. This has proven to be harder than convincing the fourteen-year-old Charlie that she was his sister.

Charlie stands and moves to the window. He rests his hand on the wall and pushes the curtains aside with his other hand. There's nothing to see in the dark. He's stalling for time. Finally he lets the curtains fall, and he rubs his face with his hand.

"As much as I wanted it to be true, I never really believed in time travel, Rae," he mutters. "Surely, you know that. Do you think I'm crazy? Really? Like a mad scientist or something?"

Rae sighs. Her body is wound so tightly, she thinks if Charlie poked her in the back right now, she'd explode. What must Chip be thinking right now?

"What I'm telling you now is I believe you." She drops her chin to her chest and then rolls her head on her neck. "I believe in time travel, because I have done it. Charlie, I *saw* Mom and Dad."

At this, he looks at her, his eyes sharp and accusatory.

"Did you talk to them?"

"No!" She wraps her hands around the back of her

neck and stands with her elbows at her ears. "No. Of course not!"

"Did you talk to anyone in 1980?"

Rae's face burns with the memory of talking to Chip. As she lay under him. And he moved inside her. She turns away from her brother and takes a deep breath.

"The guys at the bar." Her voice comes out kind of sideways and squeaky. "And a waitress—"

"I mean anyone who knows...knew you."

"You."

"Me?"

"Yes, you. I talked to you." Exhausted, Rae trudges back to the couch and sits again. "And Uncle Walt."

"Uncle Walt?" Charlie leans on the wall by the window and frowns. "Why Uncle Walt?"

"I saw him in Dixie Cream. I was getting you donuts—"

"Wait." Charlie shakes his head. He moves back to the recliner and sits down. "You went to Dixie Cream? Really?"

She nods. "And I—"

"What else? What else did you do? That we can't do now?"

"Um." She rests her elbows on her knees and leans forward to cover her face with her hands. "Shopped at Kroger's. Stayed at the Ramada Inn—"

"By the river?"

"Was there a Ramada Inn somewhere else?" she asks doubtfully.

He dismisses her question with another headshake. "What about the Mark Twain Diner?"

"Didn't eat there, but yeah, I saw it."

"Why wouldn't you eat there?"

Rae lifts her eyes to look at him when she hears the

accusation in his voice. Slowly, she raises her head and stares at him, guilty as if he's just caught her stealing from his stash of…things. Important things.

"Um." She shrugs. "Because I was never crazy about the place?"

"How could you not—"

"Charlie!" she yells. "Focus. I need your help!"

He sighs and then yawns and nods and rubs the heels of his hands into his eyes.

"Right. Right. Your laptop."

"So I—"

"What'd you get me in Dixie Cream?"

Rae drops her head back and cuts loose with a groan as she blinks at the ceiling.

"Sorry."

"You didn't believe—"

"Wait."

Head still hanging, she tilts sideways to look at him.

"Uncle Walt?"

"Mm." She winces. "He looked good."

"Did you talk to him?"

"We sort of passed each other. He said hello."

Apparently satisfied, Charlie nods for her to go on.

"I was hiding out in your closet—"

"I thought you went to Dixie Cream."

"Well, at first I was hiding in your closet. You were at camp."

"Oh man." He laughs. "How long were you in hiding?"

"I don't even know." She shrugs. "You didn't believe me. You kept rattling about a nine hundred call and how—"

He snorts and shakes his head, and he has a far away look in his eyes, and Rae wonders if he wishes he could go back just for a day. Surely, there'd be people he'd want to see again. Besides Mom and Dad and Uncle Walt.

"Yeah, let's skip that part."

"Gladly," she agrees. "I brought donuts and talked you into listening to me."

"How?"

"Um." She swallows hard. "I told you things…that no one else would know."

"Like what?"

"Well, I talked about your science fair projects…"

Charlie narrows his eyes at her. "That's all it took? For me to believe you?"

"I begged for your help to get back here."

"And you left your laptop there?" He sighs. "Okay. So what did he…I…what did I do? To get you back here?"

"Nothing." She flops back on the couch. "You went to Wisconsin Dells—"

"Oh my God, the Dells!" He laughs and drifts back into his memories. Rae decides from the look on his face that she'd rather he not share them.

"Charlie."

"Yeah." He nods. "Okay. So. You're here. How'd that happen?"

"I don't know."

"What were you doing?"

"We were watching—"

"We?"

"Um." She shakes her head. "You guys were all gone, so you told me to stay at the house. In the basement—"

"I thought you were at the Ramada—"

"I was there several nights. That gets expensive—"

"In 1980?"

"I didn't have much cash." She frowns and rubs her forehead. "Which reminds me. I owe you money."

"What?"

"I borrowed cash from your shoebox stash."

"You didn't go…" Charlie turns his nose up and shakes his head. "Snooping around in my stuff—"

"No. No." She shivers. "Of course not. I knew where you kept your money, and I borrowed some with the intent to pay you back when I got back here."

"So you were watching—?"

"*Halloween.* In the basement."

"Who's we?"

"What?"

"You said we—"

"Just someone I met. Just a friend."

Charlie stares at her wide-eyed with surprise. "You met someone? You brought a guy home to your 1980's house? Seriously? To watch a movie?"

Rae rolls her eyes when he uses finger quotes around the last phrase. She has to stand up and pace the floor so he doesn't see her blush. They'd actually been *watching* the movie, but there was the whole fishing, skinny-dipping, lovemaking afternoon thing she didn't want to discuss with her big brother.

"I got up and started wandering around. I wanted…to touch everything. To look at everything. So I'd remember it all better…when I got back here."

He nods without comment.

"And I thought we could play ping pong, so I was looking for the paddles…in the game room. The closet. And I saw Merlin." She gestured to the game on the coffee table. "And I started playing the Echo game. Chip hollered at me, I walked out of the closet, and looked up to find myself on Broadway."

"Chip?" Charlie snorts. "You dropped into 1980 and hooked up with a guy named Chip?"

"Can we not talk about that?" she asks quietly. "I need—"

"You like him?"

Rae clears her throat.

"Okay. So boom, you're back here."

"Yes."

"And Chip—is that his real name?"

"Charlie!"

"Chip is still in our house."

"I guess so," she nods, "but I would assume if he went looking for me and didn't find me, he probably...left."

"Left," Charlie repeats.

She nods and shrugs and waits for Charlie to connect the dots she's just left for him.

"Because when he didn't find you, he would think you'd been kidnapped?"

"Um."

"You told him." Charlie purses his lips. Climbs to his feet and huffs out a breath of frustration. "You told him. You know that's against the rules—"

"What rules?" she yells.

"Time travel rules!" Charlie drags his fingers back through his hair and leaves it rumpled and messier than usual.

"You just got through telling me you don't really believe in such a thing!"

"And you're telling me you were in 1980!"

"What was I supposed to do? When we went to the club, we got carded. I didn't have a place to put my license, so he—"

"You went to a club?"

She answers with a small nod. Waits for him to throw another angry fit. Stares at him suspiciously when he doesn't.

"This is unreal."

"You're telling me," she mumbles.

"So." Charlie sighs. He walks out of the room but doubles back to throw a punch at Noodie, the dummy.

"What—?" Rae shakes her head and looks from Noodie to Charlie and back to Noodie. "Really? What was that for?"

"I'm frustrated," Charlie says simply. "And he's a good punching bag."

"Yeah, and maybe he's possessed by some ghost hell bent on revenge. Ever think about that?"

"No. I don't believe in ghosts and possession."

"Yeah, well, an hour ago you didn't think time travel was real, either."

"Merlin brought you home."

Rae laughs at the absurdity of it. She's not sure which is crazier. That an electronic game from the 80s brought her back to the year 2000. Or that Charlie's comment made it sound like Merlin the Magician brought her home. If time travel can happen, maybe Merlin the Magician exists somewhere in time, too.

Charlie's gone again, and she's alone in the living room, and she looks back at Noodie. Swears he's grinning at her.

"Charlie?" she shouts. She grabs Merlin and runs from the room to find him.

"Okay." He's squatting in the kitchen doorway, hand pressed flat on the linoleum.

"Dude, if you dropped something there, I'd just throw it away. Five second rule totally doesn't apply in your kitchen."

"I didn't drop anything," he tells her.

"Then what're you doing?"

"Feeling the floor." He doesn't look at her.

"What? Like for a current or something? Or a patch of heat? Like a thermal patch conducive to time travel?"

"What?" Finally he lifts his chin to look at her.

She shrugs.

"Just speaking sciencey. You know. Your language."

"You're…" He stares at her. Apparently comes up blank and looks away.

"So what do we look for? I mean, the only time machine I can think of is the Tardis—"

"Stop."

"How did Beckett travel time? He didn't have a space ship or a—"

"You don't need a space ship. It's time travel, not space," Charlie corrects her. "And who's Beckett?"

"Hello? *Quantum Leap*? Sam Beckett."

Charlie shakes his head. "Don't remember it."

"Yes, you do. I was in love with Scott Bakula."

"What? What do vampires have to do with time travel?"

"Nevermind." She shakes her head. She has a headache now. Wishes Chip was here, because odds are he could make it go away. *Somehow*.

"Where were you?"

"Nineteen eighty. Should I spell it out—"

"In the kitchen. The day it happened. Walk me through it."

"I'm not walking you through it," she argues. "What if I go through it and end up in East Germany or something? I've gotta—"

Charlie stands slowly. Rae watches him take several deep breaths.

"Talk. Talk me through it."

Rae licks her lips and answers with an uncertain nod.

"Um. We were in the kitchen—"

"Fast forward."

"I don't know. Charlie, I don't know. I don't know where I was standing. Or what I said or did. I walked across the room to leave—"

"Like this?" He starts to step into the kitchen, but Rae lunges and grabs a fistful of his t-shirt. And shorts. "Holy tighty whities, Rae." He yanks free from her and spends a few moments adjusting himself since she'd apparently pulled a bit hard on his underwear.

"Was that a melvin?" She closes her eyes and tries to remember what they'd called it when they were kids. When someone pulled your underwear up hard and high. "Or a wedgie?"

"I thought you needed your laptop."

She nods. "I do."

"Then focus."

"'kay."

"You walked out of the kitchen."

"Yeah. The next thing I know I'm over a block walking down Broadway."

"Right…" Charlie turns to face her. Points to his left. "Over there. You were on Broadway right over there?"

"Yeah. It was hot. I was…dizzy. I felt really disoriented. I decided to find something to eat before I went to the meeting at the hospital."

"Did you have anything in your hands?"

Rae holds them up now and examines them. "What?"

"Were you carrying anything?" Charlie speaks slowly and moves his fingers like he's signing to her.

"That's rude."

"Rae."

"Um." She fills her cheeks with air and then lets it out slowly. "I had my bag. With my laptop."

"Phone in your hand?"

"No. It was in my bag, too."

"So nothing in your hands."

"I don't think so."

Charlie nods.

"What do you think?" So anxious for an answer, for a way to get back to Chip, she nearly jumps in Charlie's face. Forces herself to stand there and look at him and wait for his theory. She can't be completely still, though, so she snaps her fingers over and over again.

Charlie shakes his head.

"I got nothin', Rae."

Chapter 17

"Nothing?" she repeats, and she's impressed with her calm collectedness.

He shrugs.

"Do you know…" He looks back at the kitchen. Rubs his hand over his messy hair.

"What? Do I know what?"

"What you touched? Just before you…jumped?"

She grins. "That's kinda cool."

"What's cool?"

"I didn't say cool. I said kinda cool, and *jumping*. I *jumped*."

"Is Chip his real name?"

"Have you ever been in love, Charlie?" she asks softly. Her heart hurts. She'd always believed in love, sure, but not *instalove*. Not love at first sight. Not time jumping, bumping into the one and just knowing. The attraction had been instant. On her side. But somewhere in that short time span in 1980, she'd fallen in love with a guy with dirty blond hair, brown eyes, and a sweet laugh. She'd found the joy in the ingredients of a Happy Meal, and she'd rediscovered walking and fishing and chunky clay ashtrays. Climbing trees. Dancing.

Charlie sort of shrugs, and Rae wonders what it means, but before she can ask, he launches into a lecture.

"It can't go anywhere," he reminds her.

"What?" Her voice jumps an octave or two, and she cringes inwardly because she needs to sound innocent. *What? A time travel romance going somewhere? Of course not.* This isn't like a Jeena Jay Bell romance novel where the heroine goes crashing into the Victorian era and falls madly in love and then comes back to her present day and finds her lover's descendent and falls madly in love all over again. This is *twenty years*. Twenty years makes any future with Chip impossible.

"Rae. You can't be with him. He's probably married with kids now. If you—"

"Yeah, yeah, I know, Charlie." She nods, but she keeps her eyes averted, so he doesn't see her tears. The pressure in her throat hurts, and she rubs absently at her neck. "But I just want…"

"What?" Charlie coaxes her.

"To say goodbye."

"What about your laptop?"

"Well, yeah. That and my phone. My ID. All back in the house."

Charlie nods. "Okay. Think. What did you touch before you left? What did you do?"

"I watched you eat. I think. And I made a few phone calls. And I…" She squeezes her eyes closed to try and remember more. "I was looking at something. A new gadget you brought home."

"A new gadget?"

"Well." Rae moves her arm toward the kitchen to indicate any of his new old, broken gadgets. Charlie's gaze follows her gesture, and he stares at the table pensively. "Got it?" she asks hopefully.

"No. Just trying to remember what I would have brought home around that time."

"It was…" She licks her lips. "Let me think. You'd found…the steering column for a 1931 Bentley? Does that sound right?"

"Oh my God, yes." Charlie's grin is loaded with self-satisfaction. "Oh man. That's awesome—"

"And something from an old Frigidaire refrigerator…"

"Yeah." He nods again.

"And…a…slot machine."

"A slot machine? What?" Charlie shakes his head.

"Yeah. With the buttons and the—"

"Oh!" Charlie nods. "Oh. Yeah. This?" He hurries over to the table and digs through his treasures. Rae has always secretly considered it junk, but if it can get her back to Chip, she'll start collecting stuff, too, and treat everything like gold.

She forgets herself in the excitement and rushes toward him as he finally gives a big heave and pulls something bulky and apparently heavy from under a pile of moldy-looking material. The dull gray finish is familiar and then Rae sees the push buttons that cover the front.

"Yes!" She nods. "Yes, that was it. I was playing with that thing."

"Okay." Charlie folds his arms over his chest and nods. "Any idea what buttons you pushed?"

"Are you kidding me? I don't remember what I had for breakfast yesterday, Charlie."

"Donuts?" he suggests.

She pushes him out of the way and leans over the machine. Touches a fingertip to a button. Pulls it away quickly and looks around. Still in Charlie's kitchen.

"Maybe you need to say something," he mumbles.

"Like what? *Take me to your leader?*"

He rolls his eyes. "Like…*rabbit, rabbit.*"

"That's what you say when you wake up and you want to remember something." She waves his words away. "And I'm sure I didn't stand in your kitchen the other day and say *rabbit, rabbit.*"

"Nuh-uh. It's what you say when you wake up on the first day of the month and wish for good luck—"

Rae feels dizzy suddenly. The way she felt when she was a kid and she rode the Tom Twister at a carnival. She decides it's good she has eaten recently and then looks up to tell Charlie he's crazy. She remembers a book she read when she was a kid when the main character said *rabbit, rabbit—*

Charlie's not here. Charlie's kitchen is not here. She looks around, scared at what she will find. Gray marble floor. Fancy, certainly not the decades old linoleum in Charlie's kitchen. She turns her head a little at a time. Lets her eyes take in the scene bit by bit, lest she faint from shock or jet lag or *is it jet lag?* If she's time jumping?

The marble floor gives way to a dark industrial carpet, though for industrial carpet it's quite nice. Large, mahogany desks. Big, flat-screens, which she assumes are computers, because she doubts there is an institution or business where people sit around in suits and skirts and watch TV. Steady on her feet now, maybe, she cranes her neck to see behind her. Cubby holes. People behind counters, in those cubby holes. Kind of like *Hollywood Squares,* she decides.

The Muzak finally reaches her. She watches regular people line up at the cubbies and conduct business and then walk away. Maybe it's a type of speed confession, she thinks, and she decides maybe she feels steady on her feet, but her mind must still be back in Charlie's kitchen. In 2000.

She's in a bank, she realizes when she sees the big vault door behind the cubbies. They aren't cubbies, either: they're windows. Bank tellers.

The Muzak, something absolutely mournful, dreadful even, is not familiar to her. Women at the window line wear dresses of all shapes and colors, so there's no real clue there to when she is. Her eyes continue to slide over everyone, and she wonders if someone—security—is watching her because she must look suspicious. Suddenly, she drops her chin to her chest to see what she's wearing. She cringes. Same Mom jeans and plain t-shirt. She still clutches Merlin in her left hand.

She takes a few steps toward the door at the south end of the building. Startles when she is much closer to it, and it opens and a group of teenagers push into the lobby. Rae steps back out of their way. Looks with horror at their pants. Fleece. With cartoon characters on them. They look like pajama pants, and worse, one of the girls appears to be wearing slippers.

Quickly, the doorway clear now, Rae pushes it and rushes outside. Into a wall of humidity. Her face melts as she walks south on the sidewalk on Fifth Street. She should probably be grateful that she hasn't ended up in a winter month, since the first time this happened she was dressed for summer. But this heat and humidity is draining her. Okay, really, the time thing is killing her. And she's no closer to getting back to Chip. Whatever year this is, she's pretty sure it's not 1980.

No money. No phone. No ID. What the heck is she going to do now?

Use Merlin. Of course! She wanders slowly down the street, head bent over the electronic game. Probably, people who see her decide she is not only homeless, but crazy as well. She doesn't know for sure what year she is in now, but she's a grown woman walking down the street, studying a primitive electronic handheld game.

It doesn't work. She turns it on and off over and over again, but because this is real life, where only time travel is possible and not straight up magic, the batteries are apparently dead when they'd worked earlier today in 1980.

Charlie. She's got to find Charlie again.

The task of finding him and then convincing him that she is Rae, from 2000, and she needs his help to get to the year 2000 via 1980 is daunting, and her feet slow to the point that she almost has to drag them to move. Overwhelmed at the thought of being completely alone and exhausted from this surreal life she's been living lately, she struggles against the pressure that wells in her chest and her throat. She's not generally opposed to crying, but tears will solve nothing at this moment. Instead, she takes a deep breath, mumbles a quiet prayer to someone that she finds Charlie quickly, and gets out of there.

The library is where it should be, but the entrance has changed. Rae wanders inside, eyes on the strange things projecting upward from the floor just inside the entrance. Metal detectors? In her hometown library? Or are they there to nab anyone who tries to walk out with a book he or she hasn't checked out?

No matter to her. She's neither carrying a weapon nor planning to steal a book. She's relatively sure there are no instruction manuals on a person finding her way back to her current time, and what fictional book could possibly rival her current predicament for adventure?

She walks through the lobby. Sees the self-check out computers and likes the idea. Sees a pile of *Quincy Herald Whigs* on a table and sidles up closer to it. She glances at the date, assuming even if this is not today's paper on top, it is within a week old, and therefore the year should be correct. 2014? Her knees buckle, and she leans on the table. Curses when it wobbles under her weight. This is insane. She ambles on through to the carpeted area. Stacks straight ahead. New fiction and nonfiction to her right. The glassed-in Illinois room to her left. She's interested in the row of computers for public use that stand to the left, between her and the audio-visual department.

Currently, someone sits at every computer. Rae pops her knuckles. Sighs. Moves to the stacks to pretend to browse the latest bestsellers and really to watch the computers. She picks up a book and opens it to the teaser on the inside flap. Something about a bloody shoe print. An amateur detective. Not a fan of cozy mysteries, she lifts her eyes only to check out the computer tables. Still nothing open.

Her hands go cold when it hits her she might need to show ID or a library card to use them. Closing the book, she looks around the room again as if she's interested in the books. A matronly woman with a stark haircut and drab polyester slacks hovers near a young kid at the last computer at this end of the table. If the hair and clothing don't scream librarian, the pinched expression on her face certainly does.

Rae will have to be quick. Which will be hard because she has no idea what to look for.

She reshelves the mystery book. Wonders if they have a phone book here. Or maybe online. Of course. *That's it.* She'll look online for a phone book to find Charlie. If she doesn't find anything, she'll just have to hoof it back across town to his house in 2000 and cross her fingers.

Time both flies—every minute away from Chip goes much too fast—and crawls as she waits for her turn to grab a computer. She's wound her way through the new fiction, old fiction. Large print books. The small audio-visual section, and now from the CDs, she sees a woman begin to pack up her papers and books as if to leave her station.

What in the world is Chip doing by now? Her stomach aches with urgency and clenches around a fist of need. She can't reach him. She can't even send him a message right now. She has no idea of how much time has passed since she was pulled out of 1980.

When the woman moves from the computer, Rae steals in in a way she hopes looks smooth like a ninja, but probably she looks more like a bull rushing a red flag. No one pays her any attention as she settles her fingers on the keyboard.

Look for Charlie. She taps quickly, afraid that at any moment the pinched-face librarian will drag her away from the computer and tell her she must cough up an ID to use their equipment. She bounces her leg rapidly and finds the white pages on the computer. Feeling someone's heavy glare—afraid it's the librarian—she turns her head to the right and sees the man next to her staring at her with a deep, mean frown. Hears the squeak, squeak, squeak and slows the bouncing in her leg, and the noise lessens and then stops as she realizes she is making her chair squeak.

Charles Warner.

She sits back and lets out a pent up sigh of relief. He still lives on Vermont behind Barney's. Or whatever it's called now. *Awesome.* No one has come to evict her from the chair or to demand a driver's license or a library card. She sits up straight again and puts her fingers on the keyboard one more time.

Her stomach is now jittery like she swallowed a bucket of bees. Hands sweaty, she lifts them, wipes them on her jeans—too bad she's broke, or she'd go buy a new pair of jeans to show Charlie, take that, big brother—and then quickly, before she can change her mind, she enters Chip's name in the long, narrow box on the screen. He might not live here. Might be he moved back home. Might be he lives on the coast now with his wife and five kids and the dog. *Five kids?* Why five? she wonders.

Charlie is not here to stop her. She's not snooping, exactly. Is she? How many women get a chance to sneak a peek of their lover in the future? None, that's how many. She stretches her pinky finger and hits enter and then covers her mouth with her hand as the results pop up.

There is a Chase Andrews in Mesa, Arizona. But he knows only Martin Kessler, and he's sixty-seven so Rae looks at the next name. Chase Andrews in Clayton, Missouri. Could be, except this one is nineteen. Chase Andrews in Springfield, Illinois. Also possible. Age range given is twenty-seven to thirty-four. No.

Finally, heart in her throat, she sees Chase Andrews in Quincy, Illinois. Fifty-seven. Rae tries to breathe as she works the math in her head. If Chip is twenty-three in 1980, he is…fifty-seven…in 2014. This Chase Andrews, on the computer screen in front of her, knows Janine Andrews. Rae curls her fingers around the mouse. Clicks on Janine's name. She is fifty-five, and she shares the same address.

Chip is married. Rae stares at her hands for a moment. If Chip is fifty-seven in 2014, she's certainly aged, too, even though judging from her trip back to 1980—no one can tell, her body doesn't change when she jumps. She's forty-four here. And she's alone. And wait a minute. She's alone *now*. Here in this 2014. Where this Rae Warner doesn't belong.

She tears her eyes from her hands back to the

computer screen. What is she...what is Rae Warner doing right now in 2014? Is she married?

She shakes her head. Whimpers a bit. She can't be married. Because she's only been in love once.

And he is married to someone else. Maybe they have children. Maybe they have grandchildren. She peeks at the screen again but sees no other names listed with Chase and Janine Andrews. Her throat burns, and her vision blurs, but she remembers to clear the screen. She stands and pushes her chair in a bit too hard, and it bangs on the table, and the man next to her gives her another look. Rather than look back, she ducks her head and hurries back across the room, through the lobby, and out the door.

What's the hurry? Sure, she should find Charlie. She can't stay here anymore than she could stay in 1980. And this time, it's worse. She's alone. No money. No ID. No Chip.

Chapter 18

RAE CROSSES SIXTEENTH STREET AND LOOKS TO HER LEFT. She is walking down Maine, because York is weird and broken. And besides, Maine is closer to Oak Street, and though she hadn't meant to, she'd noticed Chip's current address.

Noticed it. As in branded it in her brain.

And since she's walking in that direction, sort of not really, she decides it can't possibly hurt just to walk by his house. Should be on the next block, she thinks, as she looks ahead. Charlie lives on Eighteenth, or within spitting distance, so she's not walking any further east than she has to. Just a few blocks north.

She'll just walk by. Take a peek. Probably see a kid or two playing in a sprinkler (if there's a kid at his house playing in the sprinkler, odds are, it's a grandchild) or something. Maybe she'll happen to cross paths with his wife as she pulls her sedan into the drive and opens the trunk to unload groceries. Whatever the case, Rae figures Janine will be lovely. And Rae can then go back to Charlie, licking her wounds, and just ask him to get her back to the year 2000.

Except the thought of just forgetting 1980, forgetting Chip there in her house knifes through her, and she actually looks down to make sure she's not bleeding. She can't just leave him hanging in 1980 without some sort of explanation. Well, okay, he knows she is from the future, but still. She needs to say goodbye to him. One last kiss. She owes him that much. She owes herself that much.

And besides, she does need her laptop. And her cell. Her ID.

A car slows to a stop just up the block, but a couple gets out. A couple who can not be Chip and Janine Andrews. This couple looks to be about twenty, tops, and they're giggling, and the girl is sipping on a soda or a milkshake or something, and Rae tries to summon some spit to swallow, but she's bone dry. She supposes if she got too desperate she could wring the sweat out of her clothes and drink it.

Someone yells as she continues to walk. A loud, angry yell. Punctuated by the slamming of a door. Another yell. Two different voices. One is distinctly male and the other female. Rae flinches and hopes she doesn't run into that couple when she walks by Chip's house. That would be awkward.

She sees the house, stares at the number on the front as if it will tell her everything she needs to know about what has ever gone on inside. And then she hears a door slam again and more yelling. She slows as she walks, but she can't just stop and stare at someone's house. It's okay, but it's not even new, and there's no breathtaking architectural detail that she could say caught her eye. Just that the only man she's ever loved lives there now with his wife.

It's possible she's married in 2014. Possible *she* has children. But she thinks she would feel that. Maybe not the love thing. But the having had children. Wouldn't she *know* that? Wouldn't she just *feel* it if she'd had children? If she were someone's mother, wouldn't there be some sort of heartstring that would pluck each time she—what? Looked at a baby? Heard a baby cry or giggle? She's indulging in crazy thoughts, and maybe this time travel trip will do nothing more than make her insane.

She stops walking when she hears another shout. This couple is fighting bitterly and publicly, and Rae's gaze sweeps the neighborhood. There's no one else around suddenly, and Rae hears the woman's cold, snippy voice saying something about being tied down for almost fifteen years with nothing to show for it and how she needs to leave to find herself. And then the male voice agrees with her and says he wants her to leave, that she needs to find herself and what had she been looking for when she'd settled for him, because obviously she'd settled and he'd never made her happy.

The couple appears at the side of the house, and the woman is tall and slender and dressed in athletic shorts and a tank top, and Rae flinches and thinks from this distance, she looks awesome dressed like that and hopes that when she is that age she will look half as good. Rae gives herself a mental shake, because she can't know that woman's age, and then the guy gestures to the car in the driveway, and it's him.

Him.

Rae is watching a fight between Chip and his wife, and she feels dirty like a voyeur for watching them and listening to their argument. The guy is walking toward her, and Rae knows she should move, but she can't. It's like her feet are set in the cement, and she can't even lift them to take the first step. The woman gets in the car and starts it, and the guy's closer to Rae. He looks haggard and old.

He is definitely Chip.

Certainly married, but not happy. His is not the face of a man who has an occasional argument with his wife. Rae would almost guess this fight is one that happens over and over again, and Chip glances at her and slows his step.

"Can I help you?" he asks with a cool, polite smile. The purple smudges under his eyes look permanent, and though he is fashionably dressed in khaki walking shorts and a white button up shirt, open at the collar, he appears unhealthy. His skin is pasty, and he's too thin, and when he takes a step closer to her, Rae sees that his eyes are dead. If the eyes are the window to the soul, Chip Andrews appears to be walking dead.

"No, thank you," she says softly and she turns and nearly walks into the driveway as his wife backs out. She holds onto Merlin with a grip that might choke him if he were a real person. Does she look familiar to Chip? Is he watching her rush down the sidewalk with that creepy déjà vu feeling stirring in his gut? Or is he just walking, hurting, alone, in what sure looks to be an unfulfilling marriage?

Charlie is not home when she finally gets to his house. She has no idea how much time has passed when she finally hurries across his front yard and knocks on his door. It's early evening, surely, as traffic had picked up while she'd walked down Eighteenth to Vermont. The sun hangs in the western sky, but Rae doesn't take the time to admire the picture it paints. She is hot and thirsty and hungry and desperate to…

To what?

Get home, she supposes.

Via 1980.

As much as it hurts to think of Chip with another woman, it is what it is. She'd still like a chance to go back to him in 1980 and tell him she'd had a wonderful time and kiss him just one last time.

She tries the doorknob, but it's locked. Rae stands for a moment and decides at least it isn't storming. And then she calls the thought back, because she's had such rotten luck maybe it will storm when it seems she will be homeless for the night. With a look around at the neighboring houses, Rae backs off the front porch and hurries to the back of the house. She trips up the small cement stoop and lunges for the doorknob, but when she rattles it, she finds that it's locked, too.

Rae groans out loud and pounds on the door. Once. Twice.

"Charlie," she sobs. "Please come home."

She doesn't fight the tears this time. Rather, she hangs her head, rests it against the door, and cries. Sheer exhaustion overcomes her, and she twists around and slides down the door to sit on the stoop.

———

"Who is that?"

She hears the voices, stirs, but sleep calls her back under. No one should be in her apartment now, anyway. Probably, she'd only left her TV on when she'd gone to sleep, and she is too tired to worry about it now. She burrows further into the pillow, and her cheek, the whole side of her face stings.

"Looks like Rae."

Charlie sounds surprised. Why would he be—

Charlie?

She sits up suddenly, body stiff and aching in places she didn't know existed, and falls off the side of the stoop; Merlin flies off the stoop the other way. She drags her knee down the cement, and finally, she's grateful for the 1980's jeans.

"Rae? What are you doing? Why are you sleeping on the stoop?"

Rae blinks at Charlie and then turns to the woman beside him. She's petite, looks like she'd be a foot shorter than Rae if she stood, and at the moment, she's not sure she *can* stand. Pretty. The woman has short, spiky blond hair, and she's wearing a cute sundress, and as Rae watches, she leans into Charlie and takes his hand.

"Rae?" Charlie says and draws her attention away from the woman.

"Oh my God." Rae sighs. She rubs her face and shakes her head. "I'm so tired."

"What are you doing?'

She shrugs. "Had nowhere else to go."

"What?" Charlie nudges her with his shoe. She does a double take when she sees that he's wearing Sperrys. Since when does Charlie own a pair of Sperrys?

"I'm tired of walking."

"What's wrong with your car?"

"Where *is* my car?"

"Parked out front," Charlie reminds her. Is she still driving that old Honda from the year 2000?

Rae shakes her head again. She crawls over the small walkway in front of the stoop and retrieves Merlin. He may be dead right now, but what if he's her lifeline? What if she loses Merlin, and she's stranded here? Broken logic, since Merlin needs new batteries, and Rae assumes with her luck, the batteries currently in the game from 1980 are most likely corroded. *Still*. She'll hang onto him, just the same.

"Honey, what happened?" The woman reaches her hand out to her, and Rae considers the hand and slips her fingers into it and lets the woman help haul her to her feet.

"Do I know you?"

The woman shoots a look of worry at Charlie, and Charlie tilts his head to look at her curiously.

"Have you been drinking? Or did you hit your head?"

"Maybe we should run her to the ER," the woman suggests.

"No!" Rae raises her hands and then slices the air with them, like an umpire calling a runner safe. "No. No ER. I haven't been drinking. I didn't hit my head. I just need your help."

Charlie looks at the woman and raises his eyebrows.

For the first time, Rae notices it is nearly dark. How long has she slept curled up in a ball on a cement stoop? She takes a deep breath and then winces and wonders when she last had a shower.

"Let's go inside," the woman says, and Charlie nods. Rae steps out of the way as Charlie moves up to unlock the door. She is about to call out to him, to be careful of where he steps or what he touches, because any or all of them could end up in Egypt and though she'd love to see the pyramids of ancient Egypt, perhaps this isn't the best time. Except that the kitchen is immaculate. Rae stands frozen in the doorway, eyeballs feeling like they might pop out of her head. The floor is slate gray tile. The ancient off-white cabinets have been replaced with new—custom-crafted?— oak cabinets, and on the slate-colored—granite?—counter-top, there is only a toaster and a coffeemaker.

"Wow." Raw hesitates to step inside. The floor looks so clean, she considers plopping down and asking for a meal there. Charlie rolls his eyes and waves her inside.

"Enough with the sarcasm," he mumbles. "What is wrong with you?"

Rae moves inside and actually shivers. The air is running, and it feels both good and too cold. She looks over her shoulder at the woman who comes inside behind her and notices the wedding ring on her finger as she closes the door.

"What." Rae shakes her head. She can't even think straight enough to ask a question. This woman is apparently her sister-in-law, and she's wildly happy for her brother. Thrilled for him, actually, and the kitchen is beautiful. Tears come again, though, because if all of Charlie's gadgetry is gone, how will she ever get back to her time?

"Lisha, would you mind getting Rae something to drink?"

Lisha? Rae looks around quickly. Who is *Lisha?* She takes a deep breath when she sees the petite blonde nod and move to the cabinets to get Rae a glass.

Charlie and Lisha.

How perfect.

"Do you have kids?" Rae asks him, and Charlie and Lisha exchange a glance. Lisha puts the glass down.

"I'll drive," she says and nods, as if Charlie's said something else.

"Wait." Rae holds up her hands. "Charlie, I'm not me. I mean, I am. But I'm not. I was here one day…fourteen years ago. And I had to leave. I had a meeting at the hospital with the director of their PR department. Do you remember that?"

"You're kidding me, right?" He shakes his head no.

"You had your…stuff…" Rae points at the table. "All over the place. You'd just been to an estate sale…in Barry or something? And I pushed some buttons on a machine… um. An adding machine. And I walked out of your house and looked up and found myself on Broadway. On the other side of the bar. Of Barney's. In the year 1980...so it was actually the Hi Hat Tavern."

Charlie stares at her silently. Finally he nods, moves his gaze from her face and over to Lisha's.

"Let's go."

"Wait." Rae takes a step back. "I know this is crazy. God, I just finally got you to believe me when I came back from then. And you were gonna send me back, and I ended up here. What year is it?"

"Honey, are you feeling okay?" Lisha steps toward her and touches her arm. Reaches up to put her hand on Rae's forehead. "Anything numb? Tingling?"

"No. Charlie, please. You found a...a car thing. A steering column. For an old car. A Bentley? I think."

"Oh my God." Charlie laughs. "Yeah. That was great."

"Do you still have it?"

"Sure. It's in the basement."

"Okay." Rae nods. "How about the adding machine you got around the same time?"

Charlie considers her question and shakes his head. "I don't think so."

"Oh man." Rae wobbles on her feet. "Will this nightmare ever be over?"

"Rae—"

Someone's cell phone rings, and then Charlie pulls the noise from his pocket and puts the phone to his ear and says hello.

Rae hears a young voice say *dad?* And she rushes to get out of the room. She can't know this. She shouldn't be here to know that her brother is married now and has at least one child. She has a nephew—the voice belonged to a boy.

The dining room is different, too. She can see the top

of the table. Only a few books are piled on it; they appear to be engineering textbooks. She moves out of the dining room to the hallway. Charlie, off the phone now, follows her to the living room.

"The last time I was here, you had that mannequin. In the corner—"

"You were here yesterday. You took Lisha—"

"No. Maybe the 2014 me was here, but I wasn't. The mannequin was there. And Noodie. Noodie was on the couch. And we were talking. I desperately need to get back to 1980—"

"Why 1980?" Charlie asks her.

"I left my laptop there."

"Anyone see you? That shouldn't have?"

Rae gives him a long look.

"If this time travel story were true," Charlie says, "it would be a bad thing if people saw you."

"It's true. I don't know how to convince you, except to beg you to believe me. It's true. We've been all through this conversation, and I know the rules. I need to get back to get my laptop."

"Where exactly is your laptop?"

"At Mom and Dad's house."

"Did they see you?"

Rae hears a phone ring again, only this time it is a landline, and the ring is louder.

"Of course not!" Rae snaps. "Can you help me?"

"Charlie." Lisha hesitates in the doorway, the cordless phone at her ear.

"What?" Charlie, irritated with Rae, looks at Lisha like she's the pot of gold at the end of the rainbow.

"Rae's on the phone. She's asking to talk to you."

Charlie looks back at Rae with a frown. Rae shrugs at

him as if to say *I told you so* as he takes the phone from Lisha and presses it to his ear.

"Can I ask you one thing?" Rae asks Lisha. There are a million things she'd like to ask, that she'd like to know. But she can't ask them. For one thing, she simply doesn't have the time. She must get back to 1980, say goodbye to Chip, kiss those sweet lips one more time, and grab her belongings and go back to the year 2000. Besides, it wouldn't be right if she knew too much about this year, when her life is fourteen years in the past.

"What?" Lisha slips her arm around her and rubs her back.

"Am I married? In this year? Have I ever been married?"

Lisha winces, and before she can even open her mouth to answer, Rae knows the answer is no. Doesn't matter if she was jilted at the altar or if she's divorced. In fourteen years, Chip will be unhappy in his marriage and Rae will be alone.

Chapter 19

LISHA INSISTS THAT RAE TAKE A HOT SHOWER, BUT RAE argues that she can't. She's got nothing clean to wear, and she's in a hurry to get back to 1980. But she's tired, and she's hungry, and her body hurts. And so while Charlie is still talking to the 2014 Rae on the phone, Rae allows Lisha to lead her upstairs to the bathroom.

"I'll leave you a robe to put on, and I'll grab your clothes and wash them for you," Lisha tells her as she pushes Rae into the bathroom and takes a towel and washrag from a cabinet. Rae wants to take the time to notice all the changes in her brother's house; it is gorgeous now, and must have cost a fortune and a lot of time to remodel, but Lisha hasn't given her time to look around.

"Maybe you could ask that Rae that's on the phone with Charlie to bring me some of her clothes."

Lisha sort of laughs, though it's clear she still thinks Rae is possibly crazy or maybe that she's had a stroke or has a brain tumor. Or maybe that she's schizophrenic. Maybe *that* would explain what's been happening. She eyes

Rae's jeans and the top and looks up at Rae then with regret and shrugs apologetically.

"Where did you get those jeans? They look like something I wore when—"

"When you were a kid?" Rae suggests. Lisha tilts her head to study her. "I got them at JC Penney."

"They went out of business." Lisha shakes her head.

"What?"

Lisha shrugs. "Well."

"Please." Rae sighs. "Help me convince Charlie to help me."

"Take your shower." Lisha pats her arm and smiles. "Soon as you pull the curtain, I'll grab your clothes and wash them. Do you…still…have you always liked meatloaf?"

"What?" Rae narrows her eyes at the woman. What does meatloaf have to do with anything?

"Well?"

"Yes."

"Great. I made meatloaf last night. I'll warm you a plate when you're done."

"Lisha."

"Hmm?" She'd been about to back out of the bathroom, but she stops now and arches her eyebrows, waiting for whatever Rae is going to say. Which, now that she has her sister-in-law's attention, escapes her. Was she going to ask how she and Charlie met? Or how long they've been married? Or tell her thanks for taking care of him?

"Thanks," she mumbles and supposes Lisha thinks she means thanks for washing her clothes and warming dinner for her, and really, Rae means all that and more. She'll wait for the whole story. She'd rather watch it play out, watch Charlie find the love of his life, than hear about it later. Now.

Lisha's smile is almost sad, but she nods and backs out of the room.

The bathroom, though redone, is still small, and it doesn't take long for the room to fill with steam. Rae peels her clothes off and feels a flash of guilt that Lisha will have to deal with the grimy, sweaty mess. She climbs into the shower and simply stands under the hot spray. Never has she appreciated anything so much in her life as she does this moment.

Except maybe the time spent with Chip.

Dancing. Driving his car. The movie. The burger at McDonald's. Making love with him at the pond.

She almost cries with joy when she squirts Lisha's salon shampoo in her hand and smells the fresh, flowery scent. Spends extra time lathering her hair and then her body, with the raspberry scented shower gel. She wishes she'd have thought to ask Lisha for a shaver, but as she rubs her hands over her legs to rinse them, she decides they don't feel too bad, and that makes her wonder again just how long she's really been gone from her present day.

This time travel stuff is over her head, and she thinks maybe over Charlie's head, too. After all, neither of them would ever have dreamt it was possible.

When she shuts the water off and pulls the shower curtain back, she sees the pile of dirty clothes has disappeared and that Lisha has left a thick pink terry cloth robe hanging on the hook on the door. Rae's not so in love with the color, but when she touches it and feels how soft it is, she sighs with pleasure and slips it on.

She doesn't want to snoop through the drawers, but she crosses her fingers and pulls one open to look for a comb. Seeing a pink one, she assumes it belongs to Lisha and quickly runs it through her hair. Next, she opens the cabinet under the sink and grabs the bottle of body lotion.

Sits on the side of the tub and rubs some into her legs and over her stomach and chest.

The house smells like meatloaf when she goes back downstairs. Charlie and Lisha sit at the kitchen table, but they halt their conversation the second Rae appears in the doorway.

"Feel better?" Lisha chirps and Rae nods, even though she suspects they think she will be *rational* now and tell them she's not actually Rae from the year 2000 but a fugitive of the law who happens to look just like Rae Warner.

"What time is it?" she asks, but what she really wants to know is what day it is.

"It's ten after nine," Charlie tells her. "Friday, June thirteenth."

Rae moans softly and wonders if the Friday the thirteenth thing is part of the problem, but dismisses the thought quickly. She'd fallen into 1980 on June thirteenth, 2000. And that was a Tuesday. Besides, time travel is sci-fi, not horror, thank God. As if real life can be tucked into a genre.

It does strike her as weird that she has stayed true to the date, though she felt like she'd been in 1980 for a good two weeks, if not longer.

"Sit down," Lisha tells her as she stands up. Rae pads barefoot to the high top table and climbs up on a chair. She watches her sister-in-law move around the kitchen with ease and speed and decides it's not a hoax. This woman lives here. She's Charlie's wife.

Rae reaches to touch Charlie's hand and eyes the gold wedding band with wonder. He snatches his hand away and rolls his eyes at her.

"You didn't used to be such a grouch," she says, and Lisha's bright laugh peals through the kitchen. "I love the house. It's gorgeous."

"Thanks. My brothers—"

Rae shakes her head when Lisha looks at her.

"Don't tell me."

Lisha narrows her eyes at her and then nods. "Right. Because you have to…go back. In time." She trills that laugh again, and when Rae moves only her eyes to look at Charlie, she sees a sloppy, love struck grin on his face.

"Can you help me?"

"I still have the adding machine," he announces. "I thought I got rid of it, but I found it downstairs."

Rae nods as a weight slides from her lungs and into her stomach. *Okay. This might be progress.*

"I'll bring it up after you've eaten," Charlie lets his eyes roam over his wife's robe, "and you've dressed again."

"Thanks." She grins.

"But we have to talk about this first—"

"Talk about what? I just wanna get back. God, my landlord might evict me."

Okay, not really, because apparently, the time jumps measure the days differently or something, but Charlie doesn't have to know that, does he?

Lisha sets a plate in front of her, and Rae eyes the meatloaf and mashed potatoes appreciatively.

"You don't like meatloaf now?"

Rae looks at Charlie with a frown. "Love it. I haven't eaten a home cooked meal…"

"Since you lived at home," Charlie finishes for her. "You didn't cook in the year 2000."

"Do I now?"

"Look. We'll try to get you back to 2000."

"No. I have to go to 1980 first—"

"Why?"

Rae isn't sure she likes this new, stern version of her brother. Sure, it's heartwarming to see him all sloppy in love, but she doesn't like that he's crabby now to her. After all, it's his fault she's in this predicament.

"My laptop—"

"You met someone there."

"I did!' Rae admits. She scoops a bite of the potatoes into her mouth and winces because they're scalding hot from the microwave. She leans sideways in her chair to move the potatoes off her tongue, but they're still hot on the inside of her cheek. Finally, she swallows them and breathes out, expecting to see flames. Or a plume of burned skin cells. "But I also left my laptop there, and I have to get it."

"You can't carry on a relationship with—"

"I'm an attorney," she reminds him. "I have confidential files on my laptop. I have to get them."

Charlie sighs and nods. "Fine."

"And anyway, I know."

"How did you get back? To your time?"

"Merlin helped me."

"You brought him with you?" Charlie sits up straight. "We just—"

"No—"

He gives her a doubtful stare.

"What? Like Merlin the magician? Really? Because bizarre time travel stories aren't enough?"

"Merlin the electronic wizard," she corrects him.

"What?"

"The game."

"Game?" Charlie shakes his head.

"The handheld game that looked like a cordless phone. You could play, like six games on it or something."

"And that got you home?"

"Yes."

"How?"

"I dunno." She shrugs. "I just know it did."

Lisha and Charlie still sneak peeks at Rae when they think she isn't looking. Maybe they are starting to believe the time travel story but still think she's crazy, besides. Rae continues to eat the dinner Lisha warmed for her and decides she doesn't blame them.

"Where'd it go?" she asks, realizing she let Merlin out of her sight.

"What?" Charlie shakes his head.

"Merlin. The game I had in my hands when I came in here."

She should have just taken it to shower with her. Well. Not shower with her. But she should have just carried it up and put it on the back of the sink or something. Face down. In case artificial intelligence might factor into time travel and insanity and Merlin the Magician. She'd hate to have Merlin see her naked and cause it to stroke out.

The thought makes her snort, and Lisha climbs to her feet.

"I think you left it in the living room. I'll check."

"You're serious about this, aren't you?" Charlie asks her.

"As a heart attack, yes."

"Have you considered that if I don't remember you jumping in and out like this, your guy, Merlin isn't—"

"My guy isn't Merlin—"

"Whatever his name is, he's not going to remember you, Rae. Whatever happened between you two, and I don't wanna know, he's not going to know you from the next ditzy blonde on the street."

The words sting, but not as much as what else Charlie says. He's right. If 2014 Charlie doesn't remember the time jump in his kitchen from 2000, the one that brought her to 2014, and if 2000 Charlie doesn't remember her talking to him in 1980, desperately seeking his help to get back home, Chip isn't going to remember her, either.

She simply nods, because she can't speak. There's a knife lodged in her throat, and it hurts to breathe, and maybe she won't. Maybe she'll just stop. What's the difference? She can't even get back to Chip now to say goodbye.

"Do you still need to go back?" Charlie's voice is gentle, careful.

"Yeah." She sniffles and blinks back the tears and looks at her big brother. Maybe she should just be happy one of them finds and holds onto true love. Maybe in the year 2014, she's happy to be an aunt.

"You sure?" He arches an eyebrow at her, as if he knows that when she gets back to 1980, she'll search for Chip just to be sure. And she'll be crushed all over again when he truly doesn't remember who she is and what they shared.

"Yeah." She nods and offers up a brave smile. "I need my laptop. I need the files for work, and there's the whole confidentiality thing." She sets her fork over her nearly empty plate. She can't eat another bite. Because her stomach is full and uncomfortable like she swallowed a bowling ball. "Besides, what if Mom and Dad found my stuff there? Wouldn't that create a ripple in time or something?"

"Is that steampunk?" Charlie grins. "Your fancy technology getting stuck back in 1980?"

"It's a four-year-old Hewlett Packard," she says and turns up her nose. "Not that fancy."

"Maybe it's not a big deal if you left it," he suggests, and even though he's been a little gruff with her—he's older now, and he has a wife and at least one child and so probably, he has more stress in his life—Rae is touched that he wants to protect her from the heartache of unrequited love. Of being forgotten by someone who means so much.

"It's okay," she tells him. "I'd rather have had that time with him than not. Even if I never see him again."

She could, though. Somehow. If she can wait until 2014, after she gets back to 2000. She knows where he lives.

And his marriage didn't seem particularly happy.

Chapter 20

Because there's no certainty that she will jump into 1980 again, or that she'll find Charlie again wherever she goes, and because she is sad to have only just met the woman who loves her brother, the goodbye is tearful and anxious. Maybe Charlie and Lisha worry that she'll be hurt, and certainly Charlie worries about her emotional state since reminding her that Chip will not remember her, and Rae is saddened by all of the above. She's not afraid of injury, but she is worried that she will end up in the wrong year again and maybe she'll never get home. And if she can't have Chip, she simply wants to retrieve her belongings from 1980 and get back home.

Charlie sends her off with Merlin and with a small wad of cash, and she tries to refuse it. He won't let her because she has no ID and no credit cards or a cell and no way to contact him. She needs the cash for food and a hotel room, if it comes to that. They'd tried to change the batteries in Merlin and found the old ones terribly corroded and gross. Charlie'd pitched the old ones and tried to clean up the small compartment before Lisha put new batteries in it.

They'd treated Rae as an invalid, insisting she rest up for her trip. As if she was going to catch a plane and head to London. The new batteries had done nothing for the game, and still when she'd touched the adding machine and Charlie and Lisha had chanted *1980* as if it were a Gregorian chant, Rae held on tight to Merlin hoping wherever she went, it would bring her home.

Not certain it would do any good, she'd punched in *1980* on the adding machine, and now she's stumbling down Broadway in a repeat of the first day of this bizarre sequence of events. She is dressed in her laundered 1980's clothing, and even though she feels as if she walks through a rain forest now, she feels refreshed and ready to get it done.

She skips Barney's this time, as Lisha had fed her well. The small soft-sided lunchbox Charlie had insisted she bring with her hangs over her shoulder by the black strap. It is packed with grapes and cheese and a candy bar and thankfully, an ice pack. Otherwise, she'd have chocolate soup by the time she got to York.

No idea what time it is or what day it is, Rae approaches her parents' house with caution. She slows her steady paces and meanders as if she is simply out for a walk with all the time in the world and not a woman hell bent on getting back to her own time.

The house appears locked up tight and empty. Chip's Camaro is not parked at the curb. Even after Charlie had warned her that he wouldn't remember her, she'd held out secret hope that he would somehow, and she could still just say a quick goodbye. The absence of his car at the curb feels like Charlie's jabbed a shiv up under her heart, and though she knows Charlie would never hurt her, the pain is so real, she feels the blood flow and the tears burn her eyes.

She steels herself for what must be done. Wonders

again what time it is and decides perhaps it will be better to come back to the house after dark when neighbors might not catch sight of her climbing the tree in the back. As much as she needs to get back to her own year, she wants to walk around town one more time. Much the same as when she'd walked through her parents' basement just— the other day?—memorizing their belongings, their things (because those things are all symbolic of something familial and something emotional to her) by sight and touch, Rae wants to walk through town one more time and study everything. Because now she knows the utter disappointment of remembering things incorrectly. If she sees things one more time, she'll commit the tiniest of details to memory and when she is back home, alone, in the year 2000, she will take these memories out one by one and hold them in her hands. That alone will hurt; she doesn't need the sharp edges of things misremembered to cut any deeper.

She starts with the theater, with a long walk from Seventeenth and York to Sixth and Hampshire. She carries her lunch box on her shoulder and Merlin in her hand, and she doesn't care if people assume she might be crazy. She walks with her head high, and she watches where she walks. She sees the bland colors of the older model cars, though she does not see any '79 Camaros. She notices guys with big combs sticking out of their back pockets, and she even sees a few people still wearing bell bottoms and platform shoes.

The marquee above the theater catches her attention, and she stands on the corner across the street, just down from the Busy Bee Mercantile building. Her mom hadn't shopped there often, but she wonders if she should walk down and see it. Still no idea what time it is—she could ask someone, but maybe it is enough that it's still daylight and therefore, she can't go climbing the tree behind the house yet—she walks. The Adams Cinema behind her, she passes Busy Bee and heads further south and then east, on past St. Boniface Catholic Church to 8th Street. She wants to go back to State Street Store, to wander through leisurely. To descend the stairs over the lower floor, see the displays come into view.

Tired, but content, she heads back toward York. It's early evening; she can tell because the sun is setting. Time enough to walk to McDonald's and grab a Coke. Other than Chip, of course, and seeing the house and her family, maybe McDonald's is her best memory here. In 2000, McDonald's has all but done away with Ronald, at least here, and the buildings are cement and turquoise and there's an indoor play place, and the old McDonald's still makes her heart happy, just as when she was a child.

She sits outside and drinks the Coke, eats the fries Charlie's cash bought her. Watches families eat and talk, as they have no cell phones or iPads to distract them. Now and then she glances toward Kroger's, to the west of McDonald's and sometimes, the mall just to the north. Years of laughter with her friends and family rattle around inside her, and she decides that if she is alone in 2014, and Charlie is happily married with at least one child, it'll do. She has a good career, and maybe she'll keep it—if she finds her laptop and gets back to her time—and she's certainly anxious now to meet her nephew and spend some time getting to know her sister-in-law.

She finishes her snack and tosses everything in the garbage can. Crosses the small footbridge over the patio to leave. The lunchbox hiked over her shoulder again, and Merlin in her hand—she'd tried to stash it in the lunchbox, but it just doesn't fit—she heads back up Broadway, eyes still greedy for memories to take back home.

When she finally reaches the house, darkness has all but settled in. The curb in front of her parent's house is still open, Chip's beat up '79 Camaro nowhere to be seen. The sadness presses in again as she moves quickly up the driveway. She's glad to have had the few days or weeks or whatever it was with him, but she does miss him, and her heart hurts for both of them knowing what the future holds.

Just for kicks, she tries the doorknob first. Charlie had left it unlocked for her when she was here, but when she and Chip had come here after going *fishing* and all that it entailed, she'd locked the door. Of course, it is locked now, and though it's an inconvenience to her, she's glad to find it locked. She'd hate to think something she'd done when she'd dropped back into 1980 might have caused any harm to any of her family when she'd left.

At least she is better dressed this time. She eyes the tree from the back door. Looks around the ground by the door. She can't climb with Merlin in her hand, although she is honestly petrified of losing it and being stuck here permanently. Still. Better to set it here by the door and then come back down and grab it, than try and carry it with her while she climbs and drop it and break it or worse yet, fall and break her arm or leg. Satisfied with her game plan—set the stuff down, climb the tree and pray that there's an unlocked window upstairs, grab her laptop and other things she'd had when she'd first come to 1980, grab Merlin, and get out. And back to 2000—she sets her lunchbox of snacks down and then cradles Merlin inside it. Too big to zip, but she feels better knowing it is cushioned, and so she dusts her hands off and turns again to face the tree.

Before she can change her mind—about anything— she crosses the yard, reaches up and finds the smooth handholds she and Charlie have rubbed into the lowest branch, and hoists herself up. She barely gets her legs up when she hears loud music blare from a car in front of the house. It's Chic, the song sounds like "Good Times," and Rae simply freezes for a moment. This—climbing this tree yet again—is not really a good time, but she'd forgotten the song and hearing it now makes her chest swell and ache with nostalgia, and finally as the song fades and the car motor rumbles and then quiets at the end of the block, she moves again.

The jeans protect her knees this time as she climbs from the tree limb to the roof. If her family is in Wisconsin Dells—are they still?—she doesn't have to worry so much about a time paradox or juxtaposition or ripple effect or whatever it is that would happen if her younger self saw her now, but she is still careful. She squats by her window, heart dropping when she sees that the window is closed. Deep breath. She wonders about it. What would it be if her younger self saw her now; what's the scientific term for that and why, exactly, is it scientific, because time travel is not supposed to really be possible?

Her hands have stopped shaking, so she slips her fingers into the slits in the screen, extra careful this time not to cut anything. She moves the screen out of the way, says a silent prayer to St. Time Traveler that the window itself is at least unlocked and flattens her palms on the glass pane. It wiggles up just a smidge, and Rae breathes a sigh of relief. It will be a pain to push it all the way up from this side, but it can be done, and so Rae works slowly and steadily, determined to get inside.

Sweat rolls down her neck and her back when she finally gets the window open wide enough that she can slip inside. She remembers to check first, but there's no one in the bed below the window. Once she slips inside and her feet hit the mattress—she hopes her shoes are clean, because she doesn't want to get anything on her old bedspread—she turns back to the window and closes it. Once she has her stuff, she'll have to go back outside, climb the tree yet again, and put the screen back so as not to arouse any suspicion.

That empty-house feeling makes her stomach hurt. Too bad she couldn't have just seen them all one more time. Instead, she does the next best thing. Shuffles through each room upstairs and catalogs everything again. Down the steps to the living room where she stops to search for the ashtray. She sees it on the end table by the sofa, and her hand hovers over it for several long seconds, and finally, she shakes her head and turns and walks away. Her mom had made a big deal of it, so she can't take it now. Besides, it's not the piece of pottery Rae really wants, but her parents.

Quickly, now, she opens the basement door, flips on the light, and then hurries down the steps. Chip is certainly gone, but then she'd known he would be. She checks the movie cabinet, the VCR—all back the way it was. No evidence anyone had been here watching *Halloween*. Next, she wanders into the game room and eyes the ping pong table. Wishes she and Chip might have been able to play one game. She ducks her head into the closet, but she is weary of going all the way inside it. She is ninety-five percent sure Merlin brought her home. But what if there's something time portal-ish about this closet? She's not ready to take any chances.

Done with the trek down memory lane, she turns back to the main living area to gather her things. She'd left her stuff here the day she'd told Chip she was from the future. When she'd shown him her phone and her laptop. The bag should be in the closet under the steps. Her heart slams to a stop and the room is so silent, she thinks it is possible her heart did stop beating, but then she hears the rapid beat, beat, beat, and she lunges for the closet door, opens it, and drops to her hands and knees to search as if the bag and laptop are still there, but have turned invisible.

Nothing. There's nothing here at all to suggest she's ever been here. Or that she'd had her belongings here. She ducks her head to cry. Sheer exhaustion. What if she's not in 1980, after all? What if it's 1979 or 1982? What if she's destined to roam years that are somewhat close to her own —as opposed to Victorian era England—but never get home? Maybe it *could* happen. Scientific breakthroughs and study and advancement, yada yada yada. Super great. But why her? Why not someone like Charlie who's always wanted to do it?

It comes to her then. Because Charlie is happily married in the future. Charlie has a family. Rae has no one.

She takes a deep breath, stands, and does a slow spin in the middle of the room. There's nothing to wait around here for. The house and everything in it is special to her, but the draw of the past is being with the people you love again. And because that's the first rule in time travel—that you can't interact with people you knew and loved in the past—there's no life for her here.

Feeling more alone now than when she'd first started this journey, when she'd decided there wasn't a spark between herself and Paul and she didn't want to lead him on, but when she'd examined her life and decided she didn't have friends in 2000, she goes back upstairs, turns off the light, and closes the basement door. Perhaps she'll get lucky, and Merlin will return her to 2000, and she'll tuck this whole incident away forever. Maybe Merlin will send her to the early 60s, and she will experience the whole fear of the Cuban Missile Crisis firsthand.

She takes a deep breath and reaches for the doorknob. And remembers eating donuts at the kitchen table with Charlie. One last puff of hope stretches her chest and her lungs. She lifts the lid on the garbage can, praying that she will not have to dig through coffee grounds or soggy cereal as she plunges her hand in to look for a Dixie Cream bag.

Finally, her fingers close on a wax paper bag. She pulls it out slowly, so as not to make a mess. In the near dark room, it is hard to make out, but Rae sees the blue and yellow symbol, and she squeals with relief and excitement, and then she shushes herself and throws the bag back into the garbage.

Still in semi-darkness, she moves to the sink to wash her hands. If there had been no bag, she might have concluded that she was indeed in the wrong year. Or even that by leaving as she had, all evidence of her ever being here had simply disintegrated or something. But maybe, her things are gone from the basement because when she'd vanished as she had, Chip realized she'd jumped time again, and he'd grabbed her stuff and run. Maybe he'd scrubbed the place of her things to protect her and to protect her family.

Maybe he *did* remember her.

Rae slips outside, locks the door, and pulls it closed behind her. She sees the lunchbox and Merlin where she'd left them, and then she stands at the base of the tree, rubbing her hands together. She has to climb the tree, yes, but it's just occurred to her, as close as she and Chip had become, as intimately as they'd been involved, she doesn't know how to track him down here. If he's a college student, she can't look him up in the phone book. There's no Internet to scour. She could go troll the college campus, but that would be weird for her and him if she ever did find him.

Shot down again, she hauls herself back onto the lowest branch of the tree and makes her way back to the roof. Trudges back to her window, replaces her screen, and then turns to face the tree and plops down on her butt. What should she do?

Wander around campus housing? She can imagine asking college kids if they know Chip Andrews. She's old, and though she doesn't look haggard—or she hadn't when this whole deal started—she'll stand out on campus. The students would be suspicious of her, and she would probably be leery of walking around there, especially at night.

She could check a phone book, but she knows that's hopeless. Chip will be gone at the end of the term, so he won't be listed there.

Go to Barney's and ask around? But that might be weird if she goes in there and starts asking around, because she's not guaranteed anyone in there now was there before. And if Charlie doesn't remember her jumping in and out of time, strangers at a bar wouldn't remember, anyway, would they?

Her feet hurt, and her back hurts, and she's hot, and so she simply sits. Stares at the tree. Wonders why she is the one who is stuck in this loop and wonders what Chip's wife meant when she'd said she'd been stuck in a marriage for nearly fifteen years with nothing to show for it.

Chapter 21

SHE WAKES TO THE SOUND OF LOUD MUSIC AGAIN. HER first thought is that it's April Fools and Y101 is playing a trick on its listeners by playing 80s music to make them think it is a new format for the station. Earlier, she'd heard Chic and now she hears "Funkytown," by Lipps, Inc. This one, at least, is fitting for her circumstances, she realizes as she struggles to sit up on the roof. Her face is sore from being pressed against the shingles. The music is gone already, and Rae looks over her shoulder at first her bedroom window and then Charlie's, but both are still dark.

When she hears a car door close, followed by footsteps, she panics. Someone is coming. What if it's her family, home from the Dells? No. Can't be. They don't come home in the dark. What if it's Uncle Walt? But why? Why would he come by the house? Wouldn't Dad have told him they were going out of town? Would he be coming by just to check on the place?

Blaring that song?

The footsteps go to the back door, directly under her. She sits completely still, afraid she will suddenly have to sneeze, and then she hears a familiar voice, struggling to whisper.

"Rae?"

Chip?

Can't be. Sit still.

She waits, but when he says her name again and suddenly, she sees his unruly blond hair as he steps out from under the porch, she sobs with relief and scoots forward, forgetting there is a bit of a slant to the roof.

"Be careful!" he reminds her.

Palms on fire now after the short slide and the quick catch, she nods. Takes a deep breath and then moves with caution back to the tree and climbs down. Chip helps her from the last drop, and then she's in his arms, and she's crying now not because he's forgotten her, but because he remembers her, and she has to break his heart.

"Where'd you go?" he whispers.

"How long was I gone?"

"Coupla days."

A fist clenches inside her stomach. *Two days?* Her family is back from the Dells. She'd taken a huge chance slinking around inside the house earlier.

"What happened?" he asks. And instead of answering him, she lifts her legs to circle them around his waist, and she cups his face in her hands and studies him. His brown eyes are warm and happy, but she sees the haunted look he'd worn in 2014. His lips are full and soft, compared to the pinched, thin polite smile he'd given her on the side-walk in front of his house.

"I missed you," she whispers and she dips her head and takes his lips in a long, desperate kiss.

"I missed you, too." He nuzzles her neck when she

finally breaks the kiss. "I was looking for you. To ask you about the movie, and then it felt like…static electricity in the air, and you were just gone."

She nods, swipes at her face, embarrassed by her tears.

"I went back to 2000," she says quietly. "And I have to go back again."

"Okay." He kisses her forehead and then the tip of her nose and sets her down. "I have your stuff in the car. I figured I'd just keep looking, checking back here for you. Didn't think you'd want them to see any of it."

"Thank you."

"Do you know how to do it now? How we get back?"

She gives him a small *sort of* nod and dodges a real answer, and they turn to walk to his car. She detours to the back door to get her lunchbox and the Merlin. Chip slides his arm around her shoulders as they walk back to his car.

Her heart swells with love and regret when she sees the Camaro. He pops the trunk, and Rae has to force herself to look away from the body of the car to the interior of the trunk. Her bag is the only thing inside. She sniffles and smiles at him and reaches for it. Because she needs to make sure she has everything in the bag to take back with her, she opens it and checks it. It's all there, even her billfold and her driver's license.

When she pulls it from the trunk and slings the strap over her shoulder, Chip closes the trunk again and turns to her. She faces him, bag and lunchbox on her shoulder, Merlin in her hand.

"So how do we do it?" His grin is that of a ten-year-old kid ready to take his first shot at the high dive. Rae wishes she could take him with her, but that very enthusiasm he wears on his face is why she can't. He is young, and he has so much life to live before he becomes that unhappy man she saw in 2014. She has no right to step in and take it from him and promise him something better. Because it isn't her decision. She has no idea if she is better for him than Janine Andrews will be when they meet and marry.

"We don't," she says softly. Tears choke her up, and she swallows hard. Reaches to stroke her fingers over his lips and his cheek. Closes her eyes at the feel of his scruff on her skin. "Chip, you might have a life you have to live—"

"Rae—"

"I'm sorry," she whispers. "I can't take you with me. I can't do that. You're young, and you have so much to do, and you might have—"

"But I want to be with you."

"You might have a wife," she says through her tears, "and you might have children."

She sucks in a quick, harsh breath when she sees him flinch. He might love her, but neither of them can ignore the possibility that he has children. He's needed in his own life; she can't drag him back to be a part of hers.

"I love you," he argues a fraction of a second too late.

She nods. "I love you, too," she tells him. "Too much to take away the next twenty years of your life so you can live mine with me."

"Rae."

She stands on her tiptoes and kisses him again and tastes the piña coladas they'd shared the first night they'd danced.

When she backs away from him, she turns on the Merlin and starts the Echo game and prays that it takes her back to 2000, because she's tired of this game, and she wants to go home.

———

FAMILIAR WITH THE DISORIENTATION BY NOW, RAE KNOWS she's jumped time again. She is on Broadway, a few steps up from Barney's, close to Charlie's house. Hopefully that location means 2000. It's dusk, and no one seems to notice that she's suddenly appeared on the sidewalk on the busiest street in town. Merlin is still in her right hand; her computer bag and lunchbox are still on her left shoulder.

Still in the 1980's clothing, she starts walking. Her feet, clad in the Keds she bought in the 80s, protest with each step. Too late now, but she remembers suddenly, she'd left her clothing—her *underwear*—in 1980. Her toiletry items she'd purchased from Kmart. She considers another trip back to fetch those things, but the thought of seeing Chip again makes her too sad, and besides there's nothing high-tech about lotion and clothing and nothing that screams Rae Warner, 2000, and so leaving them in 1980 isn't going to hurt anything.

The lights in Charlie's house don't necessarily warm her heart, because she knows he will not remember that she's coming back from 1980. That she'd been at his house earlier, twice, begging for help. The thought of having to explain it all again, of trying to make him believe it all again is exhausting, and maybe, she just won't go into it. She doesn't plan to make any more time jumps, and though the device that had apparently been responsible for her departures is in his kitchen, Charlie doesn't appear to be in any danger of being shot out of the year 2000 and into the past or future.

Still. Her car is parked in front of his house, and she can't just get in and leave without saying something to him. Instead, she opens her bag as she walks and digs for her car keys and has a moment of *heart in her throat* panic when she doesn't immediately find them. Finally, she does, and she pulls them free and unlocks her door. Pulls it open and tosses her bag down on the floor in front of the passenger seat. She doubts she will ever need it again, but for whatever reason—maybe just nostalgia, she sets Merlin in the passenger seat, and then considers Charlie's lunchbox. *That* she decides to return to him.

He answers on her first knock, and he's relieved to see her because she's been gone for a few days again, and Rae steals herself for the lie she's going to keep to herself. When he wonders if she'd hidden out to get away from Paul, she spins that tale just a tad and says that she'd simply driven to Springfield for a few days just for some alone time. She lays it on thick about how she's at a point in her life—after all, she'll be thirty this summer—where she needs to take stock and make some decisions. She tells Charlie she likes her job—the one that she probably no longer has due to her recent absences—but she's not sure that means she's happy, and though Paul is a nice guy, she's just not sure she's that interested. Charlie, being her older brother, doesn't particularly want details about her love life, or lack thereof, and so he only nods along with her and agrees that she'd certainly deserved a little rest and relaxation.

She laughs at the absurdity of the comment, because she is most certainly not rested or relaxed or recharged. She remembers the lunchbox before she leaves and slips it off her shoulder. They are in the living room, and Rae is once again sitting by his freaky dummy named Noodie, and she's uncomfortable because what if now that the time travel portion of her life is over, she is suddenly possessed by the spirit that might be currently slinking around in Noodie?

"What's that?" Charlie nods at the lunchbox.

"Oh." She hopes she sounds casual. "It's yours. I borrowed it when I left the other day."

"It's mine?" he asks with a frown. "I've never seen that thing before in my life."

Rae unzips it and takes the Snicker bar before she puts the soft-sided box still full of grapes, cheese, and the by now warm ice pack on the coffee table. She has a brief memory flash of the ashtray in her parents' living room, and then she remembers the glimpse she'd had of her mom sitting on the front porch the day she'd had to dive into Chip's car to get away from her ten-year-old self.

With a small smile, she tilts her head and frowns at Charlie.

"Really? Like you have an idea of half of what you do have stashed in this house?" She looks pointedly at the mannequin in the corner, Chiefs stocking cap pulled low, and then at Noodie. "You have more stuff in your kitchen than I have in my life."

Charlie's smile is sheepish and young, and Rae feels a pang of regret for Chip while at the same time, she's excited to know there is certain happiness to come in her big brother's life.

"What happens now?" he asks her, and for a moment, she forgets that he's forgotten the time travel and thinks that he's asking about her last trip and where she might head to now.

"What do you mean?" She shakes her head.

"Paul. The job."

"Not sure there is a job." She sighs and yawns. She should be more worried about that, and she knows it. But somehow, she feels that it will work out. After all, Charlie and Lisha had not acted as if she was destitute and home-less in the year 2014. But she can't tell Charlie that. "I'll find something."

"And Paul?"

"I'm not interested in Paul," she says quietly, but without apology. "He's a nice guy, but he's not for me."

"You'll find someone," he tells her, and Rae's bursting apart with the words she can't say. She found him, and she lost him, and perhaps her brother and her nephew will be the only men in her future life.

Chapter 22

July 2000

It amazes her that she's gone through such a monu-mental life change, and she can't discuss it with anyone. *Well.* She could tell Charlie; after all, it was Charlie's estate sale junk that had sent her leaping backwards in time. It would be a hard sell again, but she could tell him and eventually, he would believe her. But as much as she'd like to share the adventure, because it was the biggest adven-ture of her little life, she kind of likes that it is her secret. She likes that she *has* a secret, and she likes keeping the memories of Chip Andrews to herself.

She lost her job because of her unexcused absences, and though that should bother her, it had only made her giggle. Because it sounded like grade school. She'd consid-ered going to her boss and fighting for it. For the job. For her position low on the totem pole, with crazy long hours, which left her very little room for a social life. But she'd decided against it. She has other skills, after all, and she could possibly go back to law sometime in the future. Maybe. She tries to be a little more careful with those thoughts now—*in the future, back in my day*—just in case there are unseen advances in time travel and the thoughts alone might be enough to catapult her into a different year or time zone or era.

Flipping burgers doesn't appeal to her, because her parents put her through college and the present day McDonald's, though fun and always busy, lacks the charm of the past. The old Adams Cinema is sitting empty, and Rae can only hope that one day, something new and fun will find a home there. She considers retail, at least for now, and applies at the bookstore in the mall. Maybe she'll even find an instructional book on time travel. Or even just a romance novel in which the main character falls through a time portal and finds herself in the days of castles and handsome knights.

Her laptop works even after the trip back in time. She'd had to hand it over to the powers that be, of course, and so for now, when she needs a computer, she goes to the library and uses theirs. One day—careful!—she'll buy a new laptop, but until she's got a new job and an income, she figures it will be prudent to save.

For now, she buys the *Herald Whig* regularly. She reads it from front to back and pays extra attention to the classifieds. Seems that if she'd studied nursing, she could find a new job. Of if she is open to pet grooming, there's a spot just waiting for her at the Pet Wash.

Tired now, and thinking about where she can start tomorrow's job search, she jumps when her cell phone rings. Thankfully, it also still works, and though it is a smartphone, she doesn't often use the data package.

She sees Charlie's number on the screen and answers the call with a smile. Since she's come home, he's been extra nice to her, like when she broke her wrist when she was eight and he was twelve.

"Hey, Charlie," she says. She drums her fingers on the Sunday *Whig*, which is spread open on her kitchen table. A glass of wine sits close at hand, because she's found she's lost her taste for fruity drinks, but adult beverages calm her.

"I need your help," he tells her, and immediately, she thinks of the times she'd gone to him for help to get back to 2000. Her heart flip flops in her chest.

"Why? What's wrong?"

"I have a date next weekend. And I'm terrified."

Rae sits up fast and furious, as if a lightning bolt shoots through her.

"A date?"

"Don't sound so surprised."

They laugh softly, and she says of course she's not surprised. Charlie, under all the grime and junk, is a true treasure and a woman would be lucky to have him. To which Charlie tells her not to lay it on so thick.

More laughter and then she asks him, "What's her name?"

"Lisha Reed."

The aftershocks of the lightning bolt of surprise are gone now, and Rae is only happy. So this is where it begins, so soon after Rae's heart has been broken.

"You know what? I think you're gonna be fine, Charlie," she says sincerely, and she promises to be at his house next Friday afternoon to help him dress for his date.

When she hangs up, she is both happy and sad, and she misses Chip yet again. It's been over a month since she'd last been to 1980, and surely he has forgotten her by now. She didn't discuss this with Charlie, but she has a theory. Chip had remembered her because he had her belongings. She'd left nothing that belonged to her at Charlie's each time she'd jumped from his kitchen to a different year, and so each time she left, Charlie simply forgot she'd been there and went on his way.

Now that she's left 1980 for good and taken her things with her, and Chip no longer has anything that belongs to her, he has most likely forgotten her and gone on his way. Who knows? He could be well on his way to meeting Janine by now.

Rae stares at her phone for a moment. Taps the photo icon for kicks. There's not much in her life she cares to take a picture of. Not yet, anyway. If she has a nephew in the future, she assumes she will load whatever phone or camera she owns at that time with pictures of him.

The first shot she sees appears to be a selfie of Chip. A 1980's selfie of Chip Andrews on her phone. His brown eyes and his warm smile make her heart hurt so badly, she sets the phone down on its screen so she isn't tempted to pick it up and look again. She reads a story about a local golf tournament, though she knows no names mentioned, and all she knows about golf is that you use a stick to hit a ball. She reads the comics, but they don't make her laugh. She skims through more articles about things she doesn't care about, because this is her life now. Maybe if Charlie starts dating Lisha, they will become friends.

She laughs out loud because she can't hog her brother's girlfriend to hurry along their friendship without damaging his relationship with her.

Destiny sucks.

She flips randomly through the paper, restless, now. And then stops on the engagement announcements.

Destiny calls again. Maybe she should quit thinking and listen.

In the very first picture is a familiar smile and eyes that warm her even though it's black and white, and she can't see the golden brown. His arm is around an attractive woman who wears a small smile, and whose name is Janine. The write up is small. Chip, the paper calls him Chase, is a 1980 Quincy College graduate and is now a professor at Quincy University. Janine is an SIU graduate, and she'd moved here from Carbondale immediately after college. The couple plans a September wedding at Reservoir Park.

Rae cringes. *Reservoir Park*? Really? Like, on the tennis courts? The whole idea bothers her. Well, of course the whole idea bothers her: Chip marrying anyone else. But an outdoor wedding should be beautiful, and sure, September will be a gorgeous time for a wedding, but *Reservoir Park*? There are at least six other parks in town, and some of them quite bigger and better suited for hosting a wedding than Reservoir. The write up is so small, as is Janine's smile, and Rae can't help but think it's a rushed affair, and it's doomed to fail.

Of course she thinks that because of what she'd seen in 2014. The bitter fight she'd witnessed when she'd probably broken a time travel rule and walked by the house she knew he and his wife were living in. The lonely, haunted look on Chip's face. Janine's words—her complaint of being married nearly fifteen years and nothing to show for it.

A woman with children wouldn't say that, would she? If Chip and Janine have children, surely the woman would have used different words in the fight Rae overheard. Something as simple as *I'm unhappy*. Or *I don't love you, anymore*. Because a mother wouldn't have it in her to say she has nothing to show for ten or twenty or fifty years of marriage, if she had children. It would be a hurtful thing to say to the father of her children and a terribly harsh thing if her children were ever to find out what she'd said.

Maybe the marriage starts out great, but maybe it

tanks quickly. *Destiny is calling, Rae.* If there are no children, what would it hurt to fudge just a bit with the timeline? Suddenly, Rae can't wait for morning, for a new day. She's overwhelmed with excitement that she hasn't felt in years, long before last month.

Except for a few days back in 1980, when she'd been a grown woman with a terribly bad crush on a cute, sexy college kid who knew how to move on a dance floor.

Chapter 23

FRANCIS HALL, THE MAIN BUILDING ON QUINCY University's main campus, has changed some since Rae earned her undergraduate degree here. The renovations had started, of course, when she was here, but she suspects a lot more has been done since then. The third floor had been hot and stuffy, with no central air serving it or the fourth at that time. Hardwood floors. Old paint. The air was musty and thick, and the building smelled old.

Today, the third floor is carpeted and the air is frigid the same as it had been then on the second floor where her advisor's office had been. Rae tells herself she shakes because she is cold, not because she is nervous.

Nervous to possibly be messing with the space time continuum. Nervous that a time lord or time cop might show up at any moment and grab her by the arm and spin her around and ask her just what exactly she thinks she's doing. She'll risk it. She'd go on the run with him, dodge time cops the rest of her life, because there'd never be a dull moment, and who better to run with and laugh in the face of danger with than the love of her life?

She's nervous, too, that Chip will see her and look right through her.

No. He won't recognize her. He won't remember her.

But what if he looks at her and feels that same spark of attraction he must have felt for that brief moment in 1980? What then? What if it's still there and they hit it off and she and Chip find happiness and Janine Reed finds someone else to make her happy? Would that be so bad?

His office number is 332; she'd looked on the information board on the first floor and slipped by the receptionist when she wasn't paying attention. Rae stands just across the hall, stomach in her throat, and listens to him talk to someone. Maybe a student? Probably there are summer classes going on now, and Chip might be helping a student with something difficult. Or just shooting the breeze with a college kid. God knows, she'd passed some time in her professors' offices when she'd been in school.

She hasn't quite worked out what she will say to him. She's too overcome with excitement, with anxiety to pour her heart and soul into making up a story about who she is and why she is there and selling it to him. She only needs to *see* him. For him to see her. And then she'll know.

Two men walk down the hall and one glances at her, and Rae wonders if he wonders who she is and why she is here.

Why is she here? This is insanity. She should just go. Just leave now and no one will ever be the wiser. Thunder cracks outside, and she jumps and then his office door opens. Chip appears in the open door, and he's still in conversation with a kid who looks like he should be maybe fourteen, instead of apparently at least eighteen. Rae holds her breath and peeks around to find an escape route.

This was a mistake. Maybe Destiny is calling the wrong number.

And then the kid says a goodbye, and Chip says something, and Rae looks up, and their eyes meet.

He looks somewhat confused, and Rae almost sobs because she'd hoped for attraction. For love at first sight, after all.

"Hey." His smile is friendly, though a bit uncertain. He's trying to place her. And he can't.

"Hi."

"Do I know you?" He frowns and looks up at the corkboard on the wall by his door. Probably checking to see if he has another appointment, as if maybe she is a student here to see him.

"I'm Rae," she says to him and she watches him closely. "Rae Warner."

He studies her face for a long moment, and Rae nearly squirms under his gaze.

"Rae. I'm Chase. Chase Andrews." He reaches out to shake her hand. "Do we have a meeting?" he asks with another glance at his board.

"No. No," she says, and she forces a laugh. "I was just passing through, and I um..." She smiles and remembers the bulletin board behind her. "I um...got caught up looking at the board here."

He nods, but she's not sure he believes her. Then again, what reason would she have to lie? None that he knows of.

"Oh." He grins, and Rae feels that grin pluck an invisible chord in her belly, and she remembers the taste of his kiss and the feel of his hands on her body. "I'm sorry. I don't mean to stare, but you look really familiar."

She nods, and she can't swallow around the knife in her throat. This isn't going the way she'd hoped. There's nothing between them besides what's in her mind.

"It was nice to meet you," she manages to croak out. He nods and says *you too*. She starts to walk away, and he goes back into his office. The door doesn't close, but Rae is tired of chasing this dream. All through her time in 1980 and back through 2014 and back into 2000 and 1980. She has no right to do something so selfish.

She hurries downstairs, passing a small group of students who move to the side of the steps to get out of her way, and she digs her keys from her purse when she reaches the main glass doors of Francis Hall when lightning flashes, and she realizes it's raining.

Isn't that the luck? With a groan, she reaches to push the door open, and then suddenly a hand half covers hers.

"Oh." Chip sighs behind her. "Yuck."

"Mm-hmm." She sounds calm, but at his touch, her heart had jumped to her throat yet again. She doesn't tell him she should have expected this. Rain on her parade, except she doesn't even get to leave with a parade. Not even a parade of two.

"See that bar over there?" He points out the door, and though she can't exactly see it from here, she knows he is pointing at The Abbey. She nods and steels herself to walk in the rain to her car.

"Do you like piña coladas?" he asks her, and just like that, she's on fire.

"I do," she says softly, even though she knows better than to hope.

"How about a walk in the rain?"

She finally looks up at him, and his eyes seem to know her, even if the rest of him doesn't.

"Sure." She shrugs.

"Let's get a drink," he suggests. And he takes her hand to lead her out the door.

They are half-jogging through the university lot when she tugs at his hand to get his attention. He looks at her, and his hair, still on the longish side, is wet and hangs down his back in ringlets. Again Rae thinks of kissing him.

"Can I call you Chip?" she asks, and she keeps jogging, and he stops, and they collide.

"Rae?" His eyes almost pop open, and suddenly his arms slide around her waist.

She nods. "It's me."

He kisses her then, his lips soft and warm over hers. He tastes sweet and delicious, and when he pulls away, she pulls him back for more. *Destiny's calling.* Rae gathers his wet shirt in her fists to hold on and answer.

***

Thank you for reading Destiny's Calling! If you enjoyed Rae and Chip's story, please consider leaving a review on your favorite bookish/retail site.

Gettin' Hitched, Chapter 1

Mercedes Ingalls slowed her car to a stop and leaned forward to squint through the windshield at the big brick home to her right. An ornate wooden front door, flanked on both sides by ornate sidelights, gave the two-story brick house a snooty, aristocratic appearance. But the bike thrown down in the front yard and the soccer goal tipped over near the drive were clearly the mark of kids, and though Mercedes thought Nicholas Moore's kids were too young to ride bikes that size, she pulled her little Corolla over to the curb to park.

She consulted her phone again, where she'd typed the Moore address into her notes app. 4769 Stardust. Her maxi skirt felt all wrong now. If the Moore kids were old enough to ride a bike that size, somehow wearing a maxi skirt to the interview felt wrong. Maybe she should have worn khakis.

"Too late to worry about it now, Cedes," she mumbled as she swung her car door shut. The mailboxes out here were the fancy kind covered in bricks made to look like miniature houses. No numbers visible anywhere, so she couldn't be sure this was 4769. A beat-up pickup truck was parked across the street, and the garage door at that house was open. But there was no one in sight to ask if she was at Nicholas Moore's house, so she would just have to ring the doorbell and find out.

Mercedes eyed the pristine lawn as she made her way up the driveway. The bike and the soccer goal felt terribly out of place with the perfectly trimmed edges of grass and the vividly colored flowers in what appeared to be professionally done landscaping. An electronic beat pounded faintly from deep inside the house as Mercedes stepped up on the porch and lifted her hand to press the doorbell with her thumb.

She drew her hand away from the doorbell and studied the chipped robin's egg blue polish on her thumbnail. If she got this job, she could maybe start doing professional manicures again. Or at least, maybe she could afford a new bottle of nail polish. What she had now was old and chunky.

When no one answered the door—probably hadn't heard the bell with that music blaring inside—she looked over her shoulder and spotted a guy across the street. He appeared to be heading to the truck at the curb. Mercedes shifted her weight on her feet and turned to get a better look at him. Her movement must have caught his eye, because he waved and hollered hello. Deciding she might have better luck asking him about where Nicholas Moore lived, she stepped off the porch and headed back down the drive.

"Hey."

"Hi." She flashed him a smile as she crossed the street. "Any chance you can tell me which house is Nicholas Moore's?"

"This is Nick's house." The guy met her in the middle of the drive. Mercedes eyed the way his longish, brown hair curled at his crew cut shirt collar and the shock of the same curls that fell over his eyebrow. Broad shoulders filled out the faded brown T-shirt—Mercedes thought the letters across the front spelled race, but the letters, too, were faded, and given that the body under the letters appeared to be textbook perfection, she didn't want to stare too hard. Loose board shorts hung on his hips, though he was anything but scrawny. His long lean legs had been kissed by the sun—

Mercedes gave herself a mental shake. She'd been reading too many romance novels. Time to switch gears and read a thriller or a spy novel. Anything but something that talked about sun-kissed skin and finely chiseled lips and the perfect amount of scruff—

"Doorbell doesn't work," the guy told her as he offered her both a friendly smile and a handshake. "Are you here about the babysitting thing?"

"Nanny," she mumbled, wondering if this guy was actually Nick Moore. Could she be that lucky? She nodded when she realized she had barely mumbled the word and the guy was watching her curiously. Not only was his body textbook perfection, so was his face. Classic bone structure, a perfect arch in his thick eyebrows, and eyes the color of the ocean as the sun sank in the west and darkness merged with the lighter blue waters.

"I'm Parker," he told her. "Nick's brother."

Of course, this couldn't be Nicholas.

Mercedes caught herself before a disappointed sigh could slip out. It didn't matter what Nicholas looked like; she was here to score a nanny position, not a date with the dad. Who was probably married, although nowhere in the five-line job description and contact information did it say anything other than Nicholas Moore.

No matter, Mercedes reminded herself. She wasn't interested in finding a date. She wanted a job. Specifically, a job that would give her some nights and weekends off.

"Mercedes."

The guy had a firm grip, and if anything, his smile grew bigger and more inviting, but there was no telltale romance-novel zing. She didn't have a sudden urge to hold tight to his hand or to snuggle up close to him and press her face to his.

"Nick's inside. In the office."

"Okay." She nodded as the guy dropped her hand and backed away slowly. The worn flip-flops that completed his outfit screamed surfer dude, but being that they were standing in midwestern Illinois and nowhere near a coast, she doubted he had a surfboard stashed in the truck bed.

As if she would simply know where the office was once inside the house, the guy turned and headed down the drive to his truck. Mercedes watched him for a second, but she shifted her gaze back to the house and wondered what Nicholas would be like.

Should she just go on in? Parker's words and actions kind of insinuated that she should. Behind her, the truck came to life with a pretty, low rumble, bringing to mind exes who drove monster trucks and motorcycles. Mercedes chuckled as she tapped on the front door. Rather than stand here and wait and hope Nicholas heard her—she was already late—she twisted the knob and when she found it unlocked, she pushed it open just a smidge.

She peeked her head into a neat little entry way. Slate gray tiles on the floor in front of the door butted up against the snowy white carpet of the living room. A black baby grand dominated the far side of the room, though a big screen TV hung on the east wall. Two gray wing-backed chairs faced the piano, a white leather loveseat faced the TV.

Mercedes held her breath as she stepped inside. Kids lived here? And the carpet was still white?

"Mr. Moore?" she called now as she pushed the door closed behind her. "Mr. Moore, it's Mercedes. Your brother said the doorbell doesn't work."

She heard a deep male voice rambling about technology—something about design and protocol, not that she cared. The voice grew louder to her right. She looked up just as another beautiful man appeared at the end of a hallway on the east side of the house. There was a resemblance between this guy and the brother who had just left. Nicholas Moore had the same eye color; though his hair was a bit lighter, definitely shorter. A little long for business casual, but Mercedes liked the way it curled over the collar of his dress shirt.

When their eyes met, she started to say something, but he gave her a slight shake of his head. He lifted his finger to stop her and spoke again, this time talking about numbers and projections. He turned his head just enough that Mercedes saw he had a Bluetooth earpiece in his right ear. She closed her mouth, prepared to wait him out.

She let her gaze roam to a small formal dining room to her left. The ornate white marble table could seat six. The upright iron chairs covered in dove grey cushions looked pretentious and uncomfortable. Abstract art in shades of grays and golds hung on the southern wall. The longer Mercedes stared at the twisted lines and splashes of color, the more her head hurt. Instead, she turned to look her fill at Nicholas Moore while he was otherwise occupied.

He wore charcoal gray trousers—they were expensive, Mercedes could tell from looking—and a lavender dress shirt. The collar was unbuttoned; his sleeves were rolled up to reveal his forearms. A fancy gold watch decorated his left wrist, but his fingers were bare.

Which, Mercedes reminded herself, didn't mean anything. Some men didn't wear wedding rings.

Not that it mattered one way or another to her.

She noticed he was wearing wingtips and wondered if he always appeared this uptight or if it was simply the hassle of hiring a new nanny. Or…a nanny. Did they have to let someone go? Or maybe their nanny quit or moved away?

"Mercedes?"

She wondered where the kids were now. It was awfully quiet in here for children of any age, and though the description hadn't specifically said *how many* children of *what age*, Mercedes thought there should be some kind of noise.

Poor kids.

She couldn't imagine living in a beautiful, cold house like this when she was younger. She and her brother had been holy terrors when they were kids; thankfully, her parents had given them a lot of freedom to grow up and learn on their own. Some people thought she and Aaron had too much freedom. Mercedes thought some people had too much time on their hands if they needed to worry so much about how she and Aaron were raised.

"Ms. Ingalls?"

She snapped to attention at the use of her last name. Nicholas Moore pulled the Bluetooth piece from his ear and stared at her expectantly now.

"Yes."

"We can talk in the office."

If you'd like to read more about Mercedes and Nick, click here:

Gettin' Hitched, The H Books, Book 1

About the Author

Tracy is the author of the Lorelei Bluffs women's fiction series, the Williams Legacy, and several stand-alone women's fiction novels. She has recently dabbled in contemporary romance as well.

For more information about Tracy and her books, visit her website:

www.broemmerbooks.com

Also by Tracy Broemmer

Women's Fiction Novels:

Luther's Cross 10th Anniversary Edition

Fairytale (Writing as Therese Kinkaide)

Just Like Them Small Hours

Picket Fences

Two Story Home

Green-Eyed Girl

Say Everything

Come Home For Christmas

Sketching Litchfield Lake

Ever, Again

Safe as Houses

Damsel

The Valentine Suite

Every Little Thing, Lorelei Bluffs, Book 1

Two A.M., Lorelei Bluffs, Book 2

Blind, Lorelei Bluffs, Book 3

Leaving July, Lorelei Bluffs, Book 4

Hesitation Marks, Lorelei Bluffs, Book 5

Four Letter Words, Lorelei Bluffs, Book 6

See Kate, Lorelei Bluffs, Book 7

Loved You More, Lorelei Bluffs, Book 8

A Lorelei Ending, Lorelei Bluffs, Book 9

I Do, Lorelei Bluffs, Book 10

Truth Is, The Williams Legacy, Book 1

Other People's Ugly, The Williams Legacy, Book 2

Omissions, The Williams Legacy, Book 3

Contemporary Romance Novels:

Destiny's Calling: Your Future Is Waiting

Wedding Day Shenanigans

Holiday Fling

The Kiss Off

Something Like Love

Love, Nashville, The Mississippi Queen Trilogy, Book 1

Forever, Duncan, The Mississippi Queen Trilogy, Book 2

Always, Jess, The Mississippi Queen Trilogy, Book 3

Gettin' Hitched, The H Books, Book 1

Hookin' Up, The H Books, Book 2

Holdin' On, The H Books, Book 2.5

Contemporary Romance Novellas:

Indian Summer, A Novella

Dear Jaclyn Perris, A Novella

French Stuff, A Novella, originally published in the Just Coffee
Newsletter Builder

Boone's Girl, A Novella originally published in the Back to
School Anthology, Aced

Horror Novella:

The Devy Man

Women's Fiction Short Stories:

India Falls

Luther's Cross: 87,600

The Candy Cane Tree of Willow Lane

Contemporary Romance Short Stories:

Perfect Pictures, The Wine Tasting Series, Traminette

Coming Home, The Wine Tasting Series, Edelweiss

Save Me Every Dance, The Wine Tasting Series, Rosé

Marry Me, The Wine Tasting Series, Shiraz

Birthday Wishes, The Wine Tasting Series, Muscat

Dad Jeans, The Wine Tasting Series, Vignoles